SEVENTH NOVEL IN THE SOUTHERN GRACE SERIES

Finding Maisy

To Mary, Enjoy!

GLENDA C. MANUS
AUTHOR OF *SWEET TEA AND SOUTHERN GRACE*

Glenda Manus

Library of Congress Cataloging-in-Publication
Data is on file with the publisher

Text copyright © 2018 by Glenda Manus
Published in 2018 South Ridge Press

ISBN-13: 978-1-7326710-0-3

All rights reserved. No part of this book may be reproduced or transmitted in any form or by any means, electronic or mechanical, including photocopying, recording, or by any information storage and retrieval system, without permission from the author.

Printed in the United States of America
24 23 22 21 20 19 18 17 16

First Original Edition

This is a work of fiction. Any resemblance to any actual person, living or dead, business establishments, events or locales is strictly coincidental.

Cover design and formatting by Diane Turpin, www.dianeturpindesigns.com

PROLOGUE

Pastor burnout. It was something the good Reverend Rockford Williford Clark had been warned about by seasoned pros over the years when he'd gone full speed ahead tackling new programs and projects within and without the confines of Park Place Presbyterian, a church with a membership of one-hundred-fifty-four. On an exceptional Sunday, such as Christmas or Easter, the pews were overflowing, but on most Sundays, there was rarely more than ninety gathered inside the sanctuary. Built in 1912, the pews were designed to seat one-hundred-twenty-five, but the elders had joked after a recent planning committee meeting that the extra padding and love-handles on the current congregants, including themselves, 'bout filled up the pews anyway.

But Rev Rock didn't have time to worry about the pews being filled. He was running this way and that trying to keep up with the demands of a growing church. Always the optimistic one, he had scoffed at the term 'pastor burnout' when he'd heard other pastors use it. Just an excuse for a sabbatical, he'd once told his wife Liz, but now he was eating his words. Eating crow was more like it, and he had done a lot of it lately.

BAKER'S CHAPEL, a modest brick church with a tall steeple, sat atop a hill a few miles south of Park Place in the Baker's Grove Community, a barely visible red dot on the wall map in the county courthouse. The size of the dot didn't match the size of the community's heart though, and the young girl fishing in the pond behind the church had one of the biggest hearts of them all. Maisy Martin had troubles aplenty. Her best friend Sabrina had once described Maisy to a newcomer in the community as a lover of blue skies and tomato pies, a term Maisy herself would have found funny if she wasn't so busy contemplating what life would be like if her circumstances had been different. There were things she would have changed, but she knew that changes can create a domino effect and she wasn't so sure there was anything in her life that she would choose to give up if the dominoes were to fall the wrong way. Anyway, it was too late to go back and change things now, so she may as well have the attitude of the Beatitude, a term that came to her mind when she read a book she'd checked out of the library about St. Gregory of Nyssa. He was a theologian who had contributed to the writing of the Nicene Creed and his philosophy had been that, *Beatitude is a possession of all things held to be good, from which nothing is absent that a good desire may want.*

Her favorite of the Beatitudes was *Blessed are the poor in spirit, for theirs is the kingdom of heaven.* And she knew all about the poor in spirit, yes siree, she did.

CHAPTER ONE

MAISY

"I will instruct you and teach you the way you should go; I will counsel you with my eye upon you."

—PSALM 32:8

The screen door slammed shut behind me as I carried the pan of dirty dishwater outside. I stopped in my tracks and cringed at the sound the door made. Balancing the pan on the porch railing, I waited for a reprimand. I didn't have long to wait. Zell's voice boomed from the kitchen.

"Child, you're gonna tear that door off its hinges."

"I can't help it, Nana Zell; my hands are full." This chore was not my favorite, and my voice showed my frustration. But Zell didn't give an inch.

"Don't sass me Baby Girl; and don't empty that on your papa's garden. He'll tan your hide."

I walked down the back porch steps on bare feet, dodging the nails that had worked up through the weathered planks. Knowing I was out of sight and hearing distance, I rolled my eyes and repeated her words, "Don't sass me, Baby Gir-ul!" Girl was always two syllables when it rolled off Zell's tongue. The thought of the gentle old man I called Papa "tanning my hide" made me laugh, but then I felt a stab of guilt for mocking Zell who had done so much for me.

When my bare feet hit the pebbled driveway, I slowed down and gingerly made my way down the hill with a resolve to toughen up my feet before summer arrived. "Ouch, ouch, ouch," I said with each step until I reached my destination beside the road ditch. It was a royal pain carrying that pan outside every single time we washed dishes, but when I'd asked why we didn't empty it in the sink drain anymore, Nana Zell rolled her eyes heavenward. "Lord knows, Child, I've been trying to get him to fix it. It's been broken for nigh on a year now. Ask your Papa about it." He'd looked on as Zell complained, but he listened and answered quietly as he always did.

"I can't bend these old knees to get under the house anymore," he said. "The drain pipe came loose, and we just have to make do until I can find somebody to fix it." He looked so downtrodden, I almost volunteered to help him, but I remembered the big old king snake I'd seen slithering in and out from under the house and I remained silent.

I SET the dishpan down on the ground, tipped it over and watched as the murky water made its way down the embankment where it would eventually soak into the red clay soil. I took a stick and made little crosscuts in its path, watching as the rivulets trickled off in different directions. The little crosscuts reminded me of my life and I wondered what path it would lead to. Would it be the one that led to crazy? Maybe I was already well on the way—like mother, like daughter.

My feet had been tormented enough for one day, so I took the grassy path back to the house, heading for the front porch this time and slinging the remaining bits of water out of the dishpan as I walked. When I reached the steps, I sat down on the bottom one and inspected my tender feet. Satisfied they weren't bleeding, I got up and started up the brick steps. There was a fresh coat of white paint on the handrails. The floor was painted gray and it was swept as clean as a whistle. Zell was almost as particular about that porch as she was the inside of the house. I should know; it was my job to sweep inside and outside every day when I got home from school.

Papa Tom's straw hat was on the newel post where he'd put it when he came in from weeding the garden to wash up for supper. I took it down and rolled the brim around in my hands. The seam that held the brim together was frayed. It wouldn't be long before he'd be needing another one. It had an earthy smell of soil and sweat, the fragrance I always associated with my makeshift grandfather six days of the week. His Sunday fragrance was different; a mixture of Old Spice and Murray's Pomade, the cream he rubbed into his dark wiry hair to settle it down. Putting the hat on my head, I shuffled my way across the porch mimicking the way he walked. Sunday spicy, or weekday earthy, the scents would always trigger memories of the one person I could count on to have my back. It mattered not one iota to either of us that our skin colors were different. His, an inherited black, made darker from a lifetime behind a plow, and mine, white with a sprinkle of freckles from a decade of summers running barefoot behind him scattering seeds in his garden. We were kin, not by blood, but by our mutual love for one another.

Nana Zell on the other hand, seemed to be in a perpetual state of anxiety, a term I learned from Mrs. Clark, the new school counselor. I tiptoed in the house and hung Papa Tom's hat on the peg by the door. If Zell knew he'd left it outside, she would have lit into him about not taking care of his belongings. She loved us; it was just her way of dealing with things, especially the big thing of having a white fourteen-year-old girl living with them. But it wasn't anything new. I had lived with them off and on since I was six.

As I made my way across the living room floor, she met me

and took the dishpan out of my hand. "Took you long enough to empty it." She dried it off with the dish towel she was still holding. "You better go do your homework. Your teachers won't like it if you get behind. The county might come out here and try to take you away from us." I rolled my eyes like she was prone to do from time to time, but I didn't let her see me. *Taking me away* was an idle threat she used when I didn't wash my hair, change my underwear or do my homework. It would be a disgrace if any child under her care became a derelict, not her word for it but I love saying it because it's one of those words that just slides off your tongue. Derelict—derə likt. I suppose I'm a word nerd.

"I've already done my homework," I said. "I finished it on the school bus." She looked at me kind of funny, then nodded her head. She didn't always believe me, and I didn't much blame her. I had told a fib or two now and again when I was younger, but she knew I wouldn't fib about something like homework. Making good grades in school was the only path that would pull me out of a life of upheaval and uncertainty, two directions I knew too well.

"Well, let's get back to the kitchen, then. You can help me put the dishes away. It's hard for me to lift those heavy plates up on the shelf with this shoulder acting up like it is," she said, flexing her right shoulder joint up and down.

She put the dishpan back in the sink, then began placing the pots and pans under the cabinets while I put the glasses and plates away on the higher shelves. The knotty-pine cabinets matched the kitchen walls, and during my first stay with the Bakers, I became obsessed with trying to pry out one of the knots at the base of the cabinet. After a few days, I succeeded. Papa Tom found it on the floor and glued it back in without Zell ever knowing about it. He glued it so tight I gave up trying to get it back out again.

Sitting down at my usual place at the table, I watched Zell as she wiped down the stove and countertops. There were so many questions I wanted to ask her but the subject I was about to bring up was the one she always tried to avoid. She would clam up every time I mentioned it and a look of doom and gloom would settle over her face.

"Nana Zell?" It was so quiet in the kitchen, my voice seemed to echo off the kitchen walls.

Zell froze in the middle of wiping down the sink as if knowing what I was about to ask, but to her credit, she didn't ignore me this time. She hung the towel over the dish rack to dry and made her way to the table.

"What is it, child?" The words came out heavy-like.

I have a habit of saying what's on my mind without thinking it through, but I've never been that way with Zell. She has a way about her, a staring into the soul kinda' way that makes me watch my tongue when she's around. But this time I waded in, because however harsh she may look, deep down inside she's gentle. But still, I never figured out why discussing the subject of Momma's illness was off limits.

"Have you heard if Momma's getting any better? When will she be home from the hospital?"

She sighed. "I don't rightly know, Baby Girl, but soon, I 'spect. Don't you be fretting over it."

That was like telling a fish not to swim, a bird not to fly. I was always fretting over it.

MOMMA CAME AND MOMMA WENT, and I learned to go with the flow. She was the best momma ever during the good times, but a total confusion during the bad. I never questioned it in my mind much until the year I started middle school. That was the year Shelly Bumgarner sat across from me in the cafeteria one day and chanted in my face, "Maisy, Maisy, your momma's crazy", and I accidentally spit a mouthful of chocolate milk on her new pink shirt. And it was the year I realized that my life wasn't quite normal. There had been so many questions avoided and so many different excuses, I wondered if anyone would ever put the real truth in words. My thin shoulders had sagged under the weight of unanswered questions that year. And during that stressful year, Nana Zell never once told me to straighten my shoulders. I think she felt the weight too.

I remember asking her right after she tucked me in bed one night, "What's wrong with Momma, Nana Zell?" She sat in the rocking chair beside me shaking her head as if she too was puzzled. The street lamp shone through the bedroom window framing her large silhouette, and she cupped my chin in her weathered hand. The soft glow of the hallway light highlighted her soulful hazel eyes as they looked into my green ones. "I wish I knew what's wrong with your momma, Baby Girl, I surely do."

"Why can't she just be happy like we are?"

She thought about it a minute. "Happiness don't come easy for everybody," she said. "You remember the song you used to sing in Bible School?"

"Which song?"

A soft melody flowed from her lips and when it did, I remembered the song. Zell's warm, rich soprano voice has lulled me to sleep many of a night. "I've got the joy, joy, joy, joy down in my heart." I wanted her to keep singing forever, but she stopped after the second stanza. "Maisy, I know you remember plenty of happy times with your momma; you've told me about them. The joy's there, hidden in her heart, but sometimes it has trouble pushing its way up to her mind."

"Why?"

I could tell she was becoming uncomfortable with me asking questions that didn't have an easy answer. She took a deep breath and let it out slow and easy as if it would be the last breath she would ever take. "I don't know, Baby Girl. Some people are just born blue. And then there are those who are born uncommonly blue, like your momma. It's a mystery to me."

I knew she wasn't talking about the color. There was a deeper, darker term for it than blue. I had done a Google search in the school library by typing in, "happy one minute, sad the next". The first thing that popped up was "Bipolar Disorder", and by Zell's deep sigh of frustration, I figured it must be true.

CHAPTER TWO

"So it is not the will of my Father who is in heaven that one of these little ones should perish."

—MATTHEW 18:1

We'd moved in next door to the Baker's farm house right before my daddy disappeared into thin air, as my momma always said. "Here today, gone tomorrow; pouf, just like that," she'd say to anyone who would listen, giving her words a dramatic flair by blowing air upon her fingertips and sending it off towards the sky.

Daddy really hadn't disappeared; he sent money, but every so often it would come from a different address, like he didn't want to be pinned down to one place or he didn't want us to find him. He never filed for a divorce though. Maybe if he had, Momma would have moved on with her life. But every time that check came, Momma would take it out of the mailbox and start crying all over again.

His momma and daddy, my grandparents, wanted nothing to do with us. The first bad spell I remember Momma having, she called them and begged them to keep me for a little while until she felt better. My grandmother was on the other end and she was talking so loud, I could hear everything she said.

"We can't keep her," she said. "I'm sure she's crazy as a bat, just like you."

"Crazy as a bat? If I'm crazy as a bat, it's because your son drove me to it. This is your grandchild we're talking about. It's not as if I'm asking you to take a stranger in off the street."

She must have grown tired of begging because she slammed the phone down and cried. It was the summer between kindergarten and first grade, so I must have been about six-years-old. For the next week, the only thing Momma wanted to do was sleep. At first she would get up in the morning long enough to pour me a bowl of cereal and make herself some coffee; then she would go back to bed. After a few days, she didn't even do that. I don't remember her eating or drinking anything except water, but I didn't pay much attention. I watched TV and played outside. When I got tired of doing nothing, I would try to wake her up, but each time she just looked at me, took a sip of water and said, "I'm sorry, Ladybug, I really am," and she'd go back to sleep. I made do with whatever I found in the refrigerator. After that, I raided the cupboard of pop-top cans of peaches and pork 'n beans.

This went on for over a week; maybe more, I was too young to keep track.

I'd watched the old man next door plow his garden in early summer and when I saw him carrying a basket of tomatoes and cucumbers, it sure got my attention. When we ran out of milk and cereal and there wasn't anything left in the refrigerator except eggs that I didn't know how to cook and some meat in the freezer froze solid as a rock, I decided to sneak into his tomato patch early in the mornings before he was out and about. One morning, I stayed longer than I should have because it had rained the night before. My feet kept getting sucked into the mud of that red clay soil and I was having trouble pulling them out. I was concentrating on holding the tomatoes I'd stuffed in my t-shirt and pulling my feet out of the mud when I heard a deep voice behind me.

"Ah, there's the critter that's been making off with my best tomatoes! And I thought it was an old 'possum all along. You're lucky I didn't set a trap, child. It would'a snapped your toes off."

Caught red-handed, I wanted to run but my feet kept sticking in the mud. He picked me up gentle-like and toted me home while I hung on to those tomatoes for dear life.

"Does your momma know you've been taking these without asking? I bet not. If you'd told me you wanted them, I would have been glad to share. Taking things without asking is the same as stealing in the Good Book, so we're going to have a little chat with your momma soon as we get you home."

"I'm hungry!" I said, trying to squirm myself loose.

"That's what the old 'possum would say too, but he doesn't know better. You're a right smart girl, and you should." Sitting me down on a bench beside the well house, he took the tomatoes out of my shirt and hosed my feet off with the water hose. Then he took my hand and marched me up to the kitchen door, taking his muck boots off before he knocked.

"She won't hear you," I said, still trying to get away. "She hasn't been out of bed in days."

His look of determination turned into one of alarm and he knocked even harder. There was no noise coming from inside so he opened the door. Still holding my hand, he said, "Take me to your momma, child. She might be sick."

One glance at the dirty kitchen with spilled milk, dirty glasses and cereal bowls, and flies buzzing around the sink caused a look of concern, then panic to set in on his wise old face. When we stepped inside the bedroom, it was even worse. Momma hadn't showered in over a week and rarely even bothered to get up to go to the bathroom. The smell of pee was strong in the room. I'd stopped going in there because it made me gag. He grabbed me back up in his bony old arms and rushed me out the door. He put me down long enough to pull his boots back on. "You're going home with me, child. I'll send Zell over here. She'll know what to do."

He carried me into their squeaky-clean house that smelled of biscuits and bacon, and I thought I'd died and gone to heaven. A voice came from the kitchen, "You must'a got stuck in the mud, Tom. Breakfast is almost ready; all I got left to do is fry the eggs. Wash up, now."

We made our way into the kitchen. The biggest and darkest woman I'd ever seen in my life turned around and gasped when she saw me. I must have been a sight with my stained t-shirt, matted hair and dirty face. "What you gone and got us involved in, Tom Baker," she said as more of a factual statement than a question. I'm sure she's pondered over it aplenty through the years, because involved they were about to be whether they liked it or not.

The old man's voice was calming as he patted me on the back, but the look he gave Zell was desperate. "Zell, you need to go over to the old Sweeny house and check on this little girl's momma. I'll finish cooking the eggs. Me and this hungry child are going to eat breakfast."

There was no sassing back from Zell Baker that day. She took off her apron, hung it on a peg and walked out the door as fast as her short legs would allow her to go.

It was the finest meal I'd ever eaten, and I can still see Papa Tom standing in front of that harvest-gold stovetop cracking and frying those eggs in a big black iron skillet. I paid close attention to how he did it so I'd never go hungry again as long as there was an egg in the house.

NANA ZELL quickly went into action. She checked Momma's pulse and opened her eyelids, but before she even tried to wake her up, she'd scrubbed the whole house from top to bottom. Then she'd started in on Momma, holding her up and scrubbing her down in the shower under warm running water. She just stood there, too weak to protest. Clean and smelling like Dial soap, Momma finally became alert enough to sit down at the kitchen table and let Zell spoon-feed her some broth she'd warmed up from a can she'd found in the cupboard. She fluffed the pillows on the couch, turned on the TV and tucked Momma under a quilt. She went back to her bedroom to change the sheets and do the laundry. I knew all this because Nana Zell told Papa Tom all about it later that afternoon and I hung on to every word, because in my six-year-old mind, it was the most exciting thing that had happened all summer.

PAPA TOM FINISHED his breakfast while I gulped mine down and got seconds on the bacon. We washed up the dishes and fed the chickens and came back inside to watch TV.

"Your TV's bigger than ours," I said. "Can we watch *The Price is Right*? It comes on at 10:30."

"You sure are a smart one, now aren't you? Most little girls your age can't tell time." It made me proud that he called me smart and that's when I decided that being smart was a good thing.

After *The Price is Right* was over, we grew tired of waiting and walked back over to our house. The garden was still muddy so we took to the road. We found Zell making chicken soup when we stepped through the door of Momma's kitchen.

"Where did you get that?" I asked as she was stirring the pot. It smelled heavenly.

"The chicken was in the freezer, child, but it wasn't soup when you were trying to find something to eat. You have to put ingredients together to make it. Only grownups can cook, so don't you be trying it by yourself or you'll burn the house down. As soon as it's ready, I'll feed your momma. She hasn't eaten in so long her stomach is about tied up in knots."

I walked over to the couch where Momma lay. She was staring at, but not really seeing the TV.

"Are you okay, Momma?" I asked. My hand automatically went to her forehead like she always did me when I was sick. There was a different scent in the air and I sniffed it appreciatively. "You sure smell better." I pulled her pajama shirt up a little ways but I didn't notice any kind of knots her stomach was tied up in, so I pulled it back down.

Her eyes became more alert when I started talking and she put her arm out. "Ladybug, is that you?"

"Yes, Momma, it's me."

"I'm sorry, honey. I'm really sorry." Then she cried again.

"It's okay, Momma," I said, patting her on the shoulder. Old Tom was wiping tears from his eyes and I wondered what he had to cry about. "Are you sad too, Mister?" I asked.

"No, little gal," he said, straightening up and trying to take control of his emotions. "I'm glad your momma's better, that's all. My name's Tom; Tom Baker, and this here's my wife, Azelle; you can call her Zell for short."

I looked at Momma for approval. Normally she would have told me to call them Mr. and Mrs. but she wasn't saying anything now.

"Can I call you Papa Tom?" I asked. "I've never had a Papa." His eyes filled with tears again and I was sorry I ever said anything.

"Papa Tom will be just dandy," he said. "Should I call you Ladybug, like your momma did?"

I shook my head. "Only my momma calls me Ladybug. My real name's Maisy, so that's what you can call me."

"Maisy, that's got a nice ring to it. I'm glad to meet you, Maisy." He held out his hand for me to shake, and I took it, not shaking it, but marveling at how good it felt to have someone that cared. It was going to be a good day. All because I stole some tomatoes from old Tom's garden, I now had someone to call Papa.

Zell brought a bowl of soup over to where Momma was sitting up. "Fetch me a kitchen chair to sit on, Tom. I'll try to get her to eat a few bites of soup. She's a walking skeleton." As she eased herself into the small chair, I cringed, wondering if it would break, but it didn't. She held the spoon up to Momma's lips and she took a small sip.

"Her name's Mandy," I said, "Mandy Martin, and she's twenty-eight years old. I'm Maisy Martin and I'm six."

Since things had gone so well with the old man, I decided to be bold again. "Can I call you Nana Zell?"

"Lord bless you, Child; you can call me anything you want. Now let's try to get your momma to eat." I was eyeing the bowl hungrily. "Mercy, Child, I almost forgot; your bowl of soup is on the table cooling off. Go ahead, get up on that chair and eat it." She didn't have to tell me twice. That very day I decided I would be a cook when I grew up like Nana Zell. I'd already eaten two good meals in one day and there was liable to be another one at suppertime if Nana Zell was still around.

They tried to get Momma up and walk her around, but she would only take a step or two at a time. "She's weak as a kitten, Tom. She needs to be in the hospital. Me and you are too old to take care of her like this. What if something happened to her? That little girl wouldn't have a momma."

I was spooning the last drop of soup in my mouth when she came over and sat beside me. "Where's your daddy, Maisy? We've got to get your momma some help."

"He disappeared," I said, and tried to blow on my fingers like Momma did. "Pouf, just like that."

The two of them looked at each other in confusion, then back at me. "What about your Grandma and Grandpa?"

"My daddy's momma and daddy? They don't like us," I said. "They think Momma is crazy as a bat and that I am too."

"And your momma's parents; where are they?"

"They're dead. My daddy said they were goody-two-shoes missionaries and they died in the jungle before I ever got to meet them."

Nana Zell sighed. "Gracious, child. It looks like you're in a fix and we ain't far behind you." She turned to her husband. "What should we do, Tom? If we call an ambulance, they'll call Social Services and there's no telling where this child will end up."

The thought of me ending up somewhere scared me. "Please don't let them take me anywhere. Can I stay with you?"

"What if we don't tell them about the girl, Zell? I'll take her back to our house and you call the ambulance. Tell 'em Mandy is our neighbor and we found came over and found her like this. That's the truth."

"I'll have to tell 'em about the child if they ask, Tom. You know I can't lie about it."

"We'll turn it over to the Lord," he said. "He'll take care of her wherever she goes."

Zell snapped her fingers so loud I jumped. "I know what we'll do," she said. "Do you have some paper to write on, child?" I ran and tried to find a sheet of paper that hadn't been doodled on, searching every drawer. I finally found Momma's sketchbook and handed it to her.

"We'll get Mandy to write out a paper saying it's okay for us to watch the child while she's gone, and if somebody comes around trying to take her away, we'll have it as proof that she agreed."

She took the paper over to the table where Momma was sitting, half asleep, and shook her shoulders gently. Momma raised her head and looked at Zell. "Mandy, wake up now. This is important. You need to go to the hospital, and when you do, you'll need someone to take care of your baby girl. Me and Tom, we're willing to watch over her until you get home, but we'll need you to sign a paper saying it's okay for her to stay with us. If not, Social Services is liable to take her away from you for a while, you being in this kind of condition."

The term, Social Services, seemed to have found its mark and she looked from me to Zell. Putting on my best begging face, I clasped my hands together under my chin. "Pretty please, Momma.

Let me stay with them 'cause Zell cooks real good. Please sign the paper." She nodded her head, not knowing what else to do. Zell told her what to write, and she labored over the words until she finished and put the pen down.

"You be a good girl, Ladybug. I love you."

"Love you too, Momma." Her shoulders were so thin I was afraid they'd break, but I gave her the gentlest hug I knew how to do.

I looked up and Nana Zell was sniffling. She and Papa Tom were both wiping tears away, and I hoped and prayed they wouldn't end up like Momma and cry all the time.

THAT SUMMER IS one I won't ever forget. It was the most carefree time I can remember; a summer of blue skies, good food and a new grandpa that let me follow him around all over the farm. I caught my first fish, ate my first tomato pie, and I've been a fan of both ever since. I'm not sure where they took Momma that time or how long she stayed, but it wasn't close enough for Papa Tom to take me to visit, and it was so long I didn't hardly recognize her when she came home. She had plumped up, as Nana Zell said, and she was smiling. She was on some new medicine, she told us, and felt so much better. It lasted for about a year and during that time she was the best mother in the world. A lawyer from Park Place completed the paperwork for Zell and Tom to be my guardians should anything happen to her, and I know they hoped nothing would because I overheard Zell say when she didn't know I was listening, that Lord knows, she was getting too old to raise another child. She'd already helped raise two of her grandchildren and had babysat all the others until they upped and moved away, but Papa Tom shushed her and told her to see it as a blessing.

I remember one day we were sitting at the breakfast table and Momma shook a pill from her medicine bottle. "This is my last pill and I can't get a refill unless I go back to the doctor. But you know what? I don't need these pills anymore, Ladybug. Me and you are on top of the world!"

I learned quick-like that every time Momma said the words, "on top of the world", we were in for trouble.

CHAPTER THREE

REV ROCK

"Come to me, all you who are weary and burdened, and I will give you rest."

—MATTHEW 11:28

The church history brochure in the narthex of Park Place Presbyterian Church described its architectural features as an eclectic mix of Greek Revival and Romanesque designed by the visionary architect, Julius Bell. The church was completed in 1912 just two blocks off Main Street and was one of two churches built at approximately the same time on what would come to be known as Church Street. A small cottage was built in the 1920s to serve as the manse, the home for the pastor at the time and his family. Nearly seventy years later an old carriage house on the adjoining property was donated to the church and converted to become the church office. A few years after that, a new manse was built with hopes that the young pastor of the growing congregation would marry and have children.

That same pastor, albeit a few years older, was now staring out the picture window of the office at that manse. The object of Rev Rock's attention was an attractive woman in her mid-thirties who happened to be his wife. Liz was seated on the porch in one of the new rockers they had bought at Cracker Barrel. The new porch was a vast improvement over the small token porch that was original to the manse. He'd disliked that porch from the get-go. His friend Cap Price had described it perfectly.

"It's not big enough to cuss a cat on," he'd said, but Rock had never expressed his dissatisfaction to the session, the governing body of the church. Liz had been the catalyst behind getting the new and improved model. If he had asked to have a new one built, he would have surely been met with grumblings from the church leaders like, "why mess with a perfectly good porch?" But when Liz nonchalantly discussed her vision of an ideal front porch with two of the women elders, their reaction was, "Why didn't we think of that? It will add curbside appeal and make the house more pleasing to the eye."

And the best part of all, when those same two elders brought it before session, it was approved faster than a hot knife through butter. Liz could do no wrong in the eyes of his congregation and when he stopped to think about it, in his eyes either. When the work on the porch was completed, she got busy on landscaping. The new magnolias, camellia bushes, and Nellie Stevens holly gave them some much-needed privacy, where before, every car that passed down Church Street had a birds-eye view of the comings and goings at the large brick house.

Liz looked lost in thought sitting out there all alone. Little Matthew was most-likely asleep, or else they'd both be on the playground behind the church, their normal activity before he went down for his afternoon nap.

How different his life would have been if he hadn't come to his senses in his early-forties and married the beautiful Liz Logan, his widowed neighbor, younger than him by almost ten years.

He turned away from the window. Reva, the church secretary, was singing an Elvis tune while making copies of the bulletin for Sunday's service. He walked back to his office and took a quick glance at his calendar. There was nothing penciled in until 3:30. The clock above his desk said 2:55. He would have time to run over and sit with her for a short while. He had counseled many couples over the years and knew spontaneous moments together without the children can help keep marriages alive and sparkling, not that he and Liz had any trouble in that department.

"I'll be back before John and Agatha get here for their appointment," he called out to Reva.

She looked up from the copier. "Okay; if not, those two lovebirds won't mind waiting. It's downright romantic how they found each other again, don't you think?"

"Divine intervention," he said, and he closed the door behind him. Much like his love for Liz had happened.

Liz looked pleased when he walked up the porch steps. She gave him her best dazzling smile when he sat on the chair beside her. "You're home early. Do you have any more appointments?"

"I'm afraid so," he said and reached over to take her hand. "But only one more." He would never grow tired of touching her. She was as beautiful to him as the day he married her. Her warm brown hair and rosy complexion made her appear younger than her thirty-seven years. She complained now and then about not being able to lose the few pounds she'd put on while pregnant with Matthew, but to him, she was perfect. Whatever she had gained represented the love they shared by producing the energetic toddler who was now napping in his room.

"I came over to see why my daydreamer is staring off into space. Is everything okay?"

"Everything's fine. I'm just checking to see if the roses are blooming yet. They're budding, but it'll be a few more days before we have blooms."

She had created an oasis out of an eyesore with the flowers and shrubs she'd chosen. It was almost a mirror image of the front porch of the old manse, the cottage they had lived in when they first married.

"Don't forget to let me know when they're blooming. I'm so busy lately, I'm afraid I'll miss it. But look, all the work you've done has paid off. It makes me wonder why I didn't think of doing this while I was a bachelor instead of moaning and groaning about my ugly front porch?"

She smiled. "You had other things on your mind."

They both knew what those other things had been but didn't voice them. The sudden death of Liz's husband, Ron, a few years earlier, had shaken them both to the core. Ron had been Rock's best friend, and when he died, he and Liz had grieved together as friends. In time, the relationship evolved into more than friendship. Two years after Ron passed away, they had fallen in love and married. Rock had been sure he would always be a bachelor, but God knew different.

"How long has Matt been asleep?"

"Thirty minutes, maybe. The laundry needs doing in the worst way, but I need a short break." She paused, looking up at him. He could tell there was something on her mind, but he would wait until she was ready to share it.

"How are things at school? I imagine it's tough getting back into the guidance counselor routine again."

"It hasn't changed much since Jan replaced me when I left. I'd much rather be home taking care of Matthew, but at least it's only for six weeks."

"I'm sure Jan appreciates you filling in for her while she's on maternity leave. Is she coming back after summer break?"

"She is. She timed having that baby just right—six weeks before the end of the semester, then another ten weeks off for the summer. That gives her about four months to stay home with him."

"Are you ready to tell me why you were staring off into space when I walked up?"

She reached over and held his hand. "My husband has an uncanny ability to pick up on my moods." She smiled at him. "I was thinking about Maisy Martin."

"Should I know this Maisy Martin?"

"She's a student I've been counseling."

"I should have known. You're a sucker for kids, but I guess

that's what makes you good at your job. Just don't get too attached to the job. Matthew and I love having you at home."

"Don't worry! I do love the students though. Maisy is a bright child; so bright that somewhere in elementary school the administration moved her up a grade. Age-wise she should be a freshman instead of a sophomore. She'll turn fifteen in a few weeks. That means she'll be fifteen her junior year and just sixteen her senior year."

"Has she had any social issues with skipping a grade? The kids in her class must be at least a year older."

"They are, but she has a lot of friends. She's a confident kid given her circumstances."

"And what are her circumstances?"

She grinned. "I thought you'd never ask. I'm glad you walked over. The counselor needs a counselor."

"I love being needed," he said, giving her a smile back.

"Her mother is in and out of hospitals with mental health issues and each time she's hospitalized, Maisy stays with the elderly couple who live next door to them. From my conversations with her, I first thought they were her grandparents. She calls them Nana Zell and Papa Tom. They're in their early eighties according to Jan's notes. It must be difficult for them, raising a teenage girl."

"Does she seem well-adjusted?"

"Yes, she seems fidgety and nervous sometimes, but that's not unusual for children who aren't sure of where they'll be staying from one month to the next. I've seen the same characteristics over the years with the kids from the orphanage, and also with the children of the seasonal migrant workers. But she always seems happy. Jan's assessment of her in the file folder is what caused me to take such an interest in her. She said Maisy doesn't see life through any kind of filter. No matter how much it rains on her parade, she always sees the sun shining through. Wouldn't it be nice to see life that way?"

"Nice indeed." He didn't share with her that his own parades kept getting rained completely out lately, or so it seemed. He'd been grumpy and ill and acting much like a kid who'd lost his bag of candy. Just yesterday he'd grumbled out loud when someone had whipped in front of him into the last spot reserved for clergy at the hospital. He'd even thrown up his hands and shouted at the poor guy, but thankfully he didn't see or hear him. Of course, preachers aren't immune to outbursts, but when they lead to thoughts of causing bodily harm to someone, that's another story. He groaned inwardly as he remembered just last week how thoughts of wanting to strangle Brady Singleton had come to mind when the so-called landscaper drove his pickup truck across the church lawn proudly displaying the branches he'd pruned from the crepe myrtles. Pruning, my eye! Butchering was more like it. With what he'd done to those poor trees, they'd be lucky if they lived to bloom another season. He thought of the scripture passage he had used over the years from Corinthians when talking about anger issues. *Love is patient, love is kind. It does not envy, it does not boast, it is not proud. It does not dishonor others, it is not self-seeking, it is not easily angered, it keeps no record of wrongs.* Could he possibly live up to that?

He watched Liz as she continued talking about her student. His wife was compassionate and loving. He doubted seriously she would want to strangle anyone. Unless maybe him if he didn't get his act together. She was about the only person who hadn't got on his nerves lately and watching her now made him smile. She was still talking about her student. Wondering how much he had missed of the conversation, he listened a little more attentively.

"And she's so smart! Did I tell you that?"

He smiled. "You said she was bright"

She went on without missing a beat. "Her IQ score is over the top. Colleges are already recruiting her, even the Ivy League schools. If she keeps this up, she won't have any trouble getting scholarships."

Okay, there wasn't much he'd missed in his musings. He was

back on track now, or so he hoped. It wouldn't do to let her think he hadn't been listening when he was the one who had encouraged her to talk. "That smart, huh? It makes you realize environment isn't everything."

"You know, she has a pretty stable environment despite having an absent father and an oft-absent mother. She has her own bedroom in the Bakers' home and if I were to guess, I'd say she's more at home there than with her mother. And from what she tells me, they are really strict about homework."

"Does she have a good relationship with her mom when she's home?"

"It's a strange relationship, I think. She loves her mom and seems to be very protective of her; it's almost like a role-reversal. She can't depend on her mom taking care of her, but she sees it as her job to take care of her instead."

"What about relatives? Where is her father and her grandparents?"

"Her grandparents on her momma's side are dead. Maisy's dad is out of the picture. On the contact information in her school records, it lists his name, but says, 'do not call'. There are multiple phone numbers and they've all been scratched through. The last known address for him was Texas. He does send money, so she's not going without."

Rock shook his head. "Well, that's rather grand of him, isn't it? So, he pacifies his conscience by sending money."

"That seems to be the extent of it, but Maisy doesn't seem to have any animosity toward him, so apparently her mother doesn't badmouth him."

"That speaks volumes for her character."

"It does. It's so harmful when parents vent their anger to their children about the other parent. It's puts them in an awkward position feeling like they have to choose sides."

"What does Maisy's mom do for a living? I mean, she can't survive on child support, can she?"

"Her mother is an artist, and a good one apparently. She sells through a gallery in Charlotte and if she sells many at the prices they have listed, she's making a pretty good living. Maisy wears nice clothes. No fads or brand names that some of the kids wear, just basic jeans and t-shirts, and they're always clean and neatly pressed."

"So she has no family, no aunts, uncles, cousins? I guess that's possible if neither of her parents had siblings."

"Her grandparents on her father's side are still alive and live in the Old Towne neighborhood out near Granite Cove."

"Really? That's less than thirty minutes away. Why doesn't she stay with them when her mom's gone?"

"That's just it. Maisy says they'll have nothing to do with her or her mother and have refused any contact with them since her dad left. I just don't get it. She's just a child and their only grandchild. How could they do that? None of this is Maisy's fault."

"That's a tough question. Maybe there's more to it than you know, or maybe their hearts have become hardened. Things like that are beyond our scope of understanding, Liz."

"Her biggest concern is that something will happen to the Bakers."

Rock had been relieved when Liz retired. Her worst habit was letting the students' problems become her own. Gifted with a double dose of empathy, she would get frustrated when she couldn't do anything about their circumstances.

He held his hand out and she took it. "Do you ever see a problem that you don't want to fix, my sweet wife? I can see it in your eyes: you're chomping at the bit to help this child, aren't you?"

She laughed. "I've seen quite a few that I don't want to fix. If it involves adults, I'll leave those for you to fix. All school counselors feel the burdens of the students we work with. Yes, I do want to help Maisy, but I don't know how. I'm wondering if God led me to accept this assignment at school just because of her."

"He has a habit of doing things like that, doesn't He?"

"He does seem to give us more than our share."

"Maybe it's because we never say no. I'm just as guilty as you are. If you haven't noticed, I've been doing my fair share of sticking my nose into things that aren't any of my business and trying to fix things that don't need to be fixed at all."

"Really? Not you!"

He grinned sheepishly. "And as you know, it's nearly gotten me into trouble a time or two."

"I can't argue with that. And maybe that's what I'm doing."

"Not at all. Sometimes I think your heart is more attuned to God's calling than my own."

"I don't plan to get involved, Rock. I'm just concerned. Right now she needs someone to talk to. It's hard to talk about your mom's mental illness with your friends, and Mr. and Mrs. Baker tiptoe around it trying to protect her feelings, I'm sure. But she's at the age where she needs some stability in her life, and I hope she'll trust me enough to let me help."

Rock watched as a gray SUV pulled into the parking lot of the church office. "There's Agatha and John. They're early." He got up from his chair. "Whatever you do, Liz, I know it will be the right thing." He reached down and kissed her.

"Tell them to come back later," she said, with a mischievous smile. "We still have about an hour before Matt wakes up."

"Hmm, that sounds awfully tempting. I'll hurry them along."

"Go on and do your job, silly man. I'll take a raincheck. I love you!"

"I love you back," he said, breaking away begrudgingly, not wanting to leave her. There was nothing he'd rather do than spend the rest of the afternoon with her.

"Tell them I said hello."

"I will."

As he lumbered down the stairs he remembered her words, "I

don't plan to get involved", and he wondered what God's plan would be.

Agatha and John had seen him from the parking lot and waved. They got out of their car and were waiting for him to join them. He gave one last glance back at Liz. She blew him a kiss. It took every bit of his willpower to keep from turning around. The demands of his growing congregation were making it harder and harder to spend time with his family. It was a good problem to have. Many churches were experiencing dwindling church membership, but Park Place Presbyterian was an exception. They were at a point where an associate pastor was needed, but the budget didn't support hiring one.

He hadn't yet told Liz about his growing discontent. He sighed. He should ask for more help from the church leadership, but he balked at asking for help. He was a multi-tasker, happy in his ability to handle every little detail, but the increase in membership had brought couples with problems—marital problems, divorce, custody battles. It broke his heart to see those things happen and to have to counsel people he wasn't sure he was reaching.

But enough of that. Here in front of him was a couple he would find pleasure in counseling. They had known grief in the loss of their spouses, never dreaming they would find happiness again. Here they were, giddy with the feelings of love they now had for each other. Love is a marvelous thing, he thought, and once again thanked God for bringing Liz into his life. If only he could stay focused on the happy endings.

CHAPTER FOUR

MAISY

"Create in me a clean heart, O God, and renew a steadfast spirit within me."

—PSALM 51:10

Was it my imagination, or was Papa Tom breathing a little heavier as we were walking up the steps to church? We were running late because he had been slower getting ready this morning. Nana Zell hadn't even tried to hurry him, quite a change from her usual Sunday morning routine.

"Somebody needs to light a fire under your britches," she'd usually say at least three times to me or to Papa Tom while we dawdled around getting ready. Papa would just wink at me and grin. This morning all she'd said was, "I'm making an appointment for you with Dr. Walters this week. That cold you've had is lingering around too long. If you want to stay home from church and rest this morning, I'll get Glennis Mackey to drive by for me and Maisy. She won't mind."

He shook his head and answered. "I'll be fine, Zell, once I get going. Coughing all night took the wind out of my sails but Reverend Thather's sermon this morning will put it back in."

"I wish you would'a let me fix you some whiskey and hard candy syrup last night to help you sleep."

He laughed. "I can see it now; me coming into Sunday morning service with whiskey on my breath. Fine example I'd be to those young boys who stay out on Saturday night partying and imbibing of the spirits. The only spirit I'm going to allow inside me is the Holy Spirit Himself. He won't make you fuddle-minded like those other spirits will."

He looked at me as I sat on the side of his bed waiting for him to get his Sunday hat out of the closet. "Don't let nothing ever fuddle your mind, Baby Girl. You've got a fine, sharp mind and it's going to get you somewhere. Keep that Holy Spirit alive inside you and when those temptations come along, you can call on Him to get you out of any kind of mess. Will you promise me that?"

"Yes sir, Papa Tom," I promised. If the old man had asked me to promise him to reach up and grab him a star, I would have done it or died trying. My heart swelled with love for him as I watched him settle his hat just in the right spot on his head and then fold the brim slightly down over his left eye. He had been a father, a grandfather and a friend to me ever since the day we met. Sometimes I wonder what would've become of me if he hadn't found me stealing tomatoes out of his garden that day. I would have been tossed around from one foster home to another.

It's hard not to let the Holy Spirit get inside you at Baker's Chapel. Papa Tom's family had donated the land for the church back in the 1960s, and it was a pretty little spot for a church. It sat amidst a grove of old oak trees; old as Methuselah, I'd heard someone say. The Holy Spirit flows down the aisles and spills out the front door of that place, and the preacher shouts it loud and clear.

We took our seats in our usual pew. All around me were the people who had made me feel right at home from the first day I was pulled by my skinny arm down the aisle by Nana Zell. No one had seemed to notice I was the only white person in the church, and if they did, they didn't make any to-do over it. They had all been like family to me, and believe me, I needed some family since

I didn't have anyone except a momma who most everyone said was "crazy as a bat".

Right away, I spotted some of the boys Papa Tom had been talking about their drinking. Jeremy Martin and Little Rick Hawkins had got in with the wrong crowd at school and had caused their parents a heap of grief according to Zell. Little Rick had even been to jail once for possession of marijuana, and Jeremy, who had been riding in the car with him, had somehow weaseled his way out of being charged. This morning, though, they seemed to be caught up in Reverend Thatcher's sermon. He had a way with boys that age, Papa said.

Jeremy's sister, Sabrina, was my best friend, and she said the threat of jail had straightened him out. For their momma and daddy's sake, I hoped so. The whole family was sitting together in their usual pew. Sabrina saw me looking their way and smiled. We gave each other our normal finger wave so as not to attract attention. Sabrina says Reverend Thatcher has eagle eyes, but I think it has something to do with how tall he is. Even when I duck down behind Ira Parker who sits on the pew directly in front of me, he can see right over him. I've always tried to behave though, because I wouldn't want him upsetting Zell by giving her a scolding for not keeping an eye on me. She has enough on her mind as it is.

I must have been daydreaming because the next thing I realized, Sister Charlene Smith was announcing for us to sing from page 586 in the hymnal, *Swing Low*. Papa Tom looked at me sideways and gave me a thumbs-up. It was his favorite hymn, and our choir started it and we all rolled along with it until it felt like the roof was raising up high in the sky.

Swing low, sweet chariot,
Coming for to carry me home.
Swing low, sweet chariot,
Coming for to carry me home.

I looked over Jordan and what did I see?
Coming for to carry me home.
A band of angels coming after me,
Coming for to carry me home.

If you get there before I do
Coming for to carry me home
Tell all my friends I'm coming, too
Coming for to carry me home

I'm sometimes up and sometimes down
Coming for to carry me home
But still my soul feels heavenly bound
Coming for to carry me home

The brightest day that I can say
Coming for to carry me home
When Jesus washed my sins away
Coming for to Carry me home

Swing low, sweet chariot
Coming for to carry me home
Swing low, sweet chariot
Coming for to carry me home

There was a lot of swaying and a few Amens while we were singing. It's one of those songs that will either make you happy or make you sad. It brought a few tears to my eyes and to Papa's too. I wondered about my momma and what was the brightest day she'd ever seen? Had she ever had her sins washed away?

I remembered distinctly the day mine were washed away. It was when I was eleven and Momma had pulled one of her tricks again by not taking her medicine. I told Reverend Thatcher I didn't know what I believed. Would a real God keep making my momma sick when all she ever really wanted was to be well and happy? I thought he'd fuss at me for complaining about God, but all he'd said was, "Maisy, it's okay to question God and I've done it myself, but my prayer for you is that one day the Holy Spirit will come into your heart in such a powerful way that you'll have no choice but to believe. Every core of your being will believe and when that happens you'll need to feed that Spirit so it'll make you hungry for more. Because there's a hunger and thirst when you let Him come into your life that can only be fed by His Word. And that Word, Maisy, comes straight from the Bible. That will be my prayer for you. Believing won't solve all your troubles, girl, but it'll lighten your load and sometimes that's all you need."

He talked to me a long time; he prayed with me and gave me some Bible verses to read and study. In the past, the Bible had seemed like a huge chunk of words all scrambled together, but having the verses handpicked to answer my questions made them personal, just for me.

The next Sunday, I came up to the baptismal pool and asked to be dunked under. There was a lot of shouting of Hallelujah that day. It would have been best though if it hadn't been the coldest day in January that I got the urge to be baptized because that water hadn't been warmed up and I caught a cold that took me two weeks to get over.

~

I HADN'T SEEN Momma in almost two months and I was getting homesick for her. Papa said his eyes were getting too old to drive on the interstate and Nana Zell didn't have a driver's license and never had. I wondered if it would be too bold for me to ask Mrs. Clark, the guidance counselor to take me to see her. There was something about Mrs. Clark— something strong and protective that made me want to smile, and I found myself wondering what it would be like to have someone like her as a mother.

Just the week before Mrs. Clark had told me it was okay to ask for help and not to bottle things up inside me. Surely, needing to see my momma was enough reason to ask for help, wasn't it? I would do it on Monday morning. Maybe I could get to her office before homeroom started.

Zell elbowed me in the ribs. Everyone but the two of us were standing up with their hymnals. Zell was prone to keep her seat most of the time because of her bum knees, but I was expected to stand up, and I did. Papa held out his hymnal so we could share. Annie Robinson started in on the piano and we both started singing. Papa's alto started off strong and I was trying to sing louder than Bessie Hawkins behind me, but there was no competition. She sings louder than Barney Fife on a good day.

O they tell me of a home far beyond the skies,
O they tell me of a home far away;
O they tell me of a home where no storm clouds rise;
O they tell me of an uncloudy day.

By the end of the second chorus, Papa's alto had run out of steam.

PAPA TOM HAD KEPT all of us awake with his coughing on Sunday night until sometime over in the morning when Zell convinced him to let her mix up the whiskey and hard candy. He finally went to sleep, and when my alarm clock went off at 6, I had a heck of a time getting out of bed.

"Just let me sleep, please; I don't feel so good," I told Zell when she came in to check on me. But when I took one look at her tired and worried face, I hopped out of bed quick-like to keep her from having to yell at me.

"Don't worry about breakfast," I said. "I'll eat a bowl of cereal after I get dressed." She nodded and just stared off into space, which wasn't like her at all.

"Are you okay, Nana Zell?" She seemed to snap back from what she was worrying over and told me she was fine.

"I'll be making your Papa a doctor appointment this morning. Reverend Thatcher said he would take us. Say a prayer for him, Baby Girl."

"I will," I said, and for the first time I was worried myself. If the truth be told, I was always a tad worried about both of them. Papa had turned eighty-three in December and Nana wasn't far behind. And where would I stay if anything happened to them? I tried not to think about it, because when I did, it made me cry.

I ate my cereal and went out to wait for the bus. Sitting alone in the little shelter Papa had built for rainy days, I prayed like never before. The bus had to blow its horn to get my attention. Mr. Nelson, the bus driver, must have thought I was asleep. He'd be about half right, because somewhere between the prayer and the bus coming, my lack of sleep must have crept up on me and I dozed off.

Mrs. Clark was in her office when I walked by on my way to homeroom, so I stopped for a minute and waited at the door. She looked up. "Come on in, Maisy."

"Can I ask you something, Mrs. Clark?" My boldness was slipping a little, but she smiled, and I felt a whole lot better.

"Of course. Feel free to ask me anything."

I was getting my courage back after seeing her smile. "Well, there are two things actually. Will you pray for my Papa Tom? He's sick and going to the doctor today."

"I'm so sorry. Of course, I'll pray. Is it something serious?"

"It's a cold, I think, but Nana Zell is worried to death about him, so there must be something more to it." I paused to build up my boldness. "And another thing: I don't have anyone who can drive me to see my momma down at the hospital in Columbia." All of a sudden, I was at a loss for words. What would Mrs. Clark think of me asking her to drive me to the hospital when I'd only known her for three weeks?

"Maisy, I'll be glad to take you to visit your mom. Saturday would be good for me, but I'll need permission from our principal and your Nana Zell. That is, if you don't mind me taking you. You may have someone else you'd rather ask."

I breathed a sigh of relief and lifted my head up to the ceiling. "Thank you, Jesus." Then I directed my gaze to her. "And thank you, Mrs. Clark. You were the one I wanted to take me, but I didn't know how to ask."

She laughed. "Well, I think you did a pretty good job of it. I'll let you know what I can work out. Are you free this Saturday if we can get it all settled before then?"

It was my turn to laugh. "I'm always free on Saturdays. There's nothing to do in Baker's Grove."

During fourth period, the office called me out of my science class and told me to go to the guidance counselor's office. Figuring Mrs. Clark must have already arranged everything, I bounced into her office, but the minute I saw her face, I knew something was wrong.

She got up from behind her desk and closed the door behind me. "Maisy sit down for a minute if you will."

I sat on the padded blue chair. It had a small tear on the armrest; I had noticed it that morning. She sat on the other chair right beside me instead of going behind her desk. She crossed her hands in her lap and looked worried.

"Maisy, your preacher, Reverend Thatcher just called and talked to me. They admitted your Papa Tom to the hospital after his doctor appointment. He has pneumonia. Mrs. Mackey, one of your neighbors, is coming by to pick you up from school in a few minutes. Your Papa Tom is asking for you."

It felt like a dam was ready to burst out of my eye sockets, so I squeezed them shut, hoping I wouldn't cry. But when I opened them and looked up at Mrs. Clark, all I could see was someone who cared about me and how I was feeling, so I let the tears flow. "Will he be alright?" I asked between my sniffling.

Instead of glossing things over, she answered me honestly. "I don't know, Maisy. He's in intensive care. It's not considered appropriate for a school staff member to push prayer on a student, but since you asked me this morning to pray for him, we'll sit here right now and pray together if it's alright with you."

I nodded. "Can I start the prayer?" I asked, wanting to get it off the ground quickly and let God start doing His work.

"Please do." We bowed our heads.

"God, I know you're sitting up there on your throne with Jesus, but I need you to take some action on behalf of my Papa. You know him; his name is Tom Baker. He sits in Baker's Chapel every Sunday morning on the third row to the left if you're standing in the pulpit. You can't miss him; he's the one with the big smile and his favorite song is Swing Low, Sweet Chariot. He sings it loud and clear, but a little off-key. But don't mistake his liking that song to him actually wanting to go home to be with you and Jesus. He's just fine down here with me and Zell and I don't much know what I'd do without him."

"And Zell—she's your good friend, Lord. All these years she's been singing, What A Friend I have in Jesus and she means it too. She's never used your name in vain that I've heard of and she'd be lost without Papa Tom. I think she would just want to lay down and die without him. Please God. I've never asked you for anything in my life except to make my momma well, and since you haven't done that, would you please do me this one favor and fix whatever's wrong with Papa? Me and Zell, we really need him bad. Well, that's all for right now. I know you can do it. I've got someone else here with me that wants to talk to you too. Please listen to her, God. Amen."

I looked up to tell Mrs. Clark it was time for her to start but she was crying straight out. I wondered if she knew Papa Tom the way she was wiping her eyes with a tissue. She sniffed and blew her nose and started praying.

"Lord, in Heaven, you've heard this child's pleas, and I honestly can't say it any better than she can, but I ask for you to heal Tom Baker. Give him strength to get through this illness so he can come back home to those who love and depend upon him. We ask this in the name of your Son, Jesus Christ. Amen."

As soon as she said Amen, there was a knock on the door. It was Glennis Mackey and her husband, Joe. They spoke to Mrs. Clark and thanked her for praying with me.

"Maisy, I'll come by the hospital for a few minutes when I get off work," she said.

It was what I'd hoped for but hadn't asked. I was beginning to think she could read my mind.

CHAPTER FIVE

LIZ

"Love one another with brotherly affection. Outdo one another in showing honor."

—ROMANS 12:10

"I really need to do this, Rock; she wants me to be there and I don't want to disappoint her. When you pick up Matthew at Holly's, y'all go ahead and eat. There's leftover roast with carrots and potatoes in the fridge that you can reheat. Matthew can eat it if you cut everything up in small pieces."

Liz listened to her husband's response on the other end of the line.

"Yes, I'll be fine. I'll eat an apple on the way. Thank you; you're the best! I'll let them know you'll be praying too. Love you."

Liz hung up the phone and started to turn off her computer but then decided to check her email one last time to see if the principal had given her an answer. She knew it could go either way; an administrator had to be careful when making decisions about student / teacher activities away from school grounds, especially when it was a one-on-one situation. When her mail came up, she saw she had a message from him and opened it up to read it.

Liz, you won't need my permission since you're a substitute and not under contract. Just handle it with the Bakers. Lillian told me in the office that Mr. Baker was hospitalized today. I pray for a good outcome. Maisy will be devastated if anything happens to him.

Thank you for all you're doing, Liz. I'm glad to have you here, even if it is only for a short while.

*Sincerely,
Scott Williams*

She shut down the computer. That's a relief, she thought, and walked out the door, locking it behind her.

THE WAITING ROOM for ICU was empty except for Maisy and she was curled up on the small loveseat at the far end of the room with her back to the door and a book in her lap. Liz at first thought she was asleep, but then smiled as she realized she was so engrossed in her Social Studies book that she hadn't even noticed someone had walked in. She watched as she pushed a stray strand of hair behind her ear, but it immediately fell right back over her eye. Taking a deep breath of air, she promptly blew it away from her face again. When that failed to do the job, she reached in her book bag and came out with a rubber band. Pulling her long hair away from her face, she managed to get it into a messy ponytail.

Liz cleared her throat and Maisy turned her head toward the sound. Her eyes widened, and a smile lit up her face when she saw Liz.

"Mrs. Clark, you came!"

"I promised you I would." She walked over and sat beside her on the loveseat. "How's Mr. Baker?"

"He's pretty sick. He didn't recognize me when I first went

back to see him, but I got up close to him and said, 'Papa Tom, it's me, Maisy.' Then he perked up and said, 'Come here, Baby Girl.' The nurse said that was a good sign."

"That's good news," Liz said, and hoped it really was.

Despite the spark of hope from the nurse, Maisy looked worried. "He will get better, won't he, Mrs. Clark?"

Liz didn't know what to say. "If the nurse said that's a good sign, then it is. We'll just keep praying. That's all we can do for now. The healing part is in God's hands."

The door opened again, and Liz felt, rather than saw, a larger-than-life presence fill the room. She turned around. No wonder the room suddenly felt crowded. The man standing there must be at least seven feet tall, she thought, as her eyes traveled up toward the ceiling. Then she located a pair of dark brown eyes that crinkled around the corners. The eyes were below a perfectly domed and hairless head and glanced from her over to the loveseat where Maisy was sitting. Maisy jumped up from her seat.

"Reverend Thatcher!" she said. "I'm so glad you're here. Nana Zell said you'd be back." She looked at Liz and remembered her manners.

"Mrs. Clark, this is our preacher."

Liz reached out to shake his hand and he reciprocated. "It's nice to meet you, Reverend Thatcher. I'm Liz Clark, the substitute guidance counselor at Maisy's school."

"Ah, I've heard of you, Mrs. Clark. You were at the school before you married as I remember. Your name was Mrs. Logan back then, I believe."

Liz was surprised that he had heard of her. "Yes, I was. But it's been almost three years since I was there," she said, trailing off, not knowing how he knew her.

He laughed, making her feel more at ease. "I'm not a stalker, Mrs. Clark. I do a lot of counseling myself in my role as a minister to our high school students, and I remember you gained the trust and built good relationships with many of the young people in our church—boys and girls alike. You've made more of an impression in their lives than you could ever imagine. Hormones rage in those teen years and finding someone to listen and gently guide without being judgmental is a rare gift that God gives a chosen few. And from what I've heard, He gave it to you in abundance." He looked back at Maisy. "And it seems you've made another friend. I'm glad."

Liz was stunned at his compliments, but seeing that he was sincere, she accepted them graciously by simply nodding. "I'm always glad to hear success stories," she said. "I have a little boy now, so I made the decision to stay home to raise him, but when our principal, Mr. Williams, asked me to take this assignment for a couple of months, I did." She looked at Maisy affectionately. "And I'm pretty sure He had a hand in it."

"No doubt," he said. "Is there any news about your Papa, Maisy? Did you get to see him?"

"I sure did, but Nana Zell's been in there a long time now. Do you think they'll let you go back and see how he's doing? I'm afraid she's going to get tired."

"I'll go back right now, Maisy, and I'll send her back in here to give you a report and to rest up some." He turned back to Liz. "If I don't see you when I come back, I want to thank you for what you're doing for Maisy." He shook her hand again and walked out of the room.

In a few minutes, a worn-out Zell Baker walked into the waiting room, and Maisy ran to greet her. She smiled when she saw Maisy, and Liz could see the love she had for the child in her hazel eyes.

"He's doing some better, Baby Girl. His breathing is a little easier. I've just got me a feeling inside he's going to be okay."

"Thank goodness!" Maisy's eyes drifted to Liz. "See, Mrs. Clark. Our prayers worked, didn't they?"

"They did indeed."

The same brown eyes that shone with love for Maisy had a

look of relief when Zell Baker spotted Liz. "So you're the Mrs. Clark that Maisy's been talking about. She told me she'd asked you about taking her to see her momma, and I'm sorry she burdened you with that. The child doesn't think sometimes."

"It's not a burden, Mrs. Baker. It's my pleasure to take her if you'll allow it. It was my suggestion in the first place." She winked at Maisy, and she beamed. "So long as everything goes well with Mr. Baker, she and I can go to Columbia this weekend."

Zell nodded her head. "That would be right kind of you."

Liz could see the exhaustion on the older woman's face. Her shoulders seemed to carry a load that was more than she could bear. Before she could stop and think, the words just flew out of her mouth. "Mrs. Baker, I could take Maisy home with me for the next few days and you could concentrate on getting your husband well. We have an extra bedroom and it won't be any problem at all."

Maisy jumped up, holding her hands together in front of her and looked pleadingly at Zell. "Oh, please, Nana Zell! That'll be one less thing for you to worry about." She turned to look at Liz. "But do you think you could bring me to the hospital if he gets worse?"

"Of course," said Liz. She turned to Zell. "My husband is the pastor at Park Place Presbyterian. I'm sure he'd be glad to bring Maisy by when she wants to visit Mr. Baker. One of our church members is having surgery here this week anyway, so it won't be at all out of the way."

Zell looked at Liz wearily. "I'd be much obliged to you, Mrs. Clark. It would sure take a load off my mind. I'll rest better in my bed tonight. If you don't mind taking me home, Maisy will need some school clothes, and we'll pack her a suitcase. Reverend Thatcher said he'll come by to pick me up in the morning and bring me back to the hospital."

"Can I go see Papa Tom one more time before we go?"

"Go ahead and scoot in there, Baby Girl. Papa will have my

hide if I let you get out of here without him getting to say goodnight. I'll be right behind you. Then we'll go right quick-like so Mrs. Baker can get home to her family."

The two of them went out of the waiting room, leaving Liz behind. "What have I done?" she said out loud to an empty room. She was startled when the empty room seemed to answer, *"Let each of us please his neighbor for his good, to build him up."* She recognized it from Romans 15:2. If anybody needed building up, it was Mrs. Baker. She could see the worry etched across her face. Rock would understand.

CHAPTER SIX

MAISY

"But the fruit of the Spirit is love, joy, peace, patience, kindness, goodness, faithfulness."

—GALATIANS 5:22

I'd never been in a house with an upstairs before, unless you counted the pull-down ladder in our house that goes up to the attic. It would be fun to run up and down them, but I thought I'd be wearing my welcome thin if I did, especially since it was 8:30 by the time we got to Mrs. Clark's house, and their baby was asleep. She showed me to my bedroom and what a room it was! The closet was almost as big as my bedroom at home and when she hung up my few school clothes, they looked lost in there.

"There are clean washcloths and towels in the bathroom and a new toothbrush and toothpaste in one of the vanity drawers," she said.

"I brought my own toothpaste and toothbrush. I'll go back downstairs to the bathroom and brush my teeth, then come right back up, if that's alright."

"You don't have to go to the bathroom downstairs, Maisy. There's one up here. Well, really there are two up here, but you'll want to use the one across the hall. It's closer."

"You have three bathrooms in your house when there's only the two of you and a baby?"

"It does seem a little excessive, doesn't it? The house has three full baths and a half-bath." She looked a little embarrassed like she was apologizing for her big house. "But that's the way they built it, with plenty of room for a big family. When Matthew gets older, his bedroom will be up here, but for now we have plenty of room for guests as you can see." She smiled. "And we're glad to have you as a guest for the next few days."

"Thank you for inviting me, Mrs. Clark. I'll brush my teeth and get ready for bed. I've got some reading to do for Social Studies."

"I'll leave you alone then. There's an alarm clock on the nightstand. We'll need to leave here for school by 8 a.m. so you can set it accordingly. What do you like to eat for breakfast?"

"Oh, anything's fine with me. Well, maybe not anything—Nana Zell's been known to cook parts of a pig that I don't even want to know about."

Mrs. Clark laughed, and at that very moment, I decided I wanted to learn to laugh just like her. It was almost a melody, like wind chimes set off by a burst of a breeze on a clear summer day.

"I don't think I want to know about them either, Maisy. My husband cooks breakfast, so I'll tell him to surprise us; just no unexpected pig parts." She laughed again and this time I laughed the way she did. Maybe I could practice it. Her smile too, I liked her smile.

I took a shower and put on my pajamas, then brushed my teeth, all the while scrutinizing my smile in the mirror. I had good teeth and I took care of them. Momma had taught me early to brush twice a day and to floss at night, saying we couldn't afford big dental bills. I'd never had a single cavity. I'd only been to the dentist twice that I could remember, and the last time he'd told Momma my teeth were "overcrowded", and I might need braces. She'd started worrying about it right away, and to keep her from getting into a tizzy, I told her I didn't mind if my teeth were a little crooked, and I didn't. Besides, I thought, as I examined them in the mirror, there was just one little overlapped tooth and you couldn't even tell it unless I grinned real big which I wasn't prone to do anyway. I smiled at myself in the mirror to see if it was anything like Mrs. Clark's smile. It wasn't, and the more I tried, the more fake it looked, so I decided to just smile like me; it looked more natural. I'd practice the laugh later.

I did most of my reading in bed, so I took my Social Studies book out of my book bag and hopped upon the big four-poster bed, bouncing up and down to check it out. It was the softest bed I'd ever been on. My bed at Nana Zell's had seen better days. It was a little saggy in the middle and it never failed that no matter what side I started out on, by the next morning I was right slap in the middle. But it suited me just fine.

As I looked around at the unfamiliar room, I figured I'd never get to sleep. Propping myself up on all the pillows on the bed, I said my prayers. The main topic of my conversation with God was Papa Tom. When I finished, I picked up my book, but I was yawning after the first page. The next thing I knew, the alarm clock was buzzing, and I woke up with a start. My book was poking me in the ribs, I was still on the same side of the bed I started out on, and there was a huge gray cat staring me in the face.

"Where did you come from, big boy?"

He was sitting on my chest and when I spoke to him, he purred and rubbed his big head up against my face. When I got up, he got up with me and ran in and out of my legs as I made my way to the bathroom, meowing with each step. He watched every move I made while I was getting dressed.

"So much for privacy," I said, picking up my book bag and walking down the stairs. The sweet smells of breakfast wafting up the stairwell made me step a little faster and I realized I was hungry as a bear.

I could hear baby laughter before I rounded the corner of the kitchen and it made me feel happy in a way I didn't expect. I'd always wanted a baby brother or sister, I guess because I didn't want to face all our family craziness by myself, but as things turned out, it was best that my parents had stopped with just me. It was enough trouble taking care of myself much less having a baby around. But this one was different. He had happy parents who loved him.

I'm not saying that Momma doesn't love me; she does. When she's well, she makes me laugh too, but I'm not sure I've ever known a time I've laughed with such carefree abandon as little Matthew was doing, and I understood why as soon as I walked in the door. His daddy was sitting in the chair opposite his high chair waving a fork around in the air. He would put it up to Matthew's mouth, then jerk it away just as soon as the baby opened up his mouth like a little bird. Then Mr. Clark would pretend to eat the food, saying, "gobble, gobble, gobble," which would set off another round of laughter. Neither of them heard me come in, but finally Matthew looked up and saw me. "Look, Dada!" he said, pointing to where I was standing.

Mr. Clark turned around. "Good morning, Maisy. Come on in and have a seat at the table. You caught me trying to gobble up Matthew's breakfast. He took a notion he didn't want pancakes this morning, so I was trying to convince him otherwise. He's perfectly capable of eating by himself, but he loves this game."

Mr. Clark loved playing the game as much as Matthew from the way he was acting. "Thank you," I said, and sat down at the table. "It looks like it worked," I said, pointing to the little boy. He was picking up the pieces of pancake with his fingers and putting them in his mouth like there was no tomorrow. The big gray cat was underneath the high chair ready to catch any food that fell his way.

He laughed. "This boy loves a little drama to start off his mornings." He walked to the refrigerator. "Would you like milk, orange juice, or both?"

"Milk, please."

"Pancakes and bacon are warming in the oven. I'll get them after I pour your milk."

I jumped up from my seat. "Oh, I don't mind getting them myself," I said. I grabbed a potholder from a peg on the wall and walked over to the oven.

"Ah, but you're our guest," he said, setting my milk glass on the table beside my plate.

"Nana Zell says I need to carry my weight in the kitchen and not to expect anyone to wait on me hand and foot," I said, laughing at his puzzled expression.

"And I would say Nana Zell has taught you well. You can help in my kitchen anytime." I wanted to say Mrs. Clark had taught him well seeing as how he was cooking breakfast and feeding the baby, but I didn't want to get off to a bad start, so I just took two pancakes and a piece of bacon off the warm platter and put them on my plate. Mr. Clark poured two cups of coffee and set one at his plate and the other at Mrs. Clarks, and as if on cue, she walked into the kitchen.

"Looks like I'm just in time," she said. "Good morning, Maisy. Did you rest well last night?"

"Yes, Ma'am, I slept like a rock."

"You're in good company. Someone else in the house sleeps like a rock every night." She looked up at Mr. Clark and laughed. I wasn't sure what the joke was between them, but Mr. Clark rolled his eyes and looked at me.

"She's referring to me, Maisy. In case she hasn't told you, my name is Rock, and I have to endure things like this all the time."

Mrs. Clark walked over and gave him a great big kiss and he kissed her back. It was a sweet look that passed between them, and I wondered what Momma's life would have been like if Daddy had stayed and treated her like that. Little Matthew bounced in his high chair wanting attention. "He's always jealous when we kiss," Mrs. Clark explained, pulling away. "He requires a kiss from both of us before he calms down." She leaned over and kissed him on the cheek. "Ooh, what a sticky little face you have!"

Mr. Clark picked him up from the highchair. "Come on big

boy; you and I have an appointment with a washcloth and a toothbrush. You two go ahead and eat before it gets cold. Matthew and I have already eaten."

She looked at him warmly. "Thank you for everything, Rock. Now let's bless this food, Maisy. I'm famished!"

Thinking she meant for me to bless it, I bowed my head and prayed. "Bless this food to our bodies, Lord, and thank You for the hands that prepared it. Lord, bless the food my Momma will eat this morning, because she'll forget to ask you when I'm not around. Bless Papa Tom and Zell, and please make him well again. We love You and praise you in the name of Jesus, Amen."

"Amen". It was a quiet amen and a tender look that Mrs. Clark gave me, and I felt guilty wishing I could get a look like that from my own momma more often.

IT WAS nice riding back and forth to school with Mrs. Clark. She had to work late each afternoon, so I stayed in the library and did my homework. We'd go by the neighbor's house and pick up Matthew on the way home, and that little boy won my heart. We played on the floor while his mom and dad fixed dinner together, and I loved hearing him squeal with laughter. The poor cat, whose name was Theo did his best to stay out of sight, but it was almost impossible to escape when Matthew was on a mission, and that mission was pulling his tail to make him meow. Theo would jump straight up in the air every time and go skulking off like a 'possum.

IT WAS a few days before I got to see Papa Tom again, but each time I talked to Zell on the phone, she told me he was getting better. After dinner Thursday night, Mr. Clark took me to the hospital. He got off on the second floor to see one of his church members and I rode the elevator on up to the third to Intensive Care. Zell wasn't in the waiting room, so I walked on down the hall to the room and peeked inside. There was a woman lying in the bed right where Papa Tom had been. In a panic, I ran back to the nurses' station.

"Where's Mr. Tom Baker?" My heart was pounding.

"Honey don't worry; they moved him to a regular room this afternoon."

"Why did they move him?"

"Because he's so much better." She smiled. "He's on the second floor in Room 223. You can go on down to see him."

"You better believe it," I said, and ran back to the elevator.

He was sitting up in bed pretty as you please when I ran into Room 223, and I made a dash to his bedside. He grinned when he saw me. "Laud Sakes, Baby Girl. You're a sight for sore eyes."

"You too, Papa. I've missed you!" I wrapped my arms around him and I noticed that it didn't take as much to wrap as it usually did. He'd lost weight, but he felt like an oasis in the middle of the desert to me. The sweet earthy fragrance of my papa was gone, replaced by disinfectant and talcum powder, but it wouldn't be long before he'd be working his garden again. I just knew it, but to be on the safe side, I said a silent prayer as I told him how much I loved him.

I heard a noise and turned to find Nana Zell shuffling through the door, followed by Reverend Thatcher. Her face lit up at the sight of me. She wasn't much to show her emotions, but there was never any doubt in my mind that she cared about me. I jumped up and hugged her and she wrapped her arms around me. "It's lonesome around that house with you and Pap both gone, Child. Are you behaving yourself with the Clarks?"

"Yes, Ma'am."

"I can attest to that." The voice came from the doorway and we all turned around. "And our little boy is totally smitten with her." It was Mr. Clark. He walked into the already crowded room and reached out to shake Zell's hand. She took it and smiled adoringly at him. He seemed to have that effect on women, or at least with Zell and Mrs. Clark. Then he shook hands with Papa Tom who welcomed him in the room.

Reverend Thatcher shook his hand next. "Rock, it's good to see you again. I met your wife earlier in the week. You waited long enough to marry, but you got you a good woman there."

"Wait for the LORD; be strong and take heart and wait for the LORD." Mr. Clark said, smiling. "Psalm 27:14."

Reverend Thatcher returned his smile and threw a Bible verse out there himself. "I wait for the LORD, my soul does wait, and in his word do I hope. Psalm 130:5."

"Yet the LORD longs to be gracious to you; therefore, he will rise up to show you compassion. For the LORD is a God of justice. Blessed are all who wait for him!"

I watched as they had fun bantering back and forth quoting scripture about the wisdom of waiting. I'd memorized a few verses since I'd become more personal with my Bible but couldn't for the life of me just pull them up on a moment's notice like they were doing.

"Rev Rock and I go way back," Reverend Thatcher told Papa Tom. "He was the first pastor who welcomed me to Park Place when I came from New Jersey to preach at Baker's Chapel. We bumped into each other at the feed and seed store while I was looking for a mouse trap for the church office. He told me the mice grew big in this part of the world and I should get a rat trap instead. Standing at the counter with that huge trap, I wondered what I'd got myself into by moving to the South. Then he comes running up behind me, takes it out of my hand and replaces it with the mouse trap. He was laughing the whole time because he knew I had fallen for it. Then he took money out of his wallet to pay for it and since it wasn't much more than a dollar, I let him. Served him right."

"If I recall, you've got me back three times over."

"I won't deny I've played a few jokes at your expense, Reverend."

I'd not been calling Mr. Clark reverend, like I had my own preacher. I hoped he wasn't insulted, but he didn't seem the type to worry over things like that. But I hadn't come to watch preachers rattle on. My main focus was Papa Tom, so I went back and sat on his bed. "When will you get to go home, Papa?"

"I wish it could be tomorrow, but they'll probably keep me another week." He looked over at Zell. "Isn't that what the doctor said this morning, Zell?"

"That's what he said, Tom. As long as your old ticker doesn't act up again."

I looked from one to the other of them and wondered what they were hiding. As usual, I just asked, point blank. "Is something wrong with your heart?"

Papa gave Zell a stern look. "Don't worry, Child. 'Tweren't my heart causing the problems; 'twas the pneumonia."

Zell spoke up. "The doctor says sometimes pneumonia like he's had can weaken the heart muscles. So we'll stay right here just like the doctor ordered."

Reverend Thatcher spoke quietly to Zell, but I heard him. "Are you okay financially, Zell. If the church can help you with the hospital bills, let me know."

"No sir, we don't need any help. We've got insurance. Between that and Medicare, we should be just fine. Tom's just going to pretend he's on vacation up here on the second floor with people in white uniforms waiting on him hand and foot."

"Do you need me at home, Nana Zell?" I asked, although I hoped she would say no. It had been wonderful not having to get up so early to ride the bus.

"No, Child. If Reverend and Mrs. Clark don't mind, it would be a load off my mind if you could stay with them for a few more days."

"We don't mind at all, Mrs. Baker. Let's plan on her staying at least until Mr. Baker goes home from the hospital." He turned to me. "Is that okay with you, Maisy?"

"Yes Sir. I was hoping you'd say that. On Saturday, Mrs. Clark is taking me to see Momma, anyway."

Papa took my hand. "Tell your momma we love her and hope she gets to come home soon."

"I will." It was hard to know what to hope for. Sure, I wanted her home, but not if she was going to just act foolish and end up going back when she didn't take her medicine. I never knew what house I would sleep in from one month to another, and now there was one more house to throw in the mix—the Clarks'. And it was getting harder and harder getting my hopes up about Momma and then having them dashed again. Maybe if Mrs. Clark could help me get in to see one of the doctors when we went on Saturday, he could tell me how to convince her to keep taking the medicine they prescribed.

CHAPTER SEVEN

LIZ

"Therefore, accept one another, just as Christ also accepted us to the glory of God."

—ROMANS 15:7

The first half of the trip to Columbia was quiet. Maisy seemed deep in thought, but the second half, she opened up and her words spilled over like tea from a pitcher. I knew her mom kept ending up back in the hospital time after time, but I'd never thought about the fact that she wasn't taking her medication as she should. There had never been any follow-up once she was released and no other adult watching to make sure she got the proper mental health care periodically to assess her medication and make sure it was being filled. Maisy, a mere child herself, couldn't be expected to carry that kind of responsibility, and besides, no one had ever even spoken to her about it. My heart broke knowing that what she'd been through could have been prevented if Maisy's father or her grandparents had gotten involved. I seethed for a little while just taking it all in. Surely someone could be appointed to take care of this family in the absence of a clear-thinking adult.

And the child clearly needed counseling by a mental health professional; much beyond my expertise. Rock would know what to do; I'd ask him when we got home.

And then Maisy asked me something out of the blue.

"Mrs. Clark, will I end up like my momma? You know, like having the same sickness she does?"

I didn't know what to say because I wasn't sure of her mother's exact diagnosis, other than her symptoms sounded a lot like Bipolar Disorder or even Schizophrenia. I'd heard that genetics can contribute to the risk but that it's not a determining factor. Nothing in Maisy's personality pointed to it, but then again Bipolar Disorder doesn't normally show up until you're in your late teens or early twenties. During my school counseling career, I knew only one student with the disorder and she didn't show symptoms until her senior year. It wouldn't be fair to worry the child unnecessarily.

"Maisy, I don't think so, but we'll make an appointment with a therapist if it's something that's worrying you."

"I've been reading things on the internet," she said, looking at me apprehensively.

"You know, that's what I did when I got pregnant with Matthew. A pregnancy is considered high-risk for women in their mid to late thirties, and everyone seemed to think I should know that, so what do you think I did?"

"Googled it?"

"Right! And when I googled high-risk pregnancies, it scared me half to death. It worried me so much that Rock talked to my doctor about it, and he scolded me for searching the internet. There's just too much false information out there, Maisy. Everybody under the sun can post what they think about a subject, but only the professionals can give you the real details."

That seemed to appease her for the time being, but she also seemed nervous about seeing her mother, and so was I since I didn't know what to expect.

My fears were ungrounded though when a nurse escorted us into the patient family room and Maisy's mom was waiting to meet her daughter with arms stretched wide open. Maisy wasn't the least bit hesitant about running right into them. I stayed back and took a seat by the door, giving them time and space to reconnect that mother-daughter bond. It was a full five minutes before Maisy remembered I was there and motioned me over.

I wasn't prepared for the warmth and genuine sweetness that emanated from the beautiful woman in front of me. Then it dawned on me—I had been judgmental without ever having met Mandy Martin, forming my impression of her based on my knowledge of her mental illness. It was a lightbulb moment, making me realize what obstacles people with mental illnesses, however big or small, must face every day. It's no wonder they try to hide their diagnosis and don't reach out for help. Even something very treatable, like depression, can often carry the stigma of a defect in a person's personality, when in fact it is most often caused by a chemical imbalance, hormonal changes or things going on in a person's life. A physical illness gets sympathy and prayers. A mental illness is often a carefully concealed family secret that creates a hindrance in getting treatment.

So much for my reflections. In the meanwhile, Maisy and her mother were standing in front of me smiling expectantly as I was having my moment of revelation. Blushing, I reached out and shook Mandy's hand, holding on to it more for my sake than hers.

"Momma, this is Mrs. Clark, my guidance counselor at school, and Mrs. Clark, I guess you've gathered by now that this is my momma."

"I could have picked you out of a crowd, seeing that the two of you look so much alike. You have a beautiful daughter, Mrs. Martin; inside and out."

"She's something, isn't she? And look how tall you are, Maisy. We'll go shopping when I get home. Those jeans are a good inch too short." She turned back to me. "Mrs. Clark, you don't know how grateful I am that you've brought her to see me. I've missed her so much."

She teared up, but Maisy distracted her, making me wonder how often she'd worried over her mother's tears and tried to cheer her up like she was doing now. "You'll be coming home, soon Momma. You're so much better now. What does the doctor say?"

"Soon, Maisy. I feel on top of the ..."

Panic filled Maisy's voice. "Don't say those words, Momma. You'll jinx the whole thing."

I wondered what that was all about, but Mandy seemed to realize she'd said the wrong thing. "I'm sorry, honey. It's just a phrase. I've messed things up too many times for you, but I've learned my lesson. I promise I'll take my medicine when I get home. They've given me the professional help I need this time, and they're arranging for me to continue therapy when I get home instead of just turning me loose to make it on my own. That's what's taking so long. By the time the school year is over, I should be home; that's three more weeks, right?" Maisy nodded. "I'll call Zell and Tom when I know for sure. Maybe they can meet me at the bus station."

"Papa Tom's been real sick, Momma. He's in the hospital with pneumonia."

Mandy's face fell at the news. "Oh no! How is Zell holding up?"

"She's staying with him at the hospital during the day and coming home at night. Reverend Thatcher makes sure she gets back and forth. I've been staying with Mrs. Clark and her family for a few days. I'll go home as soon as Papa gets out of the hospital."

Mandy winced, and I wondered if it was because Maisy called the Baker's house "home" so naturally. She turned around to face me. "I have so much more to thank you for, Mrs. Clark."

"Please call me Liz. I feel extremely old when you call me Mrs. Clark. And in return, I'll call you Mandy."

She smiled. "Yes, it is awkward, isn't it? I think we're about the same age. Anyway, Liz, you're kind-hearted to take Maisy in like this. Everyone has shown my daughter so much love and I'm ashamed that I haven't been able to care for her myself. It's my job." She looked sad, but confident and in control. "I'll make up for it, though. Maisy, I promise you that."

Maisy didn't seem so sure, but she smiled and hugged her mother. "You don't need to make up for anything, Momma."

I was silent for a moment, not wanting to interrupt the sweet exchange between them. Then I noticed a painting on an easel where Mandy had been sitting when we entered the room. When I walked over and examined it, I was blown away at the depth of character in the subject's face.

"It's titled, 'The Unmasking'." Mandy had walked up behind me.

"I can see why," I said. The painting was of a young woman that looked hauntingly like Mandy. She had a faint smile and her lips were a bright red. The mask she held in her right hand was a sad face with black tears that dripped at the woman's feet.

"It's the first time I've done a self-portrait," she said. "I've never felt I could capture myself on canvas until now."

"I like the smile," Maisy said as she looked on. "It's not fake. It's real."

Mandy laughed. "My therapist thinks so too. He encourages me to paint and he's been privy to some of the deepest and darkest ones I've painted. It's funny, the strange ones have always been my best sellers, but I'm hoping not to be in the mood to paint many more of them."

"I love the happy ones you paint," said Maisy.

"So do I, Maisy. The studio is almost sold out, so I'll need to rebuild my portfolio." She hugged her daughter again. "I'm so ready to be home with my girl!"

"Mandy, I'll leave my phone number with you. When you find out what day you're coming home, call me. My husband and I will come down and pick you up. Maisy can ride with us. It'll be our pleasure."

My remark seemed to cheer Maisy up. "Mr. Clark is a preacher, Momma. He won't mind at all."

"Gosh, I hate to keep taking advantage of your kindness, but it would be a relief knowing I would have a safe ride home. I've taken the bus a time or two and have encountered some unsavory characters." She stopped and thought about what she'd said, then laughed. "But who am I to be talking? If they knew I'd come straight from a mental hospital, they might say the same thing."

"Maisy, when I get home, I'm going over to May's Flower Shop and buy that sign in her window."

"What sign, Momma?"

"The one that says, *Here in the South, we don't hide crazy. We parade it around on the front porch.*"

We all laughed. I've never made light of mental illness and would never use the term 'crazy' to refer to anyone other than myself, but she was genuinely amused and trying hard to break free of the bonds that were holding her back.

CHAPTER EIGHT

MAISY

"Rejoice always, pray without ceasing, give thanks in all circumstances; for this is the will of God in Christ Jesus for you."

—1 THESSALONIANS 5:16-18

I'd never seen Momma so happy, and I think it was more than just seeing me. Mrs. Clark was treating her like a normal person; like they could be best friends or something. In my recollection, no one had ever really treated her normal, not even Zell. And when I thought about it, not even me. The people in her life were always faking it, trying to make her happy, when we were really walking on eggshells. I think Momma has always sensed that.

She was telling Mrs. Clark things she'd never even told me about growing up moving from one poor country to another as the child of missionaries, never knowing what it was like to have a real home. It made me feel lucky when I stopped to think about it. I had two homes; ours and Nana and Papa's. But me and Momma were alike because I was sometimes confused about which one to call my real home.

Maybe if Momma had a friend, someone close to her age who wasn't afraid of her, she wouldn't be so apt to forget her medicine. Maybe the real friend would remind her in a nice way that it was time to get her prescription filled. I had tried, but I was just a kid.

She thought it was her responsibility to remind me of things, not the other way around and was a little resentful when I did.

Mrs. Clark even got permission for us to take Momma out to lunch to her favorite place, The Olive Garden. We talked about school, my friends, and my last report card which I just happened to have with me so I could show her I was still making straight A's.

"That's my girl! At least that's one thing I don't have to worry about, your grades. You get that from your daddy. He graduated college at the top of his class. Did you know that?"

Uh oh. I shook my head, no, and wondered where the conversation was going to lead. It was rare for her to talk about Daddy at all, but when she did, she always got sad. Mind you, she never talked bad about him, even though I thought he deserved it. Although I'm not overly fond of him because of the way he treated Momma when she needed him most, I'd be lying to say I wasn't curious about him. After all, he is my daddy. I thought about changing the subject, but she went on to another topic herself, acting like talking about him was the most natural thing in the world.

"I have to get my driver's license renewed when I get home. It expired last month on my birthday."

"I wish I could have been with you on your birthday."

"I know, Maisy." She reached over and tucked a strand of hair behind my ear. "We'll spend all our birthdays together from now on. I got the sweet card you sent."

"If you need someone to take you to the DMV, I'll be glad to," Mrs. Clark said.

"That would be wonderful," Momma said, and I could tell she was pleased as punch. Mrs. Clark wouldn't make an offer if she didn't mean it, and while they were talking, I bowed my head and prayed that the two of them would become best friends. It was my last hope and I would pray every day. I remembered a Sunday School lesson where Paul told one of those new churches he visited now and then to pray without ceasing, so that's what I would do. But I don't think God minds if I stop praying long enough to eat, sleep and do homework.

∼

MOMMA ARRANGED for us to talk to the supervisor on her hall, and we all went in together. It wasn't just wishful thinking on Momma's part; the supervisor verified that she was making good progress and as soon as the doctor could assess her and sign the paperwork for her release, she could come home. Soon, she said; no date, but soon.

It was a sad goodbye for both me and Momma, but on the way home, I hinted to Mrs. Clark that she and Momma would make good friends.

"I think so, too, Maisy. We're about the same age, and I enjoyed being with her. I'm looking forward to getting to know her."

I don't know why but hearing her say that made me cry. I wanted to tell her that my tears were happy instead of sad, but I was too busy sniffling. But she seemed to understand. She looked at me knowingly and patted my arm.

"There's a box of tissues in the dash." I got one out and blew my nose.

"Thank you. I don't even know why I'm crying."

"You need to cry sometimes. It's not a sign of weakness. It's an emotional outlet we all need to take advantage of when we need it. I cry sometimes, too. Sometimes over the silliest things."

"I guess I've seen so many tears from Momma, I try to hold mine in. I think if I cry, it'll make her sadder."

"Maisy, I don't want you to think anything you've ever done has caused your mom's tears. And you've nothing to be ashamed about. Your mother is a delightful person. She simply has an illness. It's an illness that's treatable, much like treating physical illnesses. If she could snap her fingers and make herself well, she would, but it's not that easy. The mind plays tricks on us sometimes. We get a false sense of security, like your mom has done when she thinks she's well and doesn't continue with her meds. This isn't a fair comparison, but it's a little like me trying to lose this extra ten pounds I gained when I had Matthew. After I drop a few pounds, I think I have it conquered, but then I go right back to my old habit of eating anything I want, and it creeps back up."

"I hadn't thought of it that way."

"Try not to worry about what will happen when she gets home, Maisy. The doctors seem to have their act together now, getting her the medical help she needs when she's home, so she won't fall back into the old patterns. I'm going to be in the picture too, Maisy. You and your mom are not going to fight this battle alone."

That brought on a new wave of tears. This time I just sat in that front seat and sobbed, pulling my legs up under me. This time I knew they were tears of relief and I didn't apologize for them. I just let them flow and then apologized for using up half the box of tissues. Apologies are just ingrained in my blood, I suppose. I'd spent a lifetime hearing them and giving them.

I took a deep breath and sat up straight. Mrs. Clark would help. Now I wouldn't dread Momma coming home, like I'd done in the past. But I wasn't going to take any chances. Pray without ceasing; that's what I would do. Then it hit me. The Thessalonians—that's who Paul was preaching to.

CHAPTER NINE

MAISY

"Therefore welcome one another as Christ has welcomed you, for the glory of God."

—ROMANS 15:7

It felt strange somehow going to church with mostly white people that Sunday morning. It was the first time I remembered missing a Sunday service at Baker's Chapel except one time when I had the flu.

After Sunday School, Mrs. Clark and I walked into the sanctuary. The first thing I noticed was how people dressed, or didn't dress, I guess I should say. I wore my best Sunday dress because I wanted to make a good impression in a new church. The older people were dressed nice; women in their pretty dresses and cardigans and men in their suits and ties. There wasn't a single three-piece suit in the crowd though. In Baker's Chapel, all the men wear colorful vests and ties. But here, the younger men and boys wear either khakis and polo shirts or jeans and t-shirts. The girls wear just what they would wear to school. It was a culture shock, for sure.

I spotted two of my friends from school sitting near the back, and Mrs. Clark said I could sit with them. They told me that most people called Mr. Clark Rev Rock, not Reverend Clark like I had planned on calling him. It didn't sound very respectful to call him by his first name though. Maybe I would just call him Mr. Clark after all. The service started off with a lot of reading from the bulletin. All that trivia cut down on the sermon time which made me wonder if they paid him less than Reverend Thatcher who went on for an hour or more. I watched my friends as the preaching progressed. They were passing notes back and forth to each other and I couldn't blame them. After hearing my own preacher, this was a little on the boring side. He needed to shout now and then to get people's attention.

And that choir! They could have used some help. Not a single person swayed, clapped or said amen. I couldn't help but chuckle when I tried to imagine Sister Charlene Smith getting up there and giving them a few lessons on rocking the house down. But then I started feeling guilty. This was God's house, and even though their worship service was different than ours, they were all here to glorify God. Who was I to criticize?

WE ALL WENT to the hospital to see Papa Tom after we had lunch. All except for little Matthew, and the lady across the street came over to watch him while he took his nap. Papa was happy when we walked in. The doctor had been by that morning and said he could go home on Monday.

"First time I've missed church in ten years," he said. He looked at the clock on the wall. "It's one o'clock. Y'all got out of church early today. Reverend Thatcher is just winding down right about now. I 'spect he'll bring Zell by when they're finished up."

Mrs. Clark laughed. "And we've already had lunch. I think our congregation would tar and feather Rock if he kept them past 12:15."

"I like getting out early," I said. "My stomach didn't even growl like it normally does." Everybody laughed, even though I was serious. It was true—my stomach growling was about the only thing that could wake up Mr. Thea Parker, who undoubtedly takes a sleeping pill every Sunday before church. Bless his heart. His wife used to wake him up with an elbow poke in the ribs before she died, but there's nobody to do it now except for me and my stomach.

"We went to see Momma yesterday."

Papa's laugh tapered off. He gave me a steady gaze. "And how was she, Baby Girl?"

"She's coming home, Papa." I paused. "And maybe this time it's for good."

He looked from me to Mrs. Clark. When she nodded her head, he smiled real big. "Come on over here, Baby Girl, and give me a big hug." I ran to him and hugged him as hard as his frail old bones would allow. "This time we're all going to work hard and take care of your momma. We won't let her fall again."

"Mrs. Clark will help too, Papa. With her on our side, Momma can't help but get well." I saw Mr. Clark look at his wife and beam proudly. I hope if I ever get married, I'll be lucky and get a husband like Mr. Clark instead of one like my daddy. Somebody to lift me up instead of letting me down. Poor Momma; she was always drawing the short end of the stick.

CHAPTER TEN

REV ROCK

"Wait for the Lord; be strong and let your heart take courage; wait for the Lord!"

—PSALM 27:14

Reva's fingers were tapping on her desk. "Are you going to stare out that window all day? If you don't hurry and choose a sermon title and the hymns you'll use on Sunday, I'll have to come in tomorrow to get the bulletins printed, and you know I always keep my grandbabies on Saturdays. Not to rush you or anything."

She was rushing him, but he knew he needed it, along with a swift kick to the backside if he didn't get his act together. "I can't seem to concentrate, Reva. Maybe if I stare into space long enough, my sermon will appear out of nowhere."

She gave him a look of concern that sometimes grated on his nerves but most of the time warmed his heart. She'd always treated him like her own son, even going so far as making sure he got a decent home-cooked meal every week. But that was before he married Liz. It wasn't that he didn't know how to cook; it was just no fun to cook for one.

"I'll not ask if you've prayed about it because I know you always do. You have your Bible in your hand almost every time I walk in your office, so I know it's not for a lack of inspiration. What's wrong, then?"

"I wish I knew so I could fix it."

"Well, I know what it is, even if you don't. You're just burned out, that's what. I've read about preachers doing so much for everybody else, pretty soon they start spinning their wheels and can't get out of the muck. And you fit the bill, Rev Rock. You think the church will fall apart if you don't have your hand in everything. You've got to slow down before you break down."

"And poor Liz; did you ever take her to that movie she's been wanting to see?"

He cringed. That had been weighing on his mind ever since last month when she'd come into the office and told him and Reva that she'd heard it was a great movie, and she wanted to know when he could work it into his schedule. But it had been a busy schedule. He'd had a session meeting on Tuesday night, a budget meeting with the Stewardship committee on Wednesday night, and on Thursday night, he'd met with two couples about joining the church. That left Friday night and he had fully intended to take her. They'd lined up a babysitter but their plans fell apart when Jeffrey Little's mom called and said he was in a serious automobile accident and could Rock meet them at the hospital. The "serious accident" had turned out to be a fender-bender and after an hour, Jeff was treated for a scratch or two and released.

Then Saturday was his day to finalize his sermon and after that, he simply forgot. Liz hadn't reminded him until the next week and by that time, the movie was no longer on at the cinema. Was that his fault? According to Liz, it was. She wasn't one to pout, but she let him know it disappointed her. Reva was waiting for his answer. "No, Reva. It was a busy week."

"Well you'll have to do better than that. Your wife should come before all these other people's business. You just don't know how to say *no*. Like I said, you can't do it all. Start doling out chores to other people. They think the world of you and they'd do anything to help if you'd just let 'em."

"I know they would, Reva." He also knew he needed to change the subject or she would worry and fret over him to the point of annoyance. He put on what he hoped was a convincing smile. "Let's get back to where we started. You know I always struggle a little over my sermons on Pentecost Sunday, but I have the scripture passages prepared. Ezekiel 37: 1-14 and Acts 2: 1-12."

"Ezekiel, that's the one where the Lord told Ezekiel to prophesy to the bones in the valley? I always think about the song we sang as little kids, *Dem Bones, Dem Bones, Dem Dry Bones*."

"And Reva, bless your soul, you've just given me the name of my sermon."

She looked at him skeptically. "Me?"

"Yes, you. Dem Bones for a title and we'll use the hymns, *Spirit of Gentleness* and *Breathe on me Breath of God*, if you'll just look the hymn numbers up in our hymnal." He thought for a minute. "For the last hymn, we'll sing *Come Down O Love Divine*."

"I don't remember that one."

"It's not in our hymnal. It's in the Methodist hymnal that I borrowed from Bob Hartley. Can you copy that page and insert it into the bulletin?"

"I'll just copy and paste it off the internet. We'll need to call Jenny Wilson so she can practice playing it on the organ between now and Sunday. She doesn't like things sprung on her at the last minute, no, siree."

"Thank you, Reva. What would I do without you?"

"Lord only knows!" She took the notes over to the computer and typed in the blanks she'd left for the sermon title and hymns, all the while humming a song about *dry bones*. At least she was on a mission now and wouldn't harp on him for a while.

As he listened to her hum, he felt he'd been rattling around like old dry bones himself lately. "I'll be in my office working on my sermon, Reva. Don't let anyone disturb me unless it's Liz." She nodded and kept on humming. He walked to the office and closed the door with the purpose of rereading Ezekiel and Acts 2. Maybe God's Spirit of gentleness would wash over him and renew his own spirit.

Good things had always happened on Pentecost Sunday at Park Place Presbyterian. He recalled just three short years before when the sad and bitter Miss Edie Mosher had responded to his Pentecost sermon with a changed heart. It had been nothing short of miraculous.

As he sat and read from his well-worn Bible, a familiar longing for God's Word to be revealed flooded over him and he bowed his head. "Breathe on me your breath, oh God, and allow the Holy Spirit to quicken my heart. Take away whatever is hindering me from giving my all to You. Refresh and restore your spirit within me. In Your Son, Jesus' name I pray. Amen". If only he could lay it all at Jesus' feet and it would be worked out. Where was his faith when he needed it?

He picked up the Methodist Hymnbook and turned to the index. He found, *Come Down O Love Divine* and turned to the page, reading the first stanza.

Come down, O Love divine!
seek out this soul of mine
and visit it with your own ardor glowing;
O Comforter, draw near,
within my heart appear,
and kindle it, your holy flame bestowing.

He marveled that the words were much like the prayer he had just prayed. He leaned his head against the back of the chair and breathed in and out, finally finding, if only temporarily, a sense of peace.

Back to the real world, Rock, he said aloud to himself. As he picked up his notes, the mail he'd picked up from the post office fell to the floor. As he gathered it up, the weekly newspaper from Sparta caught his attention. There it was, back-to-back showings at the new Arboretum Park Theater. The movie Liz wanted to see was playing for the next six days and his calendar was blank for tonight. He picked up the phone and dialed Zell Baker's number. He looked at his watch. It was 4 p.m. Maisy should be home from school by now.

"Hi Zell, this is Rock Clark. I hope you and Tom are doing well?"

"That's good news. He must be obeying doctor's orders. The reason I called is to see if Maisy can babysit tonight so Liz and I can go to a movie in Rock Hill. It's an early movie so we should be home by nine o'clock. Matthew is always ready for bed by seven and as Maisy knows already, he's easy at bedtime. She could do her homework here."

"Okay, I'll wait while you ask her."

In a few seconds, it was Maisy's voice who came back on the line instead of Zell's.

"Yes! You really want me to babysit? It's the first time I've ever done it."

He couldn't help but smile at her enthusiasm. He liked her honesty, and the way she had hit it off with Matthew, he had no doubts she would be a great babysitter. But maybe he should have asked Liz before he called. No, he and Liz had talked about how mature and dependable Maisy is; Liz would be fine with it.

"Wonderful, I'll pick you up at 6:15. Why don't you plan to spend the night. Great! See you then!"

He walked out of his office. He had lots of notes and a good outline for Sunday's sermon. It could wait until tomorrow to be finalized. It was time for Liz to be home and he wanted to surprise her with the news. Reva had already gone. He saw the finished bulletin on her desk waiting to be copied the next day. What would he do without her? He hoped he'd never have to find out.

It thrilled Liz that he'd made plans for the movie, and she liked his choice of babysitters. "I've missed her since she went home last week. It'll be nice to have her overnight again."

"You don't have any qualms about her babysitting? After I had already arranged it, it occurred to me that I should have checked with you first."

"Not at all. We've taken advantage of Maura and Danny across the street far too often even though they keep volunteering. And Holly has Matthew all day, so I know she's ready to have quiet time with her family when he leaves. Maisy will be perfect." She reached up and gave him a lingering kiss. "I knew you'd come through, husband of mine! Thank you for planning it all."

He held her close and nuzzled his face against hers and wondered again why he had waited until he was in his 40s to marry. Then from a place deep within his heart, he knew the answer. It was all part of God's plan for his life—to find love when he would appreciate it the most. He thought back to the scripture sparring match he'd had with Thatcher the week before. "Wait for the Lord; be strong and take heart and wait for the Lord." He was so glad he had waited.

CHAPTER ELEVEN

MAISY

"Suddenly a sound like the blowing of a violent wind came from heaven and filled the whole house where they were sitting."
—ACTS 2:2

I did a happy dance when I hung up the phone after talking to Mr. Clark. He trusted me to babysit Matthew! Ever since I read on the internet that mental illness can be hereditary, I've wondered if people were watching me to see if I would flip out or something. It had been on my mind all week. I sure didn't want to end up like Momma. Who would take care of her if I did?

Papa had been home since Monday and was getting stronger every day. Nana Zell got back in her routine of bossing us around, but it felt good to have her happy again. I went in the kitchen to see if I could help her finish supper.

"Get the plates and utensils, child," she said before I could even ask. "And put ice in the glasses if you don't mind."

"What are we having?" I asked. I usually got a whiff of whatever Zell was cooking for supper, but nothing stood out tonight.

"Baked chicken, kale, and buttered carrots."

"Kale? You've never cooked kale before, Nana Zell. And the chicken, you always fry it."

"The doctor said your papa shouldn't eat fried foods and he

needs more green vegetables. He'll have a conniption fit when he finds out I'm not seasoning these greens with fatback, but he'll just have to get used to it," she said, pouring the cooked kale into a round Corning Ware bowl with little blue flowers. "Get the pepper relish out of the refrigerator, too, if you don't mind. That'll help take away the bitterness of the greens."

It looked like I'd have to get used to it, too. I hoped the baked chicken wasn't something permanent. Nobody, and I mean nobody, fried chicken like Zell. Papa wouldn't like this one bit. "Why haven't you been cooking like this all week, Nana? He came home Monday."

"Cause he needed to be fattened up a mite, that's why. He was nothing but skin and bone. Glynnis took me to the grocery store today and helped me make a meal plan—I think that's what she called it. I don't know much about cooking healthy."

"Don't worry. Mrs. Clark has healthy cooking recipe books and I'm sure she'll loan them to us. She cooks healthy all the time. Well, except for those chocolate chip cookies Mr. Clark loves so much."

She turned toward me, and it was as if she was looking at me in a new light. "You've done grown up on me, Baby Girl," she said, and then she smiled. Nana Zell's smiles were few and far between and I felt about as proud as I'd ever felt. I finished setting the table while she put our supper in serving bowls. "Call your Papa to supper."

"Yes Ma'am. I'll go help him out of the recliner."

Just as I thought; Papa ate most of his supper, but he was pushing that kale around all over his plate, hoping it would magically disappear.

～

LITTLE MATTHEW WAS a bugger to get to sleep, contrary to how Mrs. Clark had said it would go. I guess I got him too wound up playing with his tractor that made loud noises. He finally went to sleep, not ten minutes before they got home from the movies.

"He'll be sleeping late in the morning," I said when they asked how he had done.

"He never sleeps late, no matter how late he goes to bed," Mrs. Clark said. "It'll be a miracle if he sleeps past 6:30."

And a miracle it was because when I walked down the stairs the next morning at 8 a.m., not a soul was stirring. I turned on the TV and it was a full thirty minutes before Mr. Clark came walking into the living room with a sleepy-headed little boy in his arms. "Liz has decided that we should hire you to babysit more often," he said, putting Matthew on the sofa beside me. "I can't remember a time that we've been able to sleep in on Saturday morning. I'll fix us all some breakfast, then Liz can take you home as soon as you're ready."

"Oh, I'm not in any hurry. I'll be glad to play with the baby this morning if Mrs. Clark needs to do housework."

He looked at me sort of funny, then laughed. "Are you sure you're not a grownup disguised as a teenager? Or maybe from another planet that hasn't invented cell phones yet?"

"Zell says cell phones were just made to waste time. Besides, we don't have Wi-Fi, so I'd probably never get a signal anyway."

"I think Zell has the right idea. People are forgetting how to have face-to-face conversations."

I laughed. "I have two friends at school who sit across the table at lunch and text each other."

Matthew slid his little legs down from the sofa and went running across the room. "Mommy!" Mrs. Clark had walked in and was stretching her arms out, waiting for his wild embrace.

"You are a miracle worker, Maisy Martin. This little rascal never sleeps in!"

Mr. Clark got up and started for the kitchen. "I'll get breakfast going."

"You've still got your sermon to work on, don't you?" He

nodded. "Then why don't you take your shower while I cook for a change? Maisy and I can entertain Matthew just as easily in the kitchen."

"No arguments here," he said. He kissed her on the cheek as he walked by on his way to their bedroom.

While Mrs. Clark cleaned the house and did laundry, I took Matthew to the church playground which was practically in their backyard. Abby, their seven-year-old neighbor came out to play with us, and by the time Mrs. Clark called us in for lunch, Matthew was tuckered out. It was all he could do to stay awake to eat. Mrs. Clark offered to take me home when Mr. Clark finished with his sermon, but I asked if I could stay another night. She called Zell to make sure it was okay.

I didn't bring any church clothes but seeing as how the other girls wore school clothes, I figured it wouldn't matter just that once if I did the same. I sat in the pew again with my friends and boy was I shocked when Mr. Clark started preaching. He was like a different preacher from the last Sunday I'd gone. He was animated and on fire.

Nana Zell's always telling me she's going to light a match under my backside to get me moving, and that's what must have happened to him. It's funny because the name of his sermon was; *Light my Fire*, and that's just what he did to the whole congregation as he spoke.

"After his death and resurrection, Jesus visited with the apostles often, telling them not to leave Jerusalem; something good was about to happen; that they would soon be filled with the Holy Spirit. Just think of the anticipation they must have felt! Did they know what the Holy Spirit would do? Jesus told them, but did they really understand that it would transform them in such a way that they would go out and witness for Jesus to the ends of the earth? Of course, they knew they needed something big to happen if they were going to witness far and wide. They needed power that would energize them for the long haul, power that would renew them, yes,

even transform them. This was a God-sized job and they needed quick access to God. They needed the Holy Spirit. And when it came... WOW was the word! Here it is again, from Acts 2, verses 3 and 4. Divided tongues, as of fire, appeared among them, and a tongue rested on each of them. All of them were filled with the Holy Spirit and began to speak in other languages, as the Spirit gave them ability."

I looked around. Everyone was paying attention, even Megan and Emma, my friends who had passed notes the last time. They were hanging on to his every word all the way through his summary of the sermon.

"And why, my friends, is Pentecost still so relevant today? Because it's the fire that represents the presence of Christ in our life. We not only need the Holy Spirit's power for the stormy periods in our lives, but we need Christ's very presence with us to comfort, guide and transform us. Let's all go out of here filled with the Spirit so we can share Christ's message to the entire world today and everyday throughout our lives!"

WHILE THE CHOIR was singing the last hymn, I wondered what would have happened if he'd preached the sermon title from the bulletin, *Dem Bones*. He'd apparently had a revelation at the last minute on what to preach. I've noticed that God has a way of changing our minds when we least expect it. An older man with a white shirt and purple tie pretty much summed it up on the way out from church. It must have been his wife with him. She had on a purple scarf and I thought their matching colors were kind of cute.

"That's Rev Rock for ya! It's like he's preaching a good old-timey revival sermon every time Pentecost rolls around."

"It's about time," the woman said. "He's seemed a little off-kilter lately."

Uh, oh. Maybe that's why his sermon had been a little flat the first time I came. I wondered if he even realized it. Well, he was on a roll now, maybe.

CHAPTER TWELVE

REV ROCK

"Cast all your anxiety on him because he cares for you."

—1 PETER 5:7

"I changed my sermon title at the last minute, Reva. I started all over on Saturday morning."

"You didn't preach about 'dem bones'?"

"No, I just couldn't get that one going. I titled it *Light my Fire*."

"Oh, there's a song about lighting my fire. Hmm...."

"You're right. Mid-sixties, by The Doors." He looked up to see Reva smiling. "Hey that was in your era wasn't it? How old were you in the mid-sixties?" He took a chocolate chip cookie from the plate on her desk and popped a bite into his mouth.

"That's for me to know and you to find out." She stuck out her tongue at him. "I was just a little kid when it came out, but I remember it well. You want me to sing a few bars?"

He raised his eyebrows and could tell by Reva's expression that she was amused. "Please do."

"I'm kidding. I'd sound like a croaking frog if I tried to sing it. Besides, the words may not be appropriate for a church office," she said demurely.

"Are you kidding me? You, Reva! The one who plays gyrating

Elvis music on her CD player thinks *Light my Fire* is inappropriate?"

"Ah, Elvis. I was always in love with that white boy."

He choked on his cookie and went into a fit of coughing.

She got up and whacked him across the back until he stopped.

"Don't scare me like that. For a minute there, I thought I'd have to do the Heimlich maneuver on you. You shouldn't stuff so much in your mouth at one time."

He shook his head. "And I thought you were going to beat me to death. You've got some muscle behind that wallop! Poor Walter! I pity him if he ever gets on your bad side."

"Moi?" she asked innocently, but then changed her expression as she thought of something else. "Hey, I hope your church doesn't think I made a mistake typing your sermon title!"

He smiled, sighed and looked up toward the sky, much like the apostles must have done when Jesus ascended into heaven. "Come, Holy Spirit, come."

She looked at him from the corner of her eye. "Have you gone crazy, or something?"

"No, but I might if I don't go in my office and shut the door." He walked past her, but then circled back around and picked up the plate of cookies. "And I'll need these, thank you." He patted her on the cheek, before he walked away. "Don't worry. They don't think you made a mistake, Reva. I told them it was just a last-minute change."

WITH THE DOOR closed and a mountain of paperwork in front of him, Rock slumped back in his chair. The comments from the congregants as they filed past him on Sunday after the church service had left him feeling pretty good about his sermon, but it was the honest, straightforward comment by Maisy Martin that had thrown him off guard as they ate lunch at the new Park Place Grill after church. He and Liz had been making small talk with her before the food was served. He had concluded that she was wise beyond her years. She seemed to see things others didn't see.

"I saw you sitting with Emma and Megan today. Are they friends of yours from school?"

"Yes, sir. Emma, more so than Megan. We have several classes together. But don't get me wrong. Megan's a nice girl; it's just that I don't see her often. You know, there are friends, and there are acquaintances, and Megan and I are more acquaintances, I guess you'd say."

He agreed with her philosophy. "I think you've summed it up pretty well. I'm around some of our church members more than others, like the ones who are more active in the life of the church and the ones who serve on all the committees. I have to be careful sometimes not to show partiality to those or I'll be accused of being friends to some and not to others."

"So, you can't really have best friends in your church?"

"It's frowned upon. Pastors can be very lonely people. Everyone we know is within the church walls, and we're often too busy with our pastoral duties to go outside the church to make friends."

"I thought you might be lonely."

She said it so matter-of-factly. Rock was stunned, but he laughed.

"Is it that obvious?" he said.

"And maybe a little sad, too. And believe me, I know sad when I see it."

He looked at Liz uncomfortably. "Lonely, maybe. As I said, most pastors are lonely, but I don't feel sad at all."

"Maybe sad isn't the right word. Troubled?" Then her face lit up. "Or bored? One of my teachers quit mid-term this year. She had a meltdown in class one day and said she was leaving 'cause she was burned-out. Maybe that's happening to you."

She was hitting too close to home, he thought. When he didn't say anything, Liz took up the conversation. She looked at Rock first, puzzled, then at the wise young girl across the table who was helping Matthew with his sippy cup.

"What makes you think that, Maisy?"

"Just from something I heard on the way out today. A man was going on about how much he liked your sermon, and his wife made a comment that you'd seemed a little off-kilter lately. Maybe that's it. Your sermon was good today; a whole lot better than the one you did the last time I was here."

Liz had chuckled, and Rock blushed.

"Oh no! I didn't mean it to sound that way," she said. "Sometimes I speak without thinking. I just thought you need to know whatever you were doing wrong before, you did it right today. I'm sorry."

She looked so distressed, Rock couldn't help but laugh. "At long last," he said, "someone's being honest instead of walking out the front door half-heartedly shaking my hand and saying, 'Good sermon today'. Don't be sorry, Maisy. Sometimes we adults need to see things through a child's eyes."

She had hit the nail right on the head. Feeling the Holy Spirit at work in him during his sermon preparation had convinced him that God was reaffirming his call to the ministry. On Saturday and Sunday, he felt the old passion, but where it was today, he didn't know. *Pastor burnout*—Was Maisy right? Reva had said so too. If so, where should he go from here? Tomorrow was Maisy's birthday, she had told them while they were eating lunch.

He looked in his address book and picked up the phone. When he and Liz first married, he had memorized the number. He found it, dialed it and waited for someone to answer.

"May's Flower Shop," he heard on the other end.

"May, this is Rock Clark."

She chuckled. "I know who you are, Rev Rock. I shake your hand every Sunday morning in case you forgot. And it's about time you called me. You've been slack lately."

Did she think he was burned out too? No, she wasn't talking about his sermons, but the fact that he hadn't ordered flowers in a while. "I confess I've been slack, May, but I want to make up for it. Could you send the biggest, brightest bouquet to the high school counselor's office tomorrow?"

"Well, I hope it's Liz you're sending them to. I didn't know she'd gone back to work."

"Just a temporary assignment to finish out the school year. This is the last week of school and I want to surprise her."

"Oh, I've been dying to create something with these pretty cream roses I got in today. I'll use those, along with some blue hydrangea. I'll add delphinium, Queen Anne's lace and eucalyptus in a mercury glass vase and it'll be the prettiest design I've ever done!"

Flower names were all Greek to him, but he trusted May. "Perfect!"

"It'll cost you, though. Those roses cost me an arm and a leg, but I couldn't resist 'em. They're only in season a few weeks out of the year."

"Spare no expense. As you said, I've been a slacker. She deserves more. Oh, and another thing. Could you do something age appropriate for a fifteen-year-old girl's birthday? It's from me and Liz and you'll need to deliver it to the Baker's Grove community. Hold on, let me look up the address."

"Daisies, chrysanthemums and some fillers in red, yellow and purple in a glass vase with polka-dot ribbon. It'll be bright and cheery and just $19.95 with a $5 delivery fee, a Monday Special for my favorite preacher."

"It's a done deal. Here's the address. It's for Maisy Martin who's staying with Tom and Zell Baker at 1445 Baker's Chapel Road. It's two doors down from the church, same side of the road."

"Lucky girl. The Bakers are good people. One of my friends lives on that road and her granddaughter goes to Baker's Chapel Bible School in the summer. Did you know the Bakers donated the land for that church? And I heard he bought and paid for the pews once they got the church built."

"Really? How did he have that kind of money? I thought he was a small-time farmer."

"He is now, but before he retired, he worked for the University down in Hope Springs."

"A janitor? They don't make that kind of money."

"No, a professor. Rev Rock, you of all people know better than to judge a book by its cover."

He sighed. "Yes, yes, I do, May. I just assumed...."

"You know what they say about assuming something," she said laughing.

"And that's just what I've done! Forgive me."

"Nothing to forgive. Other people have thought the same thing because of the simple life he and Zell live. He's a very intelligent man, but he doesn't put on any airs. Just the opposite, actually. He wants to relate to those around him so he can be a witness to them. But you know what? When it comes to the young men in the community, he puts his professor shoes on, and I've heard he's made a powerful impact. They really respect him."

"You know an awful lot about Mr. Baker."

"He's a good man. If you lived anywhere near him, you'd know a lot about him too. My friend adores him. Okay, enough of that. I've got to get back to work. You've just given me two big orders! I'll get Liz's to the school today, and I'll wait until school is out tomorrow to take the girl hers. I'd like to see her expression. I love it when kids get flowers for the first time."

"Thank you, May. I can always depend on you."

He hung up and banged his head back against his chair. "Lord, what is wrong with me? I'm backsliding for sure. I'm stale, I'm judgmental and I'm burned out. Whatever are you going to do with me?"

For the first time in years, all he heard was silence.

Reva knocked, waited for him to answer and walked in. "While you were on the phone, Alan Carter called from the Presbytery office. He wants to know if you'd like to play golf with him next week."

"Really? He's never asked me to play golf."

"You should do it. You could use a little break from the office. I told him you'd call him back, but he said he'd call back in about ten minutes because he'll be out of the office for the rest of the afternoon."

"Thanks, Reva. I'll answer it when it rings. Just leave the door open so I can hear it."

Hmm, he thought. Alan Carter - they had sat together at the last Presbytery meeting. He was a psychology major who answered God's call to preach but retired recently and moved to the South from New York. Now he was a supply pastor when needed and volunteered to use his psychology background to mentor and counsel pastors in the Presbytery.

The phone rang, and he picked it up. Maybe God wasn't being silent after all.

CHAPTER THIRTEEN

MAISY

"Come to me, all you who are weary and burdened, and I will give you rest."

—MATTHEW 11:28

It was the best birthday of my life! First, Max Lambert, who I've had a crush on since fifth grade ran by me in the hallway, then stopped right in front of me, making me almost crash into him. He took his Atlanta Braves baseball cap out of his backpack; there are rules against wearing hats in school or he would've had it on his head because he wears it everywhere. He looked around to see if anyone was watching and when he was sure everyone was going about their normal business, he plopped it on my head and pulled the brim down over my eyebrows. "Happy Birthday, Gator!" he said. He's called me Gator since 6th grade when we went on a field trip and I swore I saw an alligator in an old mill pond. It turned out to be a stump. My heart thumped in my chest. I've always heard about hearts going pitter-patter when you've got a crush on someone, but this was a big old thump, thump. That must be what happens when you turn fifteen. I pulled the rim of the hat up and looked him square in the eye, but he blushed and ran away. I wondered if he'd have regrets about giving away that cap later since it seemed to be his most prized possession.

When I got on the bus, I put it on my head. He sits six seats behind me, and when I turned around and tipped the cap at him, he blushed again. His best friend poked him in the ribs and laughed. He's got fair skin and it was comical seeing the red start around his collar and quickly make its way up to his hairline. Now that he no longer had on a hat, there was no way to hide it.

The second good thing to happen was when I got home from school, there was a van in our driveway that had "May's Flower Shop" in big letters across the side. It worried me a little, because the only time I'd ever seen a flower van was over at the church when we had funerals. There was no one in it so I figured they'd broken down on the road and pulled into our driveway to park. I walked into the living room and hung my book bag on the peg on the wall behind the door. Papa Tom was sitting in his recliner and was all smiles.

"Happy Birthday, Baby Girl," he said.

"Thank you, Papa. What's that truck doing in our yard?"

He pointed to the kitchen. Nana Zell was standing there and beside her was a woman holding a vase full of the prettiest flowers I'd ever seen.

"Hi Maisy, I'm May from May's Flower Shop. These are for you," the woman said, smiling.

"Who on earth would send me flowers?" I asked as I ran over to look at them.

"Read the card and you'll see."

My first thought was my daddy. I've always thought of what it would be like if Daddy surprised me and did something nice for me on my birthday. I opened the card and started reading.

"Happy Birthday to the best babysitter ever!" I read. "It's signed from Rock, Liz and Matthew Clark! How nice!" It was even better than getting something from Daddy which I never expected anyway.

May handed me the flowers and I looked around trying to find a place for them. "You can put them in your room, Child," Nana Zell said. "It'll brighten it up some."

My room could use a little brightening for sure. It was the same pale yellow as the rest of the house. "They're too pretty for just me to enjoy," I said. "They'll brighten up the whole house if we put them here in the living room."

I walked over to Nana's little table in front of the picture window and moved two photos to each side and placed the vase on the doily in the middle between the two frames. One frame holds a family picture of Zell, Tom and their children in their younger days. The other is a smaller framed school picture of me at the beginning of the school year. Momma had washed, dried and curled my hair with a curling iron that morning. It was one of her better days because I was smiling and happy and looked almost pretty. Looking up, I saw my own image in the large gilded mirror hanging at an angle over the fireplace and saw a slightly older girl in bad need of a haircut and wearing a dirty baseball cap. She had a goofy grin on her face that could pass for happy, but she could sure use a good freshening up. I took the cap off and inspected it.

"Eww, gross," was the only thing I could think of to say.

May, of the flower shop, laughed. "I hope you're not talking about my flowers."

"Oh, no ma'am! The flowers are beautiful. I'm talking about this hat someone gave me today." The hat no longer had the same appeal it had when I was standing face-to-face with the giver. It needed a good washing and I wondered if baseball caps could stand up to the spinning cycle on Zell's washing machine. It was about to be tested.

The third and best thing that happened that day was the phone call. Papa Tom and Zell go to bed at about the same time the chickens roost except in the winter when the chickens bed down too early even for them. When the phone rang at 8:30, I was at my desk studying for my last exam, so I ran in the living room and grabbed it so it wouldn't disturb them. It was Momma.

"Happy Birthday, Maisy. Honey, I'm sorry I didn't get to call before now but this is the first chance I could get to the phone. You've had a good day, I hope?"

"It's been a great day, Momma." I stretched the coiled phone cord out as far as it would go so I could sit on the bar stool at the kitchen counter. "Max Lambert gave me a baseball cap, the Clarks sent me flowers for being the best babysitter, and Zell made me a cake. She even remembered to buy candles."

"Oh, that's so nice. I wish I could have been there for your birthday, but I've got some good news for your birthday present. I'm being released on Friday."

"Oh, Momma, that's the best news ever!"

"I've already called Liz Clark and she and her husband are driving down after she gets off school Friday to pick me up."

"Can I go with them?"

"They may need you to babysit."

"That's fine. The house needs a good cleaning. I haven't been in it since you left except to get a few of my summer clothes. Nana Zell's been paying the bills from our checking account, just like she always does when you're away."

"I don't know how I'm ever going to be able to repay Zell and Tom. I can't bear to think what would have happened to you if they hadn't stepped in. You would have been in a foster home and..."

"Momma—don't go there. They did step in, and I'm fine."

"I've been so selfish, Maisy. Maybe someday you can forgive me."

"There's nothing to forgive, Momma, and look, I've got grandparents I never would have had otherwise." She gets weepy when she feels guilty about her inability to cope with her illness, so I've had plenty of practice changing subjects to get her back on a happy track again. But this time she seemed to realize what I was doing.

"Don't worry, Maisy. I won't dwell on it and I realize I'll just have to live with my illness and stay one step ahead of it by getting the help I need. I've said this too many times, but this time it will be different."

And this time I believed her. There was something different about her. She wasn't pretending to be overly happy. She seemed real—aware of the good and the bad, and very real.

"I can't wait for us to be together again, Momma. Thank you for calling me on my birthday. I'll see you Friday night. And Momma, I love you."

"I love you too, Maisy." I hung up and put the phone back on its cradle. It had been an emotional day, and I didn't know whether to laugh or cry. It was dark except for a sliver of light from the outside street lamp peeking through a raised slat on the window blinds. The light's beam landed on the far wall of the living room and bounced off the picture of the dark-skinned Jesus that had hung there for as long as I could remember. He was standing in a meadow, holding out his arms and seemed to be saying, *Come to me, Maisy, and I will give you rest*. With the weight of the world I'd been carrying around with me so long, I could use some rest.

"Maisy?"

I jumped, with the first thought in my mind that maybe Jesus was really speaking to me. But it was Zell's voice instead. I turned away from the smiling Jesus and looked to the hallway where I could just make out her figure from the light coming from bedroom. She rarely, if ever called me Maisy.

"Nana Zell, that was Momma on the phone. She's coming home."

"That's good, Baby Girl. That's real good." She held out her arms. A big snuffle made its way from my heart to my mouth, and I ran into those arms like there was no tomorrow. She held me close while I pressed my face into the shoulder of her fuzzy white robe. She smelled of Tide laundry detergent and Yardley Lavender Soap, the way I thought all Nanas should smell. The fresh scent, the warm embrace and the love that exuded from every inch of her large frame overcame me and I sobbed.

Come to me, Maisy, and I will give you rest, I heard again in my head. I guess Jesus was using Zell to fill in for Him that night and it felt awfully good to let go of the tears I'd been holding back for who knows how long. We stayed that way a full five minutes until she finally broke away and led me to my bedroom.

"Good night, Baby Girl. Sleep tight."

"Good night, Nana." I closed the book on my desk and climbed into bed and slept tight, just like Zell said.

WE FINISHED our exams the next day and the next two afternoons I spent over at the house getting things ready for Momma. Papa felt good enough to drive, so he took me to the grocery store on Thursday after I got home from school to pick up a few groceries, so we would have something at the house to eat when she got home. My hair was in a ponytail and I wore it pulled through the back opening of my freshly washed Braves baseball cap. As I walked down the cereal aisle, I tried to think how many times I had shopped like this for one of Momma's homecomings. When I was younger, Zell did the shopping, but after that she let me pick out the things we would eat. Now I was doing it all by myself, with Papa waiting in the car.

Momma liked Raisin Bran, and wouldn't you know it would be on a shelf just out of my reach. Standing on my tiptoes, my fingers barely touched the box.

"Here, I'll get that," I heard someone behind me say. The voice sounded familiar and as the hand easily reached up and picked the box off the shelf, I saw it was Max. He was wearing a blue Food Lion polo shirt.

"I didn't know you worked here," I said.

He put the box in my grocery cart. "I just started a couple of weeks ago. I've been working part-time, but I'll be working more hours when school's out."

He looked at my hat and grinned. "I see you cleaned it up some."

"Yeah, it was stinky," I said, laughing.

"It looks a lot better on you than it did me." He reached over and pulled the brim down over my eyes again. "I've got to go. I'll get in trouble if they see me talking to a customer for too long."

"Well, you were just trying to help me get something off the shelf. How can that get you in trouble?"

"They'll find a way," he said. "What are you doing this summer?"

"Momma's coming home tomorrow." Everybody in Baker's Grove knew the story about Momma, so there was no use pretending where she'd been.

"Is that good?" he asked.

"It's very good," I said, hoping I sounded convincing. "She's finally better."

We both jumped when a voice on the loudspeaker announced, "Cleanup needed in the dairy department."

"That's me," he said, and rushed off. "I'll see you at school tomorrow."

He turned around one last time before he rounded the corner and our eyes locked. "Bye," I said, and waved. He smiled and waved back. There it was again, thud - thud - thud. Why couldn't my heart just do a pitter-patter like everyone else's?

CHAPTER FOURTEEN

MAISY

"Let us hold fast the confession of our hope without wavering, for he who promised is faithful."

—HEBREWS 10:23

Friday was the last day of school, and Momma was coming home! Her car hadn't been driven for a while, so on Friday, Papa Tom drove it to Lee Robinson's Garage to have him change the oil and check the battery. Papa still hadn't gained all his strength back yet, but he insisted on doing it even though Reverend Thatcher offered. He even stopped by the car wash. Momma's car was looking nice and spiffy sitting in our driveway, just as if she'd been home all along. As it turned out, Mrs. Clark's neighbor, Maura, wanted to babysit Matthew. I could have ridden with the Clarks to Columbia after all, but I decided instead to stay at the house and be Momma's welcoming committee when she walked in the door. The pantry and fridge had been stocked, the floors had been swept and mopped, but there was still some cleaning to do. I wanted everything to look spic and span.

The house seemed still and empty with Momma gone. As soon as I walked in the door, I headed to the credenza where we kept the CD player. It had been Daddy's. He'd left it and a shoebox full of CDs when he left, most of them by Neil Diamond. It was all I had of Daddy and it made me feel like I knew him a little better because of the music he liked. Momma never talked about him much, but she played his CDs from time to time. My friend Sabrina didn't like Neil Diamond at all. She always wanted to play Daddy's James Brown CDs when she came over. But she knew how much I liked Neil Diamond and even bought me one of his t-shirts for Christmas. I popped one of the CDs out of its case and placed it in the slot. The first song to play was my favorite, but it always made Momma a little weepy when she heard it. I sang along with it as it played.

Song sung blue
Everybody knows one
Song sung blue
Every garden grows one
Me and you are subject to the blues now and then
But when you take the blues and make a song
You sing them out again
Sing them out again

By the time the song finished, I was singing loud enough to wake the dead, as Nana Zell would say. The music made the house feel more like somebody lived here. My birthday flowers looked nice on the coffee table, and I had cut some of Zell's Knockout roses to put in Momma's bedroom. The beds hadn't been slept in since she left, so I laundered the sheets along with her pajamas, then made the bed and neatly folded her PJs and placed them on top of her pillow. With a dust cloth in hand, I dusted her nightstand and the dresser that held her clothes. Some of her paintings were in the corner; some framed and some not. I thumbed through them as I dusted the ones with frames. Her artwork had always reflected her moods. At one of her art shows in Charlotte, I overheard two of the art patrons talking; a man and woman.

"It's hard to believe the same artist did these," the woman said.

"If the signatures weren't the same, I would doubt their authenticity."

Of course, I had to put my two cents in. "The same artist painted all of these," I said, feeling a little smug. "M. Martin is my mother and I watched her paint each one."

"How does she do it?" the woman in the red dress wanted to know. "Most artists paintings are along the same theme, either light and airy or deep and dark. She manages to do both, and quite well."

I wanted to say, that's just the way Momma is. Light and airy one minute and deep and dark the next but I figured that was too personal, so I just smiled and said what I'd heard other people say. "She's just gifted that way."

"She is indeed," the man said, and they walked off together, but not before I heard the woman whisper, "Maybe she has schizophrenia."

"Vincent Van Gogh was schizophrenic, you know. Let's buy one of her paintings," her friend said. "Maybe she'll be famous one day."

I was eleven years old and didn't know much about big words yet, so I had to go home and look it up in the dictionary. *Schiz·o·phren·ia, a mentality or approach characterized by inconsistent or contradictory elements.* Yep, I thought. That could be my momma.

The house was musty, so I went around spraying lilac scented air freshener until it sent me into a fit of coughing, but I recovered just in time to see the car lights flash through the window when they drove up. I don't know why, but I was nervous. Maybe it was because Mr. and Mrs. Clark would be coming inside our tiny house. Looking around the room at the second-hand furniture, I mentally compared it all to their big house and their fancy furniture and was a little embarrassed. I ran to the door just as Mr. Clark brought in Momma's suitcase. It had always struck me as a little bizarre that each time she came home from the hospital, she came in with a suitcase, all smiles, as if she'd just been on vacation. This time there was no pretense behind that smile. She held out her arms and I dove into them.

"It's good to be home, Maisy. I've missed you so much." She looked around the house and sniffed in the lilac smell. Thank goodness, it had calmed down considerably and no longer took your breath away. "The house is so clean! And look at those flowers; they're like a ray of sunshine!"

"My birthday flowers," I said, and smiled at Mrs. Clark.

She looked at her husband. "I wish I could take credit for the flowers, Maisy. That was all Rock's idea. He called the florist and everything."

Mrs. Clark was lucky to have nice man who did nice things, just because. If my daddy had been my only example of how a man should treat a wife, you can bet I would never think about getting married. But with people like Papa, Reverend Thatcher, and Mr. Clark in the world, maybe I wouldn't give up on boys, not that I had yet. I thought about the hat Max gave me and smiled. A dirty baseball cap; not much in the scheme of things, but it was sweet.

"Thank you, Mr. Clark. No one's ever sent me flowers. I'll babysit Matthew anytime."

He laughed. "Matthew will be glad to hear that." He looked around the room.

Uh, oh; is he judging our house? I wondered. But then he waved his hand back and forth.

"Liz, look at this. The layout is very similar our cottage, the old manse."

"I thought the same thing when we pulled up in the driveway, Rock. The front porch, the entryway, even the placement of the window here in the living room. I love it!"

He took a breath and then let out a sigh. "Sometimes I wish we still lived there."

"I know you do. But can you imagine Matthew and Theo

peacefully coexisting? Theo wouldn't have as many places to hide."

"It was just wishful thinking," he said. "But I love your place, Mandy. And it's the perfect size for you and Maisy."

I looked at Momma. We both stood a little taller as they were bragging on our house. And here I thought they would be judgmental. I should have known better. They're both so real.

"I'm renting it with the option to buy, but I've never felt stable enough to flat-out buy it until now. I've got a little money set aside I inherited from my parents so maybe it's time I bought it."

"It's solidly built," Mr. Clark said, "and basically the same design as ours built in the 1920s. Buying your own home is a good investment."

"I've been lucky that I haven't had to use the inheritance. If my husband hadn't kept me and Maisy on his health insurance all this time, I don't know what would have happened to us with me in and out of the hospital so much."

That was some news I'd never heard! And I thought all the time he hadn't cared about us. It made me a little bit mad at Momma for not telling me.

Mr. Clark looked as confused as I did. "I assumed you were divorced."

He looked from Momma to me.

"I'm sure he would have loved a divorce, but he never asked for one. Despite his abandonment of us, there was always something in his makeup—a sense of responsibility I suppose. Although more often than not, he ignored it. But I am grateful he kept me on his insurance. If we had divorced, I would have been dropped automatically from his policy and with my health record, it would have been hard to get insured."

"I didn't know that, Momma. I thought he was completely out of our lives except for sending child support."

"I'm sorry that I've never talked to you about it, honey, but I've never understood it all myself. The counseling I've been going through has given me a clearer picture. Your father is a complicated man. He's generous with his money but not so generous with his love. If he had been, I think I could have coped with my mental illness, but I don't blame it all on him. I wasn't easy to live with. You and I have a lot to talk about in the days ahead. We'll be going to counseling together."

"Which reminds me, Mandy," Mrs. Clark said as if she was intentionally trying to change the subject. "We've got to get you to the DMV to get your driver's license. Monday is a teacher workday, but I can take you any other day next week."

Momma laughed. "There's nothing on my calendar. I don't even know if we still have a calendar but if we do, it's clear. How about Tuesday?"

"Perfect. Let's plan to go at 10:15. Maisy and Matthew can go with us and we'll go out to lunch afterwards."

Momma looked at her and smiled. "Thank you, Liz. You don't know how much this means."

I decided it was a good idea to change the subject, so I pitched in. "I signed up for Driver's Education last week. They have a waiting list and I need to get on it."

"Maisy! You're too young to even think about driving," Momma said.

"Momma, I just turned fifteen. Remember, you can get your driver's license in South Carolina when you're fifteen."

She put her hand over her heart, pretending she was about to faint. "No, tell me it isn't true."

We all laughed. To laugh with friends was a wonderful thing, and I knew Momma had found a true friend in Mrs. Clark.

Mr. Clark looked at his watch. "I hate to rush you Liz, but I need to get home. I have a lot of research to do for my sermon."

She hugged me and then hugged Momma. "Call me if you need anything."

We promised we would. I was looking forward to having my new, improved Momma all to myself.

CHAPTER FIFTEEN

REV ROCK

Then, because so many people were coming and going that they did not even have a chance to eat, he said to them, "Come with me by yourselves to a quiet place and get some rest."

—MARK 6:31

"Rock, there are few pastors who haven't had a touch of burnout from time to time, including me." The golf club restaurant at the Sun's Up Retirement Village was empty except for five other diners. Rock and Alan Carter were sitting opposite each other in a booth. "I pastored churches for forty years, so I've had my ups and downs too. Some just won't admit it and when the rest of us go through it, we feel isolated and guilty. Have you talked to your wife about it?"

"No, I haven't wanted to burden her."

Alan wagged his finger at him. "Now how many couples have you counseled warning them against doing exactly what you're doing?"

Rock sighed. "It's one of the first things I discuss when counseling couples who are getting married. Don't keep secrets from each other. Share your joys; share your troubles."

"Okay, what's your reason for keeping this from her? Are you afraid she wouldn't handle it well or she wouldn't understand?"

"Oh, no! She's a high school guidance counselor, or she was until she had Matthew. She went back for the last six weeks of school to fill in for someone, but she doesn't plan to go back to work this fall."

"Ha! There's not much that a high school guidance counselor hasn't seen or heard."

"That's true, but Liz takes everyone's problems to heart. I'm not even sure myself how to react to my discontent right now."

"So she's not a good counselor and you don't trust her with your problems?"

"That's not fair, Alan. I didn't say that."

"No, you didn't say it, but you're implying it by not opening up to her. Women are a heck of a lot stronger than we give them credit for, Rock. My first advice to you is to go home and tell her everything you've told me. It's my guess, she's already picked up on it and is more burdened by not knowing."

"You're right. I haven't been practicing what I preach."

"Okay, we've got that out of the way. Now tell me what you think is contributing to your feeling of burnout?"

Rock laughed. "How much time do you have?"

Alan looked around the room. "Until closing time here which is about an hour and if we don't finish, we'll go back to my house. It's just two streets down. Fire away."

"I wish I could tell you, Alan. It's more of a general feeling of discontent. Sometimes I wonder if God is still calling me to preach. I'll have moments when I'm certain He does and then other moments when I just don't know. Maybe He wants me somewhere else?"

"Has He laid upon your heart another direction to take?"

"No. If He had, I don't think I'd be feeling this lost."

"How is your workload? Too much, or not enough to do?"

"Overwhelmed. We used to have a part-time youth pastor who took some of the burden off me. That worked great until he got married and needed to find something full-time. He was called to a church in North Carolina and is doing fine from what I hear."

"Yeah, it's hard to keep part-time staff. There's not enough money in it. It would be nice if there was another church nearby that you could share the cost to make someone full-time."

"There's not. And we can't afford a full-time associate, and we honestly don't need someone full-time. We're at that in-between point; too much for one pastor to do and not quite enough for two."

"Okay, since there seems to be a stalemate on that, let's work on some other problems and solutions. How many phones do you have?"

"We have one phone line in the office, but two phones. One is on Reva's desk and the other is on mine. And I have a cell phone."

"How many people have the phone number for your cell phone?"

Rock looked sheepish. "I have a feeling this isn't going to be the right answer. My cell phone number is published in our church directory, on our Facebook page and on our website; so virtually everyone has it." He paused and emphasized his next few words. "And it rings constantly. Sometimes I want to throw it in the angel fountain in our courtyard."

"That's not a bad idea. We'll get back to that. What's your calendar like?"

"Full!"

"Full of what? Appointments? Church committee meetings? Community outreach?"

"All of those and more. The growth in this area is exploding. We've had ten new members join since the first of the year and I can barely remember their names. It's embarrassing."

"That's a good problem. Your church is one of the few in the Presbytery that's growing at all. Memorize their names though. Take photos under the guise of posting new members to your website; then look at their names beside their photos every day. Back to your calendar; what kind of appointments? Do some stand out more than others?"

"Yes, some are with new members. And I've just started a confirmation class for the new confirmands. I'm on the board of directors for the Children's Home and we have monthly meetings." He paused for a minute and sighed. "And then there's marriage counseling."

Alan smiled. "I think pastors everywhere sigh a little bit when they talk about marriage counseling."

"I suppose so," Rock said. "We listen, we love, we guide, and we try to show them how God is at work in their marriage, but ultimately it's all up to the couple. Then we either rejoice with them or we comfort them."

"I prefer the rejoicing, don't you?"

"Most definitely."

"Okay, let's talk about your work space. Do you have a nice quiet place to write your sermons?"

"Most of the time. The office is busy, but Reva's good about keeping people away when I'm working on my sermons. It's getting more difficult to find inspiration within the confines of those four walls though."

"Find somewhere fresh and new. My wife's a writer and she'll sometimes go outside and just sit in her car in the driveway and write. She says it's from so many years of writing while sitting in the car-rider line waiting to pick the grandkids up from school. She never has liked wasting time, so she takes a pen and notebook everywhere she goes."

"I think I'd get talked about if I sat in the parking lot working on my sermons. Somebody would be knocking on my window."

"I know what you mean. I'd fall asleep. But you get the drift. Find an inspirational place to work on your sermon—somewhere quiet and relaxing.

"Let's get back to your staff. You have a full-time secretary. Everyone in the Presbytery knows and loves Reva. Carl Tomlinson said he'd be tempted to steal her away if she would leave you; but he's sure she won't."

Rock's mouth dropped open and he went into panic mode.

"What? I'm not going to stand by quietly and let someone steal Reva. I don't care if he is the Presbytery moderator."

Alan laughed. "Don't worry. He knows how much she means to you and vice versa. That doesn't keep him from being envious though. Carl says every report she sends in is meticulous."

"I'd have a hard time functioning without her."

"Let's hope you never have to." He closed the pad he'd been taking notes on. "That's enough to get started. I have a few suggestions."

"I'm all ears."

"Let's start with the things you can chop off from your schedule. Before you shake your head, give me a chance. Number one; take a good hard look at your calendar and clear everything that's not totally necessary. Take for instance, your church committees—do you trust the chairpersons of your committees?"

"Well, of course I do. They're all excellent leaders."

"Good! Quit going to the meetings."

"What? You're not serious? Not go to the committee meetings? How will I know what's going on in the church?"

"Hear me out. Meet with all the chairpersons and tell them what effective leaders they are. Tell them you'll pop into committee meetings now and then, but from now on, instead of wearing yourself so thin, tell them to send you a report on what they discussed and their plan of action."

"I don't know about that."

"Remember, these are just suggestions, but I think you'd be surprised at how well it will work. Also, encourage your elders to visit some of your shut-ins. They love seeing new faces anyway, especially the women. They seem to enjoy the companionship of other women, instead of feeling like they need to entertain us men. At my former church, our women shut-ins always felt like they were obligated to feed me. I doubt they'd feel that way with another woman visiting them."

"That's true with the older generation, Alan. I'll try that. Our elders are supportive, and I'm sure I can count on them to visit shut-ins and maybe even make some hospital visits. Thank you; this is making sense."

"Now for the dreaded phone problem. It can be the undoing of the best of us. Calls at all hours, day and night."

Rock rolled his eyes and nodded. "And sometimes for the craziest things. One congregant called me to come get her cat down from her utility building, because I'm the only man she knows who doesn't work, except on Sundays. Ha!"

"That's a new one, but it's true that many church people think the pastor has it made. They think preparing a sermon and preaching it on Sunday morning is all we do. My suggestion is to get a new cell phone number and don't give anyone your new number except Reva, two elders, the Presbytery office, and your wife, of course. And I see you shaking your head no, but I'm telling you, it's the only way you'll stay sane. Publish the office telephone numbers only. Have an extra office line installed in your study at home so you can check messages often. And if pushed, be honest with your church members. Ask if they would rather have limited access to their pastor or to have an ineffective pastor suffering from burnout."

"But that would drive Reva crazy. She would have so many calls, she couldn't do her job."

"Have you thought about hiring another secretary? It would fit your budget a lot better than the salary of even a part-time associate pastor. Then she or he could answer the phones, relay to you the important messages and save everyone's sanity."

"Hmm, that may just work."

"Think about it. Put these things in practice if you're comfortable with them. There are other things that would help too. Take vacations where you're only called in case of a dire emergency. Spend time with your family. Take up a sport or a hobby." He looked at Rock slyly. "Your golf game could stand some practice time."

Rock slapped his knee and laughed. "I wondered when you would bring that up."

"It's true though. Physical activity has been proven to relieve stress." He put his notebook back in his pocket and stood up. "The wait staff are staring at us. I think we're keeping them from closing shop. I've enjoyed talking to you, Rock. I'll be at a conference in Oklahoma next week. Let's meet again in two weeks; same time, same place?"

Rock stood up too, put money on the table for a tip, and chuckled. "I'll try to squeeze it in on the calendar I'm trying to clear up. Thanks, Alan. This has been helpful just to get it off my shoulders, and you've given me some good suggestions. I feel better already."

"Go home and talk to Liz and you'll feel even better." He patted him on the back. "See you in two weeks. Oh, and take a few practice swings before our next game."

They walked out to the parking lot and Rock unlocked his door and turned back around to his new friend. He wondered how old he was. Alan was fit as if he played golf every day. He looked young but had to be pushing seventy if he had pastored a church for forty years.

"You know, Alan. It's so odd you called me when you did. I was sitting in my office desperately searching for a word, any word or any sign from God about my dilemma, and then you called."

"God's funny like that. Back in the early days of the Church, the Holy Spirit used Christians to get His message out to others. He may not speak directly to me or to you, but He'll speak through the Holy Spirit, often using other Christians to do His work. Just as God reveals the Holy Spirit to me and to you to preach the gospel."

"He uses teenage girls from time to time, too. He used the bold words of one just last week to bring me to the realization that I needed help."

"Now that's a story I'd like to hear."

"I'll be glad to share it next time. Take care, Alan, and thanks again."

"God be with you, Rock, until we meet again."

"And also with you!"

Rock decided the best time to confide in Liz was after Matthew went to bed. He stayed in his study until she came to the door.

"That was fast! An afternoon of playing with Abby on the playground wears him out. We'll be doing that every day now that school's out. It sure makes bedtime easier." She walked up behind his chair and rubbed his shoulders. "You looked lost in thought when I walked in. What were you thinking about?"

"I was thinking I needed a beautiful woman to walk in and give me a good back rub. I must have extrasensory perception because it worked." She immediately stopped.

He rolled his office chair around to face her. "Why did you stop? I want more!"

"Not until you tell me what's been bothering you. It's not like you to keep things bottled up."

"I think you're the one with ESP. I was waiting until you put Matthew to bed before I talked to you. Have a seat in the other chair."

She pulled the chair closer to him and sat down. "This sounds serious."

"You know I played golf today?"

"Yes, you told me. How did the game go?"

"Let's just say that I need practice, lots of it."

She laughed. "I recall hearing those words before. Who did you play with?"

"Alan Carter."

"That doesn't ring a bell. You said he works at the Presbytery?"

"Sort of. He's a volunteer; it's not a paid position. He retired after forty years as a pastor but found he needed something to do, so he took this job."

"And what job is that?"

Scooting his chair over a little closer, he took both of her hands in his. "He's a pastoral counselor." He thought she'd be surprised, but she just stared into his eyes and squeezed his hands.

"Finally! I was hoping you'd figure out you needed help before this counselor had to tell you." She pointed to herself.

"You know how hard-headed I am, Liz. I should have confided in you earlier. But you didn't have to tell me after all. Someone else brought it to my attention."

"Who, Reva?"

He smiled. "No, but I'm surprised she didn't. It was Maisy."

Liz broke out in laughter. "Oh yes, that Sunday at lunch. She's only been to our church twice, and she noticed. See, I told you she's smart!"

"You don't have to convince me of that. She saw a lackluster sermon first, then my Pentecost Sunday sermon and she boldly called me out."

Liz smiled and squeezed his hand. "Burnout?"

"That seems like such a harsh word, but I guess it's as good as any. I'm pulled in so many directions, I don't feel like I can do anything well."

"What did this pastoral counselor propose you do about it?"

"I knew you were going to ask; that's why I've been writing down a list of his suggestions while you were getting Matthew ready for bed." He handed her the list and she slowly read over it.

"Wow! All these at one time?"

"Yep! And I plan to get started right away. Next week is our regular session meeting. I'm putting it on the agenda to discuss with the elders."

She continued reading the list. "I hope they'll be receptive. I'm especially fond of the ones about spending more time with your family and taking uninterrupted vacations!"

"I knew you'd like that. I'm already feeling better now that I've got a game plan."

"And I'm feeling better because you're talking to me about it. Please don't ever leave me out, Rock. We work better as a team."

He stood up and gently pulled her to her feet. "I didn't want to burden you, but now I see I burdened you more by holding things back. I promise, we'll work as a team." He pulled her closer and gave her a good, long kiss. "And speaking of teams...." He kissed her again. "Let's take this team of two to the bedroom?"

"I thought you'd never ask."

CHAPTER SIXTEEN

MAISY

"Search me, O God, and know my heart; Try me and know my anxious thoughts;"

—PSALM 139:23

The summer couldn't have started off any better. I had Momma, she had a friend, and Wednesday morning someone knocked on our screen door while I was eating my last spoonful of Rice Krispies.

"Someone's here to see you Maisy," Momma called from the living room. Thinking it was Sabrina, I emptied my bowl, rinsed it out and put it in the dish drainer.

"Coming," I said, as I rounded the corner, then stopped dead in my tracks. "Max! What are you doing here?"

"I came by to see if you want to go fishing in your Papa's pond? I've got two rod and reels and some worms I dug this morning." He was standing just inside the doorway and was wearing jeans and a t-shirt, and a baseball cap that said, *Gone Fishing*, with two oversized fishing hooks sticking through the visor. He was either planning to catch a shark or they were purely for decoration.

My hair was a fright; I hadn't brushed it yet, and when I tried to run my fingers through it to make it presentable, I met resistance with a mass of tangles. "Uh", I said. "I don't know."

"Go comb your hair and get dressed, Maisy," Momma said, smiling. "You can't think with your pajamas on."

"Oh, yes ma'am," I said, and ran from the room. When I reached my bedroom, I shut the door and looked in the mirror mounted on the back. "Good grief," I said out loud. The t-shirt I was wearing for a pajama top was stained with the blue paint Momma and I had used the day before to brighten up her bedroom.

"Calypso Blue", she had called it when she got home from the paint store and put the can down on the floor. "Even the name sounds happy," I had agreed, but standing there looking in the mirror at my smudged shirt, it didn't look so happy at all. I hadn't taken a shower the night before. We were both so tired from climbing up and down ladders all day, we ate leftovers for supper and went straight to bed. I pulled out my gym shorts, underwear and a clean t-shirt from my dresser drawer and went straight for the shower. Ten minutes later, I was standing in front of the mirror again, combing my wet hair. I got out my hair dryer but decided it would dry just as well outside in the sun.

When I got to the kitchen, Momma and Max were standing at the counter wrapping three peanut butter and jelly sandwiches in wax paper. She stuffed them in a brown paper bag and nodded her head at me and winked. "They'll tide you over in case you get hungry pulling all those fish in," she said. "I put some bottled water in the little cooler by the door. Y'all have fun. Oh, and if you catch a good mess, I'll cook them." She walked to the door with us. "Don't forget the sunscreen." She rummaged around in the small cabinet under the bookcase until she found it. Looking at the date, she nodded her head and handed it to me. "The date's fine. Lather it on good; especially your face since you don't have a hat."

"Oh, but I do," I said, grabbing the Braves hat from the coat rack beside the door. Max broke out into a wide grin and when I settled it on my head, he quickly pulled the brim down over my eyes, like he'd done before. "Hey, stop that," I said, "I can't see." I hit him on the arm and pulled it back up to find him grinning even more than before. We started out the door.

"Wait, you don't have on your shoes," Momma said.

"I'm going barefoot."

"There may be snakes at the pond." At the mention of snakes, I stopped and froze. Just thinking of the creepy, crawly creatures sent a shiver up my spine.

"Okay, I'll be right back," I said apologetically to Max.

"You'd better get socks too," he said. "The grass is a little tall." I was back in a flash and we were out the door with my shoes and socks in my hand. "Bye, Mom! Love you."

"Love you too. Have fun!"

I sat on the steps and was lacing up my sneakers. "Your Papa's going too," Max said, looking embarrassed. "When I got permission this morning to fish his pond, I told him I was going to ask you to go, and he said he might as well just go along with us. The sunshine would do him good, he said."

I laughed out loud. "That sounds just like Papa Tom. He probably thinks you need to be chaperoned."

He looked puzzled. "Me? Why would I need a chaperone?" Then he blushed.

"Don't worry. He's just overprotective like that. He should know we're just friends." I studied Max's face as he studied mine. It was my turn to blush. "We *are* just friends, aren't we?" I asked.

He laughed and pulled me up to my feet. "Come on, Maisy Daisy. Let's go fishing."

Normally I would have grabbed the fishing rod, taken off running and yelled, 'I'll beat you to the pond', but I got up with as much grace as I could muster and walked ahead, leaving him to carry the rods, the bait and the cooler. I had a feeling I'd lost my old nickname, Gator, but Maisy Daisy had a nice ring to it, especially when crazy wasn't tacked on to the end of it. I looked back and gave him my best smile.

IT HAD RAINED the night before and as we trampled the grass down on our way to the pond, the air had a sweet, earthy, after-rain smell. When mixed with the blooming honeysuckles, it gave off a fragrance someone should bottle up and sell. They would make a fortune.

I forgot all about being a lady when I started catching fish. I'd planned on letting Max bait my hook, but they were biting so fast, I ditched the idea in a hurry. My competitive nature took over. After a big fish straightened the hook, I replaced it and then added another hook to my line. I baited up again and then squealed like a little kid when I reeled in two fish at the same time.

"No fair," Max called out from the other side of the pond.

I walked out on the dock with Papa Tom. It's a good thing that dock can't talk. It's the one place I can go to be alone and talk out my frustrations so no one else can hear. Papa had his cane pole cast out pretty far, but he was so amused at us, I think he forgot to bait it because his cork never moved. When the fish quit biting on our side of the pond, they started in on the side where Max was fishing. We watched him haul them in for a while, but Papa got tired of standing.

"Let's go sit under the shade tree," he said, picking his minnow bucket up from the dock. "That bench is calling my name." I got up and went with him. He had built the bench some years back under a weeping willow. It was looking a little rickety, so I sat on a log beside it, checking first to be sure a snake hadn't crawled up beside it.

"How's your Momma doing, Baby Girl?" he asked when we were both seated.

I broke off a blade of grass and started chewing on it. "I don't know, Papa. Things are going so good I'm afraid I'll jinx it if I say it out loud. Do you know what I mean?"

"I do. It's been hard on you all these years. But you've got to believe in her. She seems changed; different from all the other times. When Zell and I stopped by your house after church, we could see it. We talked about it all afternoon and we've been sending up some powerful big prayers."

"I'm glad y'all came over. Mrs. Clark took her to get her driver's license yesterday. She was so excited."

"I could have taken her, but I'm happy she's got a new friend. Everybody needs a friend."

"Papa, I've been wondering. Did you ever know my daddy?"

"I didn't get to know him, Maisy, but right after you moved here he came over to borrow some tools and returned them a few days later. He seemed a nice enough fellow, but a mite immature. At the time, I didn't know about you and your momma. After a few months went by, I noticed his truck was no longer there. The first time I met you was when I caught you barefoot and ankle deep in mud stealing those ripe tomatoes out of my garden." He grinned. "And I'm glad you did. Just look what me and Zell would have missed out on if you hadn't been hungry that day."

"I've been thinking of trying to find him, but when I typed his name in Google a few weeks ago, about a thousand men named Chris Martin showed up in the data search. I don't know how to narrow it down."

"Some people don't want to be found, so don't go hunting more trouble than what you already got. You've got to search your own heart before you can see what's in the heart of others. So instead of looking for your daddy, maybe you should focus on finding yourself."

I smiled. "But I know who I am. Why should I try to find me?"

"If we ever reach a point where we're not looking to change and to grow, then we've grown stagnant, just like this old pond does in hot weather. See the green moss building up in the shallow spots?" He pointed to the shallowest end of the pond. We'd been avoiding it all day because of the green icky stuff.

"There's a cool spring feeding the pond, but it's not moving fast enough to keep the water fresh in this heat. It's the same with us, Baby Girl. We need fresh water to live, so God designed us to thirst to keep from becoming dehydrated. It's the same with our spirits; there's a built-in spiritual thirst in all of us and it takes Jesus to fill it. But what about those other people in need? To help them, we've got to have the spirit within us and we can only keep it fresh and alive if we keep drinking from the One who gives the living water. Your momma needs you, and someday your daddy might too. Yes ma'am, you know who you are, but you've got to keep up. Never let yourself grow stagnant."

Looking at his kind old face brought tears to my eyes and I got up from the log and hugged him. "I love you, Papa."

"I love you too, Baby Girl. You've been a blessing in this old man's life."

I sat back down on the log and pulled up a reed with seed heads on the top. Tying the thin shoot into a loop, I pulled it back with a pop, sending the seeds hurtling off into the air like Papa had shown me how to do when I was just a kid.

He laughed. "You've still got the touch. Let's see if I can out-distance you." We spent the next few minutes popping the seeds up into the air until he finally conceded that I was the winner, which he had always done even when I was the clear loser. But I wasn't finished talking about Daddy. Lately I'd been obsessed with wondering about him.

I opened the cooler. "Speaking of thirsty, would you like some water?"

"I don't mind if I do. Fishing makes a man thirsty."

"And a girl, too," I said, taking a long drink. "I don't even remember what he looks like, Papa. It seems like I'd remember being that I was four-years-old when he left. If he was to walk up to us right now at this pond, I wouldn't know him from Adam's house cat. And I don't remember what his voice sounded like either, but I have a vague memory of sitting on a man's lap and him reading me a book. He had something written on his arm, maybe a tattoo, and there was a heart beside it."

Papa smiled. "That was your daddy. If I'm not mistaken, it was your momma's name written inside the heart."

I looked up. "So, he loved her at one time, I suppose. It makes me wonder when he stopped." I poked a stick I'd found into the mud and when I took it out, the hole quickly filled up with water. It made me think about my momma and if Daddy's leaving poked a hole in her heart that had never been filled up with anything.

"Trouble is, I don't know how I should feel about him. I've always felt resentful because of the way he treated Momma, going off and deserting us. It's not that I dislike him—I've just never found much reason to like him, if you know what I mean." Papa looked at me, not saying anything, but just nodded his head. "Momma says he's never asked her for a divorce and he's kept us on his health insurance all these years. If he hadn't, she'd be in a pickle with all those hospital bills. Do you think it means he still loves us?"

"There are different ways people love, Maisy. Could be that's the only way he knows how to love, by providing financial support for the two of you. Maybe it's the only kind of love his own momma and daddy ever showed to him. We learn by example, but that's not an excuse for staying the same and never learning anything better. We can rise up above our circumstances. Just look at you, child. You've had trouble enough in your own little life, but you've become a responsible young lady and you've made us proud."

"It's all because of you and Zell. Momma said she didn't know what would have happened to me if not for y'all taking me in."

"Not us, Baby Girl. It was God leading you into our tomato patch that morning. We just followed His directions."

"Why haven't we ever talked like this before? You know, about Daddy?"

"Maybe because you weren't ready, and I wasn't going to bring it up until you started asking questions. I wish I could tell you more, but I honestly don't know. Maybe there's some reason it's on your mind now more than ever, like something God is working out in your own heart."

We both turned around when we heard footsteps stomping in the grass behind us. It was Max with a big old grin on his face, and a string full of catfish. "Looks like you'll be eating good tonight," Papa said. "Between the two of you, you've got a right nice mess of fish."

"Momma said she'd cook them if we caught enough," I said. "Why don't you and Zell come over for supper? And you too, Max."

"Well, I don't mind if we do. Zell will be happy about not having to cook for a change."

"I'll come too, Max said. "But speaking of food, I'm hungry. Let's break out the peanut butter and jelly sandwiches."

"There's one for you too, Papa," I said. Max pulled the cold water out of the cooler and I opened the brown paper bag Momma had packed with sandwiches.

Papa cleared his throat. "And I don't suppose you two have noticed this picnic basket?" He pointed to a shady spot under the other weeping willow tree a few feet away. "When I told Zell what we were doing, she fried the batch of chicken she'd laid out for tonight saying we would be having fish for supper anyway. Then she commenced to making fried apple pies to beat the band. But I suppose you two would rather have a peanut butter sandwich, wouldn't you?" he asked with a twinkle in his eye.

"I say the ducks can have the PBJs," and I started stuffing them back in the bag. "We'll wait until after we eat, or they'll be pestering us for more. What about you, Max?"

"I've never turned down fried chicken and apple pies," he said. He ran, not walked and brought the basket to the shade tree we were under.

"Hey, look!" I said pulling things out of the basket. "She even packed a quilt for us to sit on while we eat." I unfolded it and Max helped me spread it on the ground.

"Man, this is like a real picnic," he said, rubbing his hands back and forth. He sat down on the quilt looking a little like a hungry coyote ready to devour the roadrunner.

"Wait," I said, holding my arm out like a school crossing guard. Max and Papa both looked up. "We need to clean this icky fish smell off our fingers before we eat," I said, pulling the wipes Momma had packed out of our bag and passing them around.

Papa watched as we finished cleaning our hands. "Now, let's ask the good Lord to bless this food." He waited until we'd bowed our heads. "Lord, we thank you for all you've given us—these fish and the fine meal they'll make tonight. Thank you for the friendships we share and for the way you've blessed our lives by bringing us together. We ask you now to bless this food to the nourishment of our bodies and bless the hands of Zell who made it. In your Son's name we pray. Amen."

Max and I said our amens in unison and started digging in. We'd worked up an appetite, especially him. It was funny watching him wolf down two pieces of chicken and start in on the apple pie. Wile E. Coyote never had it so good.

IT WAS ALMOST 6 o'clock and Momma was trying a new recipe from the cookbook I had borrowed from Mrs. Clark. She was nervous. Everybody said Zell Baker was the best cook in Baker's Grove, and I could vouch for that since I'd had the benefit of being a first-hand witness. In all the years we'd been neighbors, Momma had never cooked for Papa and Nana Zell. Zell had cooked for us plenty of times. Max and Papa had cleaned the fish after lunch and I brought them home. Momma seasoned them with salt, pepper, garlic and lemon juice, then sprinkled parmesan cheese all over them and waited until Nana and Papa knocked on the door to put the skillet in the oven. I was sulking around a little bit. After I'd gone to all the trouble of washing my hair, putting on a sundress, and spritzing myself with Momma's perfume, Max's boss called at the last minute and asked him to work. I was even wearing my sequined flip-flops, a big change of dress from my normal bare feet, t-shirts and shorts.

The coleslaw and baked sweet potatoes were already on the table and I filled up the iced tea glasses just as Momma pulled the fish out of the oven. Nana Zell took one whiff and smiled. "Something smells awfully good, Mandy Girl." She stretched out gur-ell just like she did when she called me Baby Girl. I could tell Momma was pleased with the compliment and I wanted to give Zell a big old hug. She could be a little grumpy at times, but she had always been sweet and gentle with Momma.

With everything on the table, we sat down and held out our hands to one another to say grace. Papa said the blessing with his own personal touch. *"Lord, we thank you for the food we are about to share, the cabbage and potatoes you have so generously provided from our garden and the fish from our pond. We ask you to bless young Max, who shared his bounty but couldn't be with us tonight. And Lord, we especially thank you for Mandy who lovingly prepared the food, so it will nourish our bodies in a healthy way. What a fine family you've given us, Lord, and we are grateful for these two who let us share their table. In Jesus's name we pray. Amen."*

Momma beamed as Papa Tom declared the fish as good as he'd ever tasted. Zell looked on in astonishment as she watched him eat four pieces, and then hurried to catch up thinking he was going to eat them all before she got her fair share. "This is delicious," Zell said between bites. "I've been trying to cook healthier, but old habits are hard to break. I even bought a pack of turkey bacon but it don't hold a candle to pork, no siree."

"Maybe you just need some new recipes," Momma said.

"I'm not much good with recipes," she admitted glumly. "I

tend to make the same things over and over. I think I could make them blindfolded. It's been a long time since I've even looked at a cookbook." Everyone was finished eating so I started clearing off the table while Momma talked to Zell.

"This fish recipe will be a good place to start since both of you seem to like it. It's only got five ingredients." She called off the ingredients. "Be sure to brush it with a little olive oil before you add the parmesan, or it will dry out." She picked the cookbook up from the barstool behind her and thumbed through it. "Look, it's even got a section called Heart Healthy, and it gives you little tips on things to substitute to make it healthier; like olive oil instead of lard or butter." She flipped to another page. "Here's a brownie recipe I think you'll like. It uses applesauce instead of vegetable oil, and egg whites instead of whole eggs. It says to avoid ingredients like palm oil, and partially hydrogenated oils in processed foods.'"

I had put the dishes in the sink and sat back down at the table. Momma flipped through a few more pages, then looked up at all of us. It was a minute before she spoke again.

"There's even a section about foods that may cause depression and what to avoid. For example, sugars, artificial sweeteners, trans fatty acids, processed foods; all of those can cause mood swings in children and adults. It says it's much better to eat fresh fruits, vegetables and unprocessed meats." She closed the cookbook.

"I never knew that before, so see, Zell—we're all in this learning process together and we'll do what we have to in order to stay healthy, even if it kills us." We all laughed.

"Maybe Maisy and I could come over once a week and we could all cook healthy together."

"I sure could use some help," Zell said.

I looked at Momma in wonder. Six months ago, she would have never mentioned the word depression. Even though every person in Baker's Grove knew she had it, she had never admitted it by speaking the word out loud. You couldn't much blame her though. It doesn't seem to matter how much people learn about it, they always look at you like—well, like you're crazy. I had seen the look, I had heard the whispers. I had even experienced the pain with Shelly Bumgarner's "Maisy, Maisy, your momma's crazy" chants. That was the first time I'd ever let anybody see me cry.

I was proud of her. She was coming out of a shell that had been wrapped as tight as a roly-poly pillbug. One that made her curl up inside it and roll along instead of walking tall and straight with a purpose in life.

I had a momentary glimpse of how things could be for her—that she would be alright. But there, niggling in the back of my mind was another image saying, "hold up, Maisy; it's too early to tell." Just then I looked at Papa studying me with his wise old eyes and even though he was silent, I could hear him say, "where's your faith, Baby Girl?" Sometimes I think he can read my mind. Or maybe I can read his.

CHAPTER SEVENTEEN

CHRIS

"My soul is in deep anguish. How long, LORD, how long?"
—PSALM 6:3

To the average eye, the man in the black t-shirt with a receding hairline was just one of many veterans calmly waiting his turn to be seen by a doctor. What they couldn't see was that his blood pressure was high, and he was close to having an anxiety attack from the waiting. The smell of medical antiseptics had always made Chris Martin feel faint. No one else in the room seemed bothered by it. They were all calmly reading magazines or texting on their cell phones while he was sitting up straight taking deep breaths, hoping to overcome the feeling before he fainted.

To take his mind off why he was there, he looked at his surroundings. In front of him was a large framed portrait of the clinic's major benefactor, a businessman who gave back to the community that had contributed to his success. The room was pleasant enough. Textured pale yellow walls, beige blocks of carpet, alternating orange and mustard-yellow chairs; fifteen of them if his count was correct. He couldn't see around a small dividing wall so there may have been more. It was enough to make him feel like he was in an autumn landscape—not too bad for a veteran's medical center. Completing the scene was a wall-mounted TV tuned to a do-it-yourself channel where the host was completing a curb-appeal project.

Fear was nothing new to Chris. Throughout his whole life, he'd been streamlined for the tough-guy image by a drill sergeant of a father and he'd followed the old man's footsteps by joining the Marines. After the September 11th terrorist attacks, his unit had been sent to Afghanistan as a military offensive to try to overthrow the Taliban.

He'd watched helplessly as his best friend lost a leg when he stepped on a landmine right in front of him. Back home, after his tour of duty was over, Chris had softened and taken on a different persona when he fell in love with and married the beautiful but fragile Amanda McKay. Her fragility was not physical, but emotional. He had known her mental frailties before they married, but he thought all she needed was someone to love her. And it seemed to work. There were some mild episodes, but his coddling and care would return her to an almost manic joyfulness. It was infectious and made him as happy as it made her.

His parents never warmed to Mandy, though. His father looked upon her fragile nature as a weakness and his mother would never accept any woman who was untying her son from her apron strings. He knew their attitude toward her hurt Mandy, but she pretended it didn't. Shortly after they married he took a job on an oil rig in Texas and they moved. It felt liberating to break free from his parents' perpetual leash around his neck.

Ten months into their marriage, he and Mandy were ecstatic when a drugstore pregnancy test confirmed their suspicions that they themselves would be parents in a few short months. It was difficult not having the support of loving parents to share their news. His were bitter and suspicious by nature, and hers had been killed in an uprising in a village in East Africa. But at least they had each other and it seemed all would be well. But it wasn't.

After Maisy was born, Mandy seemed fine, but as the stress of motherhood wore on her, she became unpredictable, sullen most of the time and she would get angry at him over the slightest things. It was like she transferred all the love inside her from him to their baby. At the time, he didn't realize her symptoms pointed to something called postpartum depression; he didn't even know there was such a thing. Instead of spending time at home trying to make life easier for Mandy, he had distanced himself from his wife and baby and worked all the overtime hours he could get.

After a couple of years, oil prices dropped, and the oil rigs stood idle. They both decided they should move back to South Carolina where construction was booming so he could find work. They rented a house outside of Park Place in the community of Baker's Grove. Mandy was better, but she was still wrapped up in their daughter. He felt slighted. He worked for a while, but when oil prices went up and the oil rigs became fully operational again, he left one day telling Mandy he was going back to Texas but wouldn't be gone long. The weeks turned into months and after a while he just didn't go back home at all. Somewhere along the line, he had matured enough to know he had been wrong, but by then, he was too ashamed to return to his family. In hindsight, he now realized his mental health had suffered too as a result of the things he'd seen in Afghanistan. If he'd gotten treatment, maybe things would've been different. So many maybes.

Chris had worked hard and sent a fair share of the money to Mandy, trying to make up for his not being there. He had also started a college fund for Maisy, but money was not a good substitute for a missing father. It was likely she didn't remember him. How foolish he'd been. He had not been around to watch his little girl grow up and now he was paying the price. It had been over ten years and she'd just turned fifteen.

"Mr. Martin?" He jumped at the sound of his name being called. "Dr. Blakeney can see you now."

"I'm sorry; I was in another world. Have you been calling my name long?"

"Only a dozen times," she said. His mouth fell open, and she laughed. "I'm kidding, just twice. I could tell you were in deep thought."

He followed as she led the way down a maze of corridors, finally coming to a stop at a door with a teal ribbon stuck to it. He had noticed them posted on other doors they had passed.

"Why the ribbons everywhere?"

"It's Ovarian Cancer Awareness Month," she said. "Since this is an oncology clinic, we show our support to our veterans during the months dedicated to bring attention to the various forms of cancer." She knocked on the door in front of them.

"Come in."

Dr. Blakeney was sitting at his desk with a file folder in front of him. He looked up as they entered the room.

"Come on in, Chris. Pull up a chair."

The doctor looked weary and Chris figured it must be draining on oncologists to have to give bad news all day long. When he'd received the call yesterday, he'd known by the urgent tone of the voice on the other end that something was wrong.

"Give it to me straight, Doc. Don't hold anything back."

"It's not good news, Chris." He shuffled things around on his desk and pulled out the MRI image of Chris's spine. "The cancer is back and this time it's spread." He held the image to the light. Chris pulled up a little closer in order to see the image better.

"What we're looking at are metastatic spinal tumors of the cervical spine, involving the C4, C5 and C6 vertebral bodies. There's also some significant compression of the spinal cord, which over time will weaken its structure if left unchecked. But that's not all." His finger moved down the MRI a few inches. "See all the shadowing here?" He turned to Chris. "You asked, and I'm not holding anything back. This isn't what I wanted to see."

Chris wasn't surprised. Over the last three months, the pain in his back had grown steadily worse until he could no longer lift the heavy loads on the rig. His job as a supervisor didn't let him off the hook. The men would lose respect for him if he didn't carry his share of the work.

"So no more working on the oil rig?"

"Not unless you've got some cushy job doing paperwork."

"No such luck." He leaned forward. "What's my prognosis? I need to plan for the future." He stared long and hard at the doctor who seemed to be avoiding his gaze by looking down at his files again. "Or maybe to plan for the absence of a future."

Dr. Blakeney looked back up. "I'm sorry, Chris. I didn't intend for my silence to worry you. I was just thinking what our next steps should be. I want to do a biopsy of the tumors to see what we're dealing with before I can answer you. If it was an isolated tumor, I'd lean toward thinking it's benign, but it's not isolated as you can see by the image. The biopsy will tell us how aggressive it is and will determine our treatment schedule. Radiation, surgery and chemotherapy are all options."

"Do you think this spread from my lung cancer last year?"

"More than likely. Lung cancer will often metastasize in other parts of your body, and the spine seems to be the main target when it does." He pulled out his prescription pad. "How much pain are you experiencing?"

"A lot. My back, my neck; even my right leg, all the way down."

The doctor scribbled something on the pad in front of him. "This is the strongest I can give you. I need to warn you though; it's an opioid so you should never drive or operate machinery while taking it. And don't tell others you're taking it. It's a shame, but some people would kill for this stuff." He ripped the sheet off and handed it to Chris.

Chris took it from him. He ran his fingers through his short hair and noticed again how little was there. He'd had a full head of hair before he lost it all during his previous chemo treatments.

"I'm going to ask you this upfront, Doc, and I want a truthful answer. You're pretty sure it's aggressive, aren't you?"

Dr. Blakeney took a deep breath, then let it out. "I think it is, Chris. If you have some things to settle in your life, I urge you to do it now. And if you're so inclined, start praying and ask everybody you know to do the same. I started before you even walked in the room."

It had been years since he had prayed, and he wasn't sure he even knew how anymore. Just the mention of prayer made him feel uncomfortable, so he changed the subject. "What if I decide to forego treatment of any kind?"

"That will be up to you, but I hope you'll wait until we do a biopsy before you make a decision."

He got up from his chair, wincing with pain as he stood up straight. He reached out and shook Dr. Blakeney's hand. "You set the appointment and I'll be there."

When he got to the parking lot and opened the car door, he was met with a blast of heat coming from inside. The black interior of his jeep didn't bode so well with the extreme heat of a Texas sun bearing down upon it. He felt weak and nauseous, so he turned the air conditioning up full blast and sat there in the parking lot until his nausea subsided.

He took his VA card out of his pocket to put it back in his wallet, but when he opened it up, something fluttered to the floorboard. He picked it up. It was a faded photo of an attractive young woman holding hands with a five-year-old little girl with wavy hair. It had been in the last letter she'd sent him ten years ago.

"Mandy," he said in a forlorn voice, then rested his head on the steering wheel and sobbed. A few minutes later, he heard a rap on his window. He looked up and saw it was an older man wearing a Vietnam Veteran hat.

"Are you okay?" the man asked. Chris gave him a thumbs-up sign, composed himself and drove away.

∼

As the plane started its gradual descent over the foothills of the Blue Ridge Mountains, Chris Martin was thankful he'd been assigned a window seat. He marveled at the distinct hazy blue hanging over the valleys of the majestic peaks they had just flown over en route to their Charlotte, North Carolina destination. There was something ethereal about the blue color, but he remembered reading it was all a matter of perception and it had a scientific explanation. Tiny particles of hydrocarbon released by the pine trees and the thick blanket of vegetation react with ozone molecules to produce the hazy effect. Add in the blue sky shining on the dark, solid mountain and from a distance, the scattered light gives it a ghostly blue appearance.

He had flown first to Oklahoma City where the Proust Oil Company had their headquarters to sign his exit paperwork. Working on an oil rig was a hard, backbreaking job but it had paid well. In his fifteen years with the company, he had accumulated a healthy financial portfolio and his beneficiaries would be taken care of. It grieved him that he wouldn't be leaving a legacy of love and respect, but at least they would know he had planned and cared for them in other ways, wouldn't they?

After the biopsy revealed the cancer was aggressive, the doctor had ordered other scans and found it had spread throughout his body. It was difficult but he made the decision to forgo any more treatment since it wasn't likely to improve his chances of survival. He would live out whatever time he had left without the chemo fog clouding up his mind.

It didn't take him long to pack his few belongings and ship them back to his parents' house in South Carolina. The lease on his furnished apartment was up anyway, so the only thing he had to worry about was getting rid of the odds and ends he'd accumulated. His neighbor was kind enough to take them off his hands to give to a charity shop in Houston.

He was consumed with thoughts of seeing Mandy and Maisy one last time. They wouldn't exactly welcome him with open arms, even if they knew he was dying. It was selfish of him to even think about it. "Get over yourself, Chris."

"Pardon me?"

He hadn't realized he had spoken aloud. The older man seated beside him had been reading a book since they boarded the plane but was now looking at him expectantly. "I'm sorry. I have a habit of talking to myself. I didn't mean to disturb you."

"You didn't disturb me at all," he said, closing the book. "If you think you talk to yourself now, just wait until you get my age. I do it all the time."

Chris had noticed the title of the book—*The Gift of Compassion*. What did he have to lose? This guy had heard it all.

"I'll never get to be your age," he said matter-of-factly.

The man laughed. "Sure you will; I'm not *that* old. Or at least I don't think seventy is old, but I imagine it is to you. You're what; forty maybe?"

"Close. I'm thirty-nine. My birthday is in December, but I doubt I'll be around for it. I'm dying."

The man's look of surprise was quickly replaced by a look of concern. "Where are you headed, son?"

"I'm moving back home. Just south of Charlotte across the state line. Park Place, South Carolina. Have you ever heard of it?"

"I have indeed. I live in Sun's Up Retirement Village. The Park Place post office is exactly 5.2 miles from my driveway. The interstate is 2.1 miles further, and if you think I have an obsession about measuring miles, you'd be right." He took a business card out of his shirt pocket and handed it to Chris.

"My name is Alan Carter. I'm sorry I've been preoccupied with my book this whole trip. It sounds like you might have needed an ear to talk to."

Chris smiled. "Some things are best left unsaid. I don't know what possessed me to blurt it out."

"I think I do."

"You do?" He looked again at the book in the man's hand. "I

noticed the book in your hand, but honestly, I didn't think much about it, if that's what you were thinking."

"Or maybe, because I was reading a book, it made you feel more comfortable with talking to yourself, thinking I wouldn't be listening anyway. Whatever way you choose to look at it, I'm pretty sure God had a hand in it."

Chris looked down at down at the business card. "What is a Presbytery? Are you a preacher?"

"A Presbytery is a governing body within The Presbyterian Church. And I guess you could say, once a preacher, always a preacher, but I'm retired from the pulpit except on sporadic occasions when I'm asked to fill in. I found retirement boring, so I now volunteer to counsel and mentor those who still preach."

Chris squirmed in his seat. The last person he wanted to be seated on the plane with was someone who was going to preach to him. "It sounds like a noble calling, but I don't think you could help me. I'm not a preacher who needs mentoring."

"You're right. I doubt I could be of any help to you."

Chris breathed a sigh of relief. "Thank you for understanding."

Alan Carter smiled. "But I know someone who can."

"Can what?" Chris said, puzzled.

"Someone who can help you."

Chris rolled his eyes. "I knew I shouldn't have been talking to myself. It always gets me in trouble."

Alan's eyes twinkled. "How about sharing your phone number. I have someone I'd really like you to meet. I think you'll end up helping each other."

Chris pulled out his cell phone. "I don't know why I'm doing this. Maybe it's because you seem to be a good-natured sort." He pulled up his own number on the screen and pushed it in Alan's direction. "But I want to warn you, I'm beyond help."

Alan entered it in his own phone. "Son let me tell you something. While you're still on God's green earth, you're not beyond help."

When the man in the seat beside him looked up from his phone, Chris noticed he had startling green eyes that looked as if they could stare straight down into a man's soul. Instead of finding it unsettling, he found it somewhat comforting, and for the last short leg of the plane ride, he found himself sharing his story, and even carrying their conversation inside the coffee shop of the airport for another hour. The whole story from start to finish, leaving nothing out in telling him what a lousy husband and father he'd been. Alan Carter just listened, never offering to judge or condemn, and as Chris drove out of the airport in his rental car, he felt some of his burden had been lifted. Then he remembered he was going to see his parents and his shoulders visibly drooped. He hadn't told yet them his cancer had spread. He wondered if they would even care.

CHAPTER EIGHTEEN

REV ROCK

"Be careful then, how you live; not as unwise but as wise."
—EPHESIANS 5:15

Rock had just locked the office door when he heard the phone ring. He started to go back inside, then remembered what Alan Carter had said, so he let it ring as he walked across the parking lot. Before he reached the sidewalk leading to his front porch, his cell phone was ringing. He looked down at the number; Alan Carter. It had been less than a week since he'd seen him; did he want to meet again so soon?

"What's up, Alan. I thought you were at a conference this week."

"I was. I just got in from the airport and I have a favor to ask. There's someone I'd like you to talk to."

"I don't think so."

Rock smiled as the voice on the other end was silent for a moment. "You don't think so? You haven't given me a chance to tell you about it."

"You told me I need to start saying no. I'm just following your advice."

"Well, you didn't follow my advice about changing your cell phone number, so I'm not letting you off the hook so easy."

"Touché." Rock sat down on the bench beside the angel fountain in the courtyard. "Okay, hold on. I was walking home from the office. Let me get a pen out of my satchel. I'm going to set the phone down for a second so don't think I hung up on you." The quiet, gentle sound of running water from the fountain was soothing to his soul as he dug around inside his satchel for pen and paper. The bench was set back inside an arbor with clematis growing up from each side and meeting overhead in the middle with its tentative finger-like branches. The fragrance was subtle, not overbearing. Tucked away in the middle of a labyrinth of shrubbery, the space was designed for privacy where a person could go for quiet, reflective moments, but it was rarely used. With pen and paper in hand, he picked the phone back up and held it to his ear. "I think I've accidentally stumbled on the perfect place to work on my sermons, so I'm glad you called."

"See, I knew you'd be glad to hear from me!"

Rock laughed. "Okay, bring it on. Who is it you want me to contact?"

"His name is Chris, and I just realized I didn't write down his last name. He's just moved back here after spending several years in Texas. He's hurting inside and out. He's struggling with guilt. He's hurt the people he was supposed to love and protect, and he's dying."

"I think a lot of us die a little inside when we're feeling guilt weighing us down."

"That's not what I meant, Rock. He's literally dying; he has cancer."

"Oh, I see. And before he passes away, he's trying to make amends. Is it for his own sake or for theirs?"

"Maybe a little bit of both, but I don't think he even plans to contact them. He says they'll never forgive him anyway."

"He underestimates human compassion and forgiveness then, doesn't he?"

"I'm afraid it's a bit foreign to him. There's a lot of backstory here, Rock. I hope you can make some time to talk to him. If you find you can't, let me know and I'll carve some time out of my own schedule, but the Lord put it on my mind to hand it over to you."

Rock sighed and rolled his eyes heavenward. "Well, since you put it that way, I don't think I have a choice. I'll call him. Who am I to argue with God's plan?"

He was expecting a light-hearted comeback from Alan, but he didn't get it. Instead, he heard raw emotion in the voice on the other end. "You don't know how relieved I am to hear you say that, Rock. Who are we, indeed? I'm sorry to have to pass this cup to you but thank you for taking it nonetheless."

Rock said his goodbyes and pushed the End Call button on his phone. He sat there a moment and thought about their conversation. What did Alan mean by *passing this cup*? He didn't hear the expression used often except in the context of scripture where cups are mentioned numerous times. He thought about the Old Testament where the cup is used as a symbol for our lives. The cup of the 23rd Psalm, *my cup runneth over*, speaks of the many blessings from God to mankind, but in Isaiah 51:17, the prophet Isaiah warns God's chosen people that they *have drunk the cup of the Lord's fury*. In the New Testament, Jesus plead with his Father to take away the cup of the cross. Rock's own understanding was that in Jesus' humanness, He was alluding to those words of Isaiah and knew He would have to bear God's wrath and judgment for mankind and suffer horribly.

Rock realized he himself had been asking for his own cup to be emptied of overwork and frustration. What a little cup compared to the cup of Jesus, and how often we try to pass our cups of unpleasantness to someone else. But in doing so, Alan had given him these thoughts to ponder. He thought about the analogy of the cup half empty and the cup half full. He would have to remember that in reality, his own was overflowing with blessings.

CHAPTER NINETEEN

MAISY

"And do not forget to do good and to share with others, for with such sacrifices God is pleased."
—HEBREWS 13:16

My toes pushed hard against the weathered plank boards to keep the swing in motion as I sat there snapping green beans from Papa Tom's garden. Momma was sitting in the porch rocker, and as she pulled the strings off the beans and filled her pan, she poured them in mine for me to snap. I was doing a pretty good job of keeping up if I do say so myself.

"Ouch," I yelled, and put my pan down beside me.

"What's wrong," she asked. "Another splinter? I think you need to wear shoes when you're swinging."

I picked the splinter out of my toe and moved over into the middle of the swing where the planks were smoother. So far, the splinters I had encountered were the only casualties I'd suffered from a barefoot summer. I looked up at her and smiled. It was the first time we'd ever attempted to freeze and can vegetables from the garden. She'd never felt up to it before, always either going wide open or crashing. There had never been much of a middle ground with Momma. But here she sat peacefully carrying on a natural conversation.

"Shoes?" I said, acting shocked at her request. "My feet have grown wild and carefree." I wiggled my toes. "I don't think shoes could contain them."

She laughed. "In that case, maybe we should just work on those boards; file them down or something."

"I'll ask Papa about it tomorrow. He'll know what to do."

"You're a big help to him in the garden, Maisy. He told me yesterday he couldn't have handled it without you."

"I worry about him, Momma. He stops every ten minutes just to catch his breath. Today I just told him to sit in the shade while I picked the beans and okra, and he didn't even argue. He said to pick all we could use because tomorrow he's going to let the neighbors come in and get what they need. I'm glad because I'm about gardened out, and Nana Zell is all tuckered out from so much canning."

"I've enjoyed canning and freezing this summer, but we have all we need." She held up the basket the beans had been in. "Look, it's empty. I'll help you finish snapping them and we'll call it a day. They'll keep in the refrigerator for a day or two." We quickly snapped the last of them and poured them into the large pot I'd been putting them in.

It had been breezy earlier, but when the sun set, the air grew sticky and still. Still enough to hear the mosquitos buzzing around my head. The crickets and cicadas were making their night noises and I thought how nice it was living tucked back on a little country road with only an occasional car passing by. I picked up the pot of beans and started walking toward the screen door. "I'm going inside; the mosquitos are starting to bite." Momma closed the door behind us and I set the container of beans upon the counter. "How many pints do you think we'll have when we finish canning these?"

"Eight or ten; maybe more. We'll hold off canning them until tomorrow afternoon late. Liz called today and asked me if I wanted to go shopping in Rock Hill with her. Would you like to come?"

"Does she need a babysitter?"

"No, Holly and Abby are going to the new water park across the river. She's taking Matthew along."

"I think I'll pass then. Maybe I'll ask Papa to go fishing. It'll keep him out of the garden."

"That's sweet of you, Maisy. You're always putting others first." I smiled, not letting on I might have an ulterior motive. It would be Max's only day off work and I was secretly hoping he might come fishing too.

THE NEXT MORNING, we were eating breakfast when we heard a knock on the door. "It can't be Liz this early," Momma said. "It's only 8:30. She said she wouldn't be here until 9 o'clock. Can you see who it is, Maisy, while I wash the breakfast dishes?"

"Sure." I walked into the living room and could see a familiar baseball cap through the small glass window at the top of the door. I unlocked the door and the storm door and invited him in. "It's just Max, Momma," I yelled back into the kitchen.

He stooped down and looked me straight in the eye, and I stifled a laugh. "*Just* Max, is it? Who were you expecting; the queen of England?"

"You'd sure make a funny looking queen," I said, letting the laughter spill out.

"Well, invite him in," Momma called from the kitchen.

"He's already in," I called back.

Momma came to the door. "Have you had breakfast, Max. We have two pancakes left, but I can make you some more."

"No ma'am. It sounds good, but I've already eaten. I came by to see if Maisy could go fishing."

"Aha! You must have read her mind from afar. She's already planned to go fishing with her Papa." She looked at me suspiciously, then at Max. "Am I missing something here?"

Max looked confused. "Missing what, ma'am?"

"No, Momma. I didn't invite Max to go fishing, but he just now invited me. Can I go?"

She smiled. "Only if Papa Tom goes along. I'll call him and make sure he can go before I leave."

"I've already asked him, but you can call him anyway," Max said. "I just thought it was the right thing to do."

Momma nodded and smiled. "I like you, Max. Maisy's lucky to have a good friend like you."

He blushed and looked down at his feet. "Thank you, Mrs. Martin. I guess I'm lucky to have her for a friend too." He looked at me and grinned. "Freckles and all." I hit him hard on the arm.

"By the way, Mrs. Martin. Were you waiting for someone to pick you up?"

"Not this early. Why do you ask?"

"When I walked across the field from Mr. Baker's house, I saw a man in a car parked on the other side of the road. He was looking at your house, but when he saw me he looked down at what appeared to be a map, then he drove off. It was probably someone who took a wrong turn."

Momma looked worried. "Maybe I shouldn't leave. I don't like the idea of a strange man hanging around with Maisy here alone."

"I won't be alone, Momma. I'll stay with Nana Zell until you get back. I'm sure it's nothing. No one drives down these roads unless they're lost."

"What did the man look like, Max?"

"I didn't get a good look at him. He appeared to be a little stooped over, like maybe he had a bad back or something. And he didn't have a lot of hair, you know. Like maybe he was going bald."

Momma looked relieved for some reason. I guess she didn't think bald people were as dangerous as men with hair. "Okay, just be sure you stay with Zell and Tom until I get home, Maisy. I'll give you a call when I get back."

"Let's go fishing then," I said, pulling my cap down from the peg.

"What about lunch?" Momma asked. "You'll get hungry."

"Oh yeah, I'll fix us a sandwich."

Max held up a paper bag. "I packed lunch this time; I hope you like sardines."

"Yuck! No way." But I put my cap on and started for the door. It wouldn't kill me to eat sardines one time in my life. Or would it? On second thought, I turned around and headed for the kitchen. "Maybe I'll bring a pack of Nabs, just in case."

"Chicken!" he said.

"Sardine Man!" I said back.

I CAUGHT three fish right off the bat when we got settled in at the pond. But then they quit, cold turkey. "We got too late of a start," Papa said. "When the weather's this hot, they only bite early in the morning or late afternoon."

"So, they've quit for the day?"

"No doubt."

"Let's go back to your house, then. I'm about to burn up. Momma says I should stay with you and Zell until she gets home. Max saw a man parked on the road near our house and I guess she thinks he'll kidnap me or something." I laughed nervously. It did sort of spook me now that I thought of it.

Papa turned to Max. "What kind of car?"

"It was a Chevy Impala. I didn't get a real close look, but it could have been a rental car."

"White?"

"Yes sir, it was."

"I saw that car making a couple of passes by the house yesterday. You don't see many strangers coming this far down the road. I didn't think too much of it then; I figured he must be lost, but with you seeing him again today, I don't know. I'll call around and ask the other neighbors to keep an eye out." He snapped his fingers. "I just thought of something. I heard the Haywood family is selling off a few acres across the creek now that Mr. Haywood's passed. Maybe it's a real estate agent."

"Yes sir, I'll bet that's it," Max said, but I saw him and Papa Tom exchange glances. They weren't fooling me. They just didn't want me to worry, which made me worry all the more.

We made it back to the house and Max took the string of fish from me. "I'll clean the fish and bring them in when I'm finished."

"Thank you, Max. I'll let Zell know we're back and see if she has lunch ready." I watched Papa Tom as he clutched the handrail leading up the steps onto the porch. He took one step, then waited and took another, and kept going like that until he reached the top. I thought how frail he looked and said so to Max.

"Well, he is pretty old, Maisy. That's the way old people get."

"You don't think he's going to die, do you?" I asked. "He's the closest thing I've ever had to a grandpa, well, even a daddy, actually. I can't stand to think about losing him." The thought brought tears to my eyes. I brushed them away, not wanting Max to see them. But he did and put the fish down on the steps. He opened his lunch bag, pulled out a napkin and handed it to me.

"Everybody has to die sometime, Maisy, but I think he's got a lot of life left in him. He just hasn't got his strength back from being sick, but he looks better than he did a month ago."

I wiped away the tears and put the napkin in my jeans pocket. I was embarrassed he'd seen me cry. I picked the fish up off the steps. "I can clean my own fish, thank you."

He took them out of my hand and grinned. "But you don't want to, do you?" I rolled my eyes and he laughed.

We both jumped at the clap of thunder. It seemed to come out of nowhere and was followed by smaller rumbles in the background. I looked up and saw that the sky had changed from bright blue to a deep gray in a matter of minutes.

"Yike's!" I said. "Look at those clouds; looks like a thunderstorm is coming up." Pretty soon there would be lightning strikes and there was nothing that scared me more than lightning. Max must have sensed my uneasiness. He handed me his lunch bag. "You'd better go inside; it's getting ready to rain. Take this in and add it to whatever Mrs. Baker has for lunch."

"Ha, like they're going to eat stinky sardines!"

MAX FOLLOWED Maisy into the house, and they did eat the sardines. Even Zell going so far as to brag on the brand Max had bought. "This is the best kind," she said. "I can't find them in the grocery stores anymore."

"Yes ma'am. Dad gets them from a wholesaler. We have a whole case of them at home, so I'll bring you a couple of packs the next time I come over."

Needless to say, I didn't let a sardine pass my lips. Two tomato pies had just come out of the oven when we walked inside. "You must have known I was coming, Nana Zell," I said as I sat down at my usual place at the small kitchen table. Max sat down beside me.

Nana looked at me and nodded her head. "Lord a'mercy, child. I always make two when you're here. You can eat a whole pie by yourself." She set them on the table while they were still steaming. I breathed in the savory aroma of onions, basil and grated cheese on a layer of tomatoes baked in a deep-dish pie shell. She sliced it and put the biggest portion on my plate. I could hardly wait for Papa to bless the food before I dug in.

"Yum," I said as the melded flavors reached the back of my tongue. "Nana Zell, you're the best!"

As Zell beamed at the compliment, I realized at that moment how much she truly loved me, and the feeling was every bit as savory as the tomato pie. After we ate, I washed the dishes as Zell dried. I looked out the kitchen window and saw blue skies. The storm left just about as fast as it came up. I lifted the dishpan full of water out of the sink and started out the door.

Max looked at me funny. "Where are you going with that?"

"I'm taking it out. Their sink doesn't drain right, so we always empty it outside."

"What's wrong with the sink, Mr. Baker?"

Papa explained. "And my knees won't let me crawl under the house," he said, as if he was embarrassed about it.

"And I'm not fond of that big old king snake living under there," I said, "or I would have fixed it."

"Do you have all the hookups? I've helped my dad with plumbing repairs around the house. I could try doing it for you."

"It's all in a bucket under the house, Max. That's as far as I got."

Max looked at me. "Come on Maisy, you can hold the pipes up while I join them together."

"Huh-uh. Not while the snake lives under there."

"That snake's a whole lot more scared of you than you are of him. He'll be hiding in a corner somewhere if he's even under there."

"But it's been raining; it'll be wet under there." I was using every excuse I could think of.

"I'll get you a flashlight," Papa said, not wanting to let the opportunity get gone. He looked at me and grinned. "It doesn't rain under the house."

How could I refuse?

IT DIDN'T TAKE MORE than twenty minutes, but I stuck like glue to where Max was working, thinking maybe he would protect me from the snake. "Quit shining the light all over the place, Maisy. You need to shine it on the pipe where I can see what I'm doing."

"I'd rather see what the snake's doing," I said, giving the perimeter one last shine.

"We'll be under here all day if you don't cooperate."

I was eager to get back into the daylight, so I did what he said, and we got it done. But on the way out, I was sure I heard something slithering and I crawled as fast as I could. Max just laughed.

Nana Zell was pleased as punch and found every excuse to run water in the sink. She even took the Sunday best dishes off the shelf, declaring they needed a good cleaning.

Papa tried to pay Max, but he wouldn't take it. "I could have fixed it faster if Maisy hadn't been searching high and low for that snake. Just consider it a favor for letting me fish in your pond. If you ever need anything else done, let me know."

"We need something done at our house," I blurted out. "I'd planned to ask you what to do about it, Papa Tom."

"What is it, Maisy?" I'd noticed he'd taken to calling me by my name occasionally which made me feel happy and sad all at the same time, if that makes any sense.

"Momma says the plank floor under the swing set needs smoothing out. I get splinters in my feet every time I push the swing."

"Well, we can solve that problem easily enough," Max said, with a smug look on his face.

"Oh yeah? How?"

"Just put your shoes on before you swing."

I stuck out my tongue and he laughed. His laughter made me think of honey straight out of Papa's beehive being poured over hot buttered biscuits. Be still my heart!

CHAPTER TWENTY

REV ROCK

"Brothers, do not be children in your thinking. Be infants in evil, but in your thinking be mature."

—1 CORINTHIANS 14:20

There was nothing Rock enjoyed more than watching the antics of their boy at the kitchen table. It was more fun than a three-ring circus or a bull-riding rodeo, both of which he had seen and loved.

They were finishing dinner and Matthew was chasing garden peas around on the tray of his high chair, squealing gleefully when he captured the slippery things and popped them in his mouth.

Rock laughed. "It doesn't take much to amuse him, does it?" He turned to Liz, but she seemed lost in thought. This time she wasn't participating in the circus nor the rodeo and he waited, knowing she was about to reveal something he'd rather not hear.

"She's not going to be happy about it. You wait and see. I think she'll be insulted."

"What are you talking about? Who could be insulted over our son eating garden peas?"

"Not that, Silly. We were talking about Reva."

"That was thirty minutes ago. Why wouldn't she be happy? I thought she would be thrilled we're hiring her some help."

"Reva's very competent, Rock. She doesn't need any help

doing her job and you know it. You should have talked to her before you got it approved through session."

"But I'm the one who needs the help."

"Then that's the way you should approach it."

Rock was worried. He hadn't even considered Reva would be upset about hiring additional office staff. "Heavens to Betsy; I didn't know this would be such a big deal."

"She'll be jealous, too. She's like a mother hen where you're concerned, and she won't take kindly to someone else honing-in on her golden boy."

This was going to be more complicated than he thought. "Golden boy, ha. I think I'm more like a troublesome son. Maybe I should just forget it. Or maybe *you* could come to work in the office." He knew he sounded a little whiny, but what was he to do?

"Huh-uh! No way would I do it. But you do need someone."

"Well, what am I going to do? Tell me, please?"

Liz smiled. "Don't I always?"

"The last thing I want is for Reva to get mad and quit on me. People at the Presbytery are chomping at the bit to hire her out from under me anyway."

"Reva's not the quitting kind, Rock. But unless you handle it right, she'll pout about it for weeks."

He groaned. "That may be even worse. When those hands go up on her hips and she fixates those eyes on me, I'm ready to crawl under my desk. I don't want to face that again, so tell me how to handle it, Mrs. Clark."

"How did you ever manage your church without me?"

"I honestly don't know. I guess I was flying by the seat of my pants."

"Okay, we're going to play a bit of a mind game here."

"That's what you counselors thrive on." His eye roll was definitive, but she ignored it.

"Well, you've got to do it quickly, before the word gets out. And you've got to make her think it's her idea. And for heaven sakes, don't use the word secretary! It's such an outdated expression. Office assistant or administrative assistant sounds much better. You'll also need to use one of those terms when you post the position."

"You're so smart, Mrs. Clark." He wanted to do another eye roll but knew it would be wise to stop at one.

"Stop buttering me up. I am not going to talk to Reva for you."

"Drat."

"When you talk to her, tell her the kind of help you need and ask her if she'd like to do it instead of what she's doing now. Tell her you'll give her a raise if she'll take it."

"We voted to give her a raise anyway. Alan Carter scared me when he said she might be offered another job."

"Great! She'll get a raise either way. But be sure to offer her the position. She'll turn it down because she loves what she's doing and she's comfortable in doing it."

"What if she doesn't?"

"Doesn't what?"

"Turn it down."

"Would that be so bad?"

"No, I don't guess it would. She practically walks on water. I haven't found anything she can't do." And she does it so well, he thought. Especially her talent for making him feel like a little boy being scolded by his mama when he did something off-the-wall.

"And she would have a hand in hiring the new person and training them, so see, you don't have a problem at all, whichever way it turns out."

He leaned over and kissed her on the mouth. "You're a genius, Mrs. Clark. And a beautiful one to boot." And he meant it.

She kissed him back, lingering in his embrace. "Thank you, Mr. Clark. But I'm still not talking to Reva."

"Drat," he said, pulling away. "You would do it so well."

Matthew started banging his hand on the highchair tray. "No mommy!"

Rock reached over and planted a kiss on top of the baby's head. "Okay, okay, we'll share our kisses with you too, silly boy." He pushed his chair back and stood up, ready to take him out of the high chair.

"Unless you're in the mood to be pea-green, you'd better use a washcloth on those little hands before you pick him up."

"And what a messy face!" Rock said, walking to the sink to get a paper towel. "If kids came with pamphlets about what to expect from them, our population on earth would decline by leaps and bounds."

HE COULD SEE trouble waiting around the corner when Reva placed her hands on her hips when he brought up the subject of hiring additional staff. "And what makes you think I need help?"

"You don't need help, Reva. It's me that needs help. Alan Carter suggested it." He realized he was whining again but this wasn't going according to plan. He'd just told Reva about the new position, but he must have said something wrong. Where was Liz when he needed her?

"You sure do! And if you think for one skinny minute I'm going to take that job, you've got another think a'comin'. Raise or no raise, I do very well just like I am, thank you very much."

Maybe this wasn't going so bad after all; at least she admitted he needed help. He didn't want to mess things up by saying anything. What was it Liz said? Make her think it was her idea.

"Tell me what I should do, Reva. You always know what I need better than I do." It wasn't a lie. She was always one step ahead of him.

She put her head in her hand. "Let me think it over a minute. It's a shame you don't have enough money to hire an associate pastor." She tapped her fingers on the desk and shook her head back and forth.

"One thing you really need is someone to screen your calls. And your blasted cell phone; you need to get rid of the thing! Since when did people start expecting preachers to be at their beck and call anytime, day or night? Back in my day, if a man of the cloth wanted to get away from it all, he just went fishing and there was no way to find him."

"We can cancel the church cell phone account, put in another land line, and me and Mr. or Mrs. Whosoever you hire for this job will field your calls. That'll take a load off right then and there." She pulled a notepad out of her desk. "Hey, I'm on a roll! I can think of dozens of things this person could do to help you out. We'll just put our heads together and write out a job description." She looked up and smiled. "And whatever you do, don't advertise for a secretary. That term is so outdated!"

He stood there in total amazement with his mouth wide open. It was just what Liz had said. Then it hit him. "Hey! Have you been talking to Liz?"

She did a huge belly-laugh. "Maybe," she said, still snorting as she tried to settle down. "Who wants to know?"

Rock sighed. "And you purposely made me squirm," he said, not thinking it was funny at all. He turned on his heels and walked to his office, muttering, "It's bad when your wife and your secretary gang up on you."

She called to him as he was getting ready to close the door. "Office assistant, if you please. I've decided I don't want to be called a secretary anymore."

He rolled his eyes, threw up his hands and almost, but not quite, slammed the door. But the minute the door clicked shut, there was a sharp rap from the other side and he reluctantly reopened it. There was Reva standing with her hands on her hips again and he wondered how she got up from her chair so fast.

"Don't hide yourself in there like a pouty child, Rev Rock. We've got work to do. And what happened to your sense of humor, pray tell?"

"It seems to me like you and my sweet wife have been in collusion behind my back." As soon as he said it, he wished he could take it back. He *was* acting like a pouty child.

"Reva, I'm sorry. It just surprised me that Liz talked to you about the new position. She told me, in no uncertain terms, that it was up to me to tell you."

"Well, if you must know, I'm the one who called *her* this morning while you were visiting Eli Cunningham in the hospital, so don't blame her."

He felt like a complete heel, or more like a worn-out heel with a wad of chewing gum stuck to the bottom of it, sticking to the floor each time he picked up his feet. And speaking of feet, he had surely inserted his in his mouth and he didn't like the taste of it.

"Reva, I…"

She interrupted him in mid-sentence. "There's no need to apologize again. You've been acting like a cat with his tail caught in a screen door these days, and that's why I called Miss Liz to find out what we could do about finding you some help. It was then she told me about the job position. And like I told her, there's no way I'm going to learn a new routine in my old age. I like things just like they are." She held up the notepad she'd brought into the room. "Now, if you've got nothing else to say, let's get to work making out a job description and figuring out who we're going to hire."

He felt like a child who had just been sent to his room, but that was just fine with him. "Yes, ma'am!" He was glad to have someone else in charge for a change. He pulled up a chair so Reva could sit beside his desk, and then he sat down in his. When he picked up his pen, a little white note card fell to the floor and he picked it up. It was his handwriting and he'd written Alan Carter's name, then Chris with a question mark and a phone number. Oops, it was the man Alan said was dying. He'd almost forgotten. The poor man would be dead before Rock had a chance to call, and once again, he felt inadequate. "Lord, help me and help this Chris, whoever he is," he pleaded silently.

"What's that?" Reva asked. Maybe he'd said it out loud. Or maybe Reva could read his mind now. It wouldn't surprise him one bit.

CHAPTER TWENTY-ONE

CHRIS

"For everything there is a season, and a time for every purpose under heaven."

—ECCLESIASTES 3:1

Chris moved in with his parents when he came home, but quickly realized living with his mother would make what little time he had left miserable. He visited an assisted living center, but it was depressing, and he wasn't quite ready to make the step. He started looking for a temporary apartment, one he could rent month-to-month.

Dr. Blakeney had recommended a homeopathic doctor in Charlotte since Chris had decided to forego chemotherapy, and the treatment he'd received so far was helping. Dr. Patterson was weaning him from the narcotics, and had put him on the drug, *Aurum Mettalicum*, which was helping with the pain and giving him a boost of energy. The narcotics had made him too groggy to make clear decisions and too sleepy to get out of bed, which the doctor explained could quickly lead to loss of muscle strength, more pain, and a weakened condition. It was by no means a cure, but a treatment that would make his final days, weeks or months more bearable. He also couldn't drive while taking the narcotic and it was his goal to see his little girl one last time. And Mandy—the guilt of what he'd done to Mandy was worse than the dying. He must see Mandy.

He'd been so close. For two days, he'd sat in his car near their house hoping for just a glimpse of them. He moved his car from time to time to keep from looking suspicious, but a teenaged boy had paid him too much attention for comfort, so he drove away, not wanting to cause alarm. On his trip back through Park Place that morning, he'd decided on a whim to ride down Main Street and see how much the town had changed since he'd been gone. He was surprised when he saw all the old buildings were now filled with merchants. It was one of the few small towns that hadn't succumbed to new malls and shopping centers.

At the end of South Main, as he started to make a left turn, an inconspicuous sign stared him in the face, *Miss Marple's B&B - Rooms for Rent*. He immediately drove into the driveway and knocked on the door. It was one of those *aha* moments, and if he'd still been a believer, he would have thought God had purposefully led him there. He had knocked on the door and explained his plight to Mrs. O'Malley, the owner, and she had shown him way more compassion than his own mother was even capable of. She said she had one room vacant on the top floor, but better still, there was an apartment in the basement. It could be accessed from a little driveway which ran behind the house, so he wouldn't have to climb up and down stairs.

He met John, Mrs. O'Malley's fiancé, and Anna, a young nurse who was renting a room on the second floor. The clincher was something the nurse had said. She said it matter-of-factly, not sugarcoating anything. There would be a time, she said, when his condition would weaken to the point he wouldn't be able to care for himself. The apartment would be large enough for a live-in caregiver if he opted to go that route rather than checking into Hospice. That sealed the deal. He paid for his first month's rent, went home and packed his belongings and moved in that very afternoon. His mother was livid, but he didn't care. He had spent the first half of his life trying to please her and the last half avoiding her. He'd moved back in out of desperation, but he wasn't desperate enough to stay there. Her animosity toward Mandy and his daughter had driven a wedge in their relationship that could never be repaired.

CHAPTER TWENTY-TWO

MAISY

"My intercessor is my friend as my eyes pour out tears to God; on behalf of a man he pleads with God as one pleads for a friend."

—JOB 16:20-21

The sound of Momma's alarm clock woke me up. I'd been hearing it for several minutes and it had somehow woven its way into my dream of riding a Ferris wheel at the county fair with Sabrina. I thought the alarm was a warning that the ride was about to break down, so I was startled when I sat up in bed. My bedside clock read 9:00. I jumped up wondering why Momma had let me sleep so late. We had a joint appointment with the counselor at 10:00 and it was a twenty-minute drive to Rock Hill. I'd have to hurry and get ready.

I started to brush my teeth, but the alarm was driving me crazy, so I went to her bedroom to turn it off, figuring she must have walked outside to get the newspaper. When I walked in, I saw she was still asleep. I turned off the alarm and shook her shoulders.

"Momma, didn't you hear the alarm? We're going to be late for our appointment if you don't hurry and get up."

She raised her head from the pillow and looked at the clock, then lowered her head again, groaning loudly. "Help me, Ladybug; I'm so dizzy, I can't hold my head up."

I panic every time she calls me Ladybug, because over the

years I've learned it's a sure sign something bad is about to go down. Every major spell she's had, that's what she called me. I ran to the bathroom for a wet washcloth. When I came back I raised her head and put an extra pillow under it, then I started washing her face with the cool cloth.

"What's wrong? Momma. Come on, please get up!" She looked at me and tried once more but collapsed back on the bed.

"I can't, Maisy. Everything's a blur." Thank God she'd called me Maisy this time. Maybe it wouldn't be so bad after all. I spread the cloth across her forehead and picked up the phone beside her bed. I would have normally called Nana Zell, but she would just call for an ambulance and I didn't want Momma going back to the hospital. Besides, this time was different. She had at least tried to get up. All the other times she had made no effort at all. On the third ring, Mrs. Clark answered. Our phone number must have shown up on her cell phone. Her voice sounded concerned.

"Mandy, I wasn't expecting you to call. I thought you and Maisy would be on your way to your counseling appointment by now. Is everything okay?"

"Mrs. Clark, it's me, Maisy. Something's wrong with Momma. Can you come over right now?"

"What is it, Maisy? What are her symptoms?"

"She can't get out of bed. She's dizzy and says everything looks blurry." I paused for just a second. "And she called me Ladybug."

"I'll be right there, just as soon as I can run Matthew by Rock's office. Try not to worry; I've got the doctor's number on speed-dial and Mandy authorized me to talk to him on her behalf. I'll call him on the way." She hung up without saying goodbye.

I picked up Momma's hand and held it. "Everything's going to be alright, Momma. Mrs. Clark is on her way over." She seemed to relax. I left her there while I brushed my teeth and hurriedly changed clothes since I knew we'd be going to the hospital. It was a routine I'd been through many times. Before I got my hair combed, Mrs. Clark was knocking on the front door. I'd forgotten to unlock it. Hurrying to open it, I stubbed my toe hard on a chair I'd pulled out the night before to change the overhead light bulb. That's what I get for not putting things back where they belong.

"Ouch, I'm coming, Mrs. Clark." I hopped on one foot to open the door, and she came rushing in. I sat on the arm of the sofa and grabbed my foot. Whoever knew a stubbed toe could hurt so bad.

"Are you okay, Maisy? What's wrong?" She knelt down beside the sofa and picked up my foot. Suddenly, the stress I had been under since I found Momma like that started to sink in. I started shaking all over.

"I'm okay," I said, but my trembling voice said otherwise. "I think I might have broken my toe." I don't know why I said it, maybe because she was being so kind, and I was craving sympathy.

She gave me a hug, then examined the toe I pointed to. "It doesn't look broken, but I'll get you some ice from the freezer, and then I'll go check on your mother."

"Please, I'm okay. Just take care of Momma."

"Is she still in bed?" I nodded. "The doctor returned my call while I was driving over. He said it could be a side effect from one of her meds. I'll need to see her medicine bottles. Do you know if she records her dosage each day?"

"I think so. She has a notebook on the kitchen counter right beside her medicine. I just check each day to make sure she doesn't need refills on any of them. I don't want her to run out. We've been down that road before."

"I know you have, Maisy. I'm glad you're keeping up. It makes it less awkward for me to have to remind her. I told her I would when we left the hospital, and I do, but sometimes I feel like I'm intruding. She's done so well. I'll go in and check on her; you bring the notebook and the meds. Be sure to get an ice pack for that toe while you're at it." I flexed my toes and found out it didn't hurt anymore. If felt so good to have someone in control.

When I got back to the bedroom, she had Momma propped up on a pillow. She was still weak, but she was talking.

"I couldn't remember if I had taken the dose I take before supper. Zell was here." She stopped talking and looked all tuckered out, so I picked up where she left off.

"Nana Zell knew we'd been freezing corn, so she cooked a big meal and brought us half of it. She stayed and talked while we ate," I explained.

"And I didn't write it down in my notebook," said Momma. "It's become such a routine now to just take it with my meal, sometimes I take it without thinking, but it's rare that I don't write it down." She coughed and looked up at Mrs. Clark. "My mouth is so dry; can I have a drink of water?" Mrs. Clark got the water bottle off the bedside table and held Momma's head a little higher and Momma drank about half of it.

"That's better," she said. "My thinking was that it would be better if I took two of the pills rather than none at all, so I waited until right before I went to bed and took it."

"Which drug was it, Mandy?" She pointed to one of the bottles. Mrs. Clark nodded her head. "That's it then. When I explained your symptoms to Dr. Benton, he thought this one could be the culprit. It's a typical overdose reaction."

Momma looked alarmed. "An overdose? I couldn't have possibly taken over two, total."

"He said just one extra pill could cause an overdose. That's a powerful antipsychotic drug. The good news is that it will wear off if we get some food and lots of water in you."

I jumped up. "I'll go cook some breakfast."

"That sounds good. In the meanwhile, do you have some cookies or crackers that I can start feeding her now?"

"Yes, ma'am. Nana Zell brought some homemade blueberry muffins when she brought our supper, and Momma loves those muffins." She nodded. It was the first I'd seen a hint of a smile all morning. I would call and reschedule our appointment later.

CHAPTER TWENTY-THREE

REV ROCK

"What good is it, my brothers and sisters, if someone claims to have faith but has no deeds? Can such faith save them?"

—JAMES 2:14

"She's going to be fine, Rock. She thought she'd missed a dose, but she hadn't. So she took an extra pill before she went to bed. All the symptoms pointed to an overdose. Thank God the doctor walked me through it. When I left after lunch, she was fine, but it was such a scare for Maisy. Poor child, I didn't realize it, but she's still on pins and needles, not quite trusting that her mom will stay well."

"That's understandable from her past experiences."

She walked over to the office refrigerator and took out a bottle of water. "Where's Reva?"

"She went to the bank and the post office. She'll be back in a few. We're beginning to schedule interviews."

"That's great." She smiled. "So, you had to call in the big guns for Matthew? Did he give you a lot of trouble?"

"Only when he was ready for a nap, and thankfully Maura came over with a peach pie right about the time he started throwing a temper tantrum. She was more than happy to take him with her. It was amazing to watch the transformation in him when he saw her. Reva and I had worn ourselves out trying to get him to take a nap, but when she picked him up, he snuggled up on her shoulder and was out like a light."

"She has a calming influence on him, alright. I'm sure he sensed that you two were stressed. I'm sorry I had to leave him here when you were both so busy."

"Don't be sorry. You were where you were needed." He reached for her and pulled her into his arms. "You have such a heart for giving, one of the many things I love about you."

She pulled back and smiled up at him. "And all this time, I thought it was my cooking!"

"Well that too," he said. "That's why I have this extra paunch around my waistline to worry about."

She looked around the kitchen. "Where's the peach pie Maura made? I could use a slice right now. I spent so much time feeding Mandy that I forgot to feed myself."

Rock looked sheepish. "What's left is in the fridge." At her expression, he rushed on. "But don't worry, there's a big piece left for you."

She raised her eyebrow and gave him the look his mother would always give him when he was in trouble. "One slice left? What happened to the rest of it?"

"Well, let's see." He looked everywhere but in her eyes. "Reva and I both had a slice when Maura brought it in, then the UPS guy came in while we were eating, and I politely offered him a piece. Then I had another slice for lunch." He shrugged his shoulders. "And, somehow it just disappeared. I'm just as surprised as you are."

The shrug did it for Liz, and she laughed. She patted him on the stomach. "Your little paunch is just fine with me, but don't blame it on my cooking. It's all these other good cooks around here that you need to worry about." She walked to the fridge.

"Now where's my pie? I'm famished!" She pulled it out and set it on the counter. "Ah, there are two slices left. I'll have one and put it back in the fridge for you to have tomorrow."

Just as she took the plastic wrap off the top, the bell on the front door jingled. "Knock, knock, it's just us." She and Rock looked up as Agatha and John walked in. "It's our last counseling session. It's hard to believe we'll be getting married in a little less than three weeks."

"It's gone by in a flash, hasn't it?" Rock said.

John looked at Agatha and smiled. "It's been six months today that we became engaged. I think it's appropriate that we're having a July 4th wedding since fireworks exploded as soon as I saw Aggie again after all these years."

Agatha blushed. "He's a hopeless romantic; he always was." Rock was as sure as he'd ever been that this couple would have a happy marriage.

Liz had been partially hidden behind the open refrigerator door when they came in, and when she closed it, Agatha looked around and saw her.

"Oh Liz, it's good to see you. I didn't realize you were here." She eyed the pie on the counter. "Ooh, what is that? Peach pie? I love peach pie!"

Rock saw his wife's crestfallen look. He started to come to her rescue, but before he could, she had recovered. "Well, you're in luck. There are two slices left. I'll make a fresh pot of coffee and you two can eat it while you're talking to Rock. Or there's some cold milk in the fridge if you'd rather have it."

"Oh no, I love it, but it doesn't love me. If I eat one more dessert, I may not fit into my wedding dress."

Rock smiled as a look of relief flooded Liz's face, but he didn't stay smiling for long. John was looking longingly at the pie with its buttery crust and crisp edges. "I'll have a slice, if you don't mind," he said. "And a glass of milk if it's not too much trouble."

Liz grinned. "No trouble at all," she said. It was Rock's turn to look crestfallen and he could have sworn that Liz was smirking at him. So much for that last piece of pie.

"Let's go into in my office. John, you can eat your pie while we talk."

~

WHEN THEY'D FINISHED their counseling session, Agatha stayed seated. "Rock, there's something I'd like to ask you to do. We have a guest at the B&B who needs some spiritual guidance. Do you think you could come by one day and talk to him?" Rock groaned inside. He was ready to go home to Liz and Matthew. This was exactly the kind of thing people kept throwing at him, as if he had time for his own flock, much less a stranger. Then he felt like he'd been sucker-punched as the scripture passage, James 2:14 dropped into his mind like a hot potato. *What good is it, my brothers and sisters, if someone claims to have faith but has no deeds? Can such faith save them?* Was he becoming too busy to help someone in need?

"Who is it, Agatha?" he found himself asking.

"I wasn't even going to say anything, Rev Rock. I know you're stretched too thin already, but it's been weighing on my mind, so I had to.

"I took him in as a border without checking references—something I had vowed never to do—but I felt so sorry for him. When he first arrived, I kept hearing in my mind a verse from Proverbs. *Do not withhold good from those to whom it is due, when it is in your power to act."*

John smiled. "Good one, Aggie. Proverbs 6:27. I've always thought of it as when we have both the opportunity and the ability to act in someone's favor, who are we to say no?"

Rock felt sucker-punched again. Agatha's initial thoughts had been just the opposite of his, the minister in the room. She'd understood right off the bat, whereas his thoughts had been only of himself and his own set of problems. And John's affirmation of her point made him feel like more of a heel.

"Tell me what I can do." he found himself saying.

"His name is Chris, and he's dying."

Again. He was going to turn into a virtual punching bag if this didn't stop. Chris—there couldn't be two people in town named Chris who were dying, could there? He'd told Alan Carter he would call him, and he still hadn't.

"I asked him if he had a church home and he said he hadn't been to church in years. I think somewhere along the line his faith has been shaken. Or it's possible he's not a believer, but he didn't sound skeptical or offended when I asked him about it."

"I'll be glad to talk with him, Agatha. Has he moved in yet?"

"Yes, he moved in last week. He only had two suitcases with him, and he said he was traveling light from here on out. It sounded so final, I wanted to cry." She dabbed at her eyes and John put his arm around her and spoke up.

"He stayed pretty much to himself the first few days, but now he's eating breakfast with us and even comes into our library to read. Last night, I was playing chess with Kevin and I noticed he was reading one of Aggie's grandfather's theology books. He had quite a collection. I tried to strike up a conversation with him about the book he was reading, but he closed it up and said he was tired and needed to go to bed. I'm planning on getting my books out of storage when we leave here today. I have some that are more up-to-date and easier to understand in case he tries to delve into one again."

It had slipped Rock's mind for a moment that John was a retired pastor and when the lightbulb went off, John seemed to intercept it.

"I'm more than willing to try to help the young man, Rev Rock, but Agatha has it in her mind that it should be you." He laughed. "Maybe she thinks I've lost my touch."

She put her hand on his arm. "You know that's not it, John. It's just a strong feeling I have that this is meant for Rev Rock to do. I don't always understand these feelings, but I've learned to trust them." She squeezed his arm. "Just like the feeling I had when you proposed to me. I knew it was the right thing to accept."

He took her hand. "Then I'll trust your feelings too, because you sure made the right decision on that one." They all laughed.

"You're right, Agatha," Rock said. "It is my job. I'm ashamed to say it but Alan Carter, another retired pastor, asked me to call this Chris when he first got to town, and I haven't done it. It's got to be the same person. Alan was returning from a conference when he met Chris on the plane. I think it's been laid upon all of our hearts that it's my job to do, and I'd better get on with it. I may not have much time."

"What is it you think you're supposed to do?" Agatha asked.

"Guide him to the Lamb," Rock said, with more positivity than he felt.

"If I can help in any way, please feel free to ask," John said. Rock could sense his sincerity and felt encouraged by it. "After all, God brought me to Park Place and although I thought it was because of this sweet woman here by my side, it may be twofold." He paused as if trying to decide if he should go on, and then he did.

"Rock, I know what a toll pastoring takes on a man's family life; I've been there. In the six months I've been attending church here with Aggie, I've gotten to know this congregation and I would be very comfortable helping you make pastoral visits to the hospital or wherever I'm needed. I could be your pulpit supply anytime you feel the need to get away; and the best part about it is, my services are free. It was what I had intended to do all along after retirement. It will work here just as well as it would have in my home town in Indiana. And I'm not just making an idle, empty or an appeasing kind of offer—I'm sincerely offering my help in any way you could use me."

Rock wanted to get up and hug him but wasn't sure how John would react to it. He wanted to cry tears of gratitude, but didn't want to look foolish, so instead he stood up and said, "Thank you, Jesus!"

He walked out of his office with them and while he and John discussed ways that he could help out, Agatha and Reva talked about their grandchildren. They all stopped talking when the outer door of the office opened again. Holly McCarthy stood at the door for a moment before entering. As they all stared at her, she asked timidly, "I hope I'm not interrupting anything?"

Rock walked over to meet her. "Of course not, Holly. We were just talking about how God answers prayers in unexpected ways. You're a prime example of that with your miraculous recovery."

She smiled. "I am, indeed. I wasn't in any condition to pray at the time, but all of you lifted me up in a big way and I'll always be grateful."

"You've met John, haven't you?" She nodded. "And of course, you know Agatha."

"Yes, I was privileged to be a guest at Agatha's house when she hosted our Stewardship Committee meeting last month." She smiled. "The weather was perfect for an afternoon tea in her garden, and we were all impressed when John served the tea, fancy little sandwiches and all."

Agatha's face softened. "I do have a keeper, don't I?"

"Definitely. The wedding date is coming up soon, isn't it?"

"The fourth of July," Agatha said with a chuckle. "A firecracker kind of day. It falls on Sunday this year, so we're having it right after church services. The whole congregation is invited."

"I'm looking forward to it," Holly said. She turned to Rock. "I wanted to talk to you and Reva for a moment, but it can wait. I'll come back tomorrow morning."

"Oh no, please stay," John said. "Aggie and I were on the way out the door." He looked at his watch. "Oops, as the old saying goes, time flies. I have a fitting for a tuxedo in twenty minutes. We've got to hurry."

They said their goodbyes and Rock closed the door behind

them. Holly laughed nervously. "I was almost hoping they would stay. I was about to chicken out on what I came to talk about."

Rock looked at her reassuringly. She was a walking, talking miracle, this young woman standing before him. Three years ago, Holly had been diagnosed with brain cancer in her hometown in Ohio. The young unwed mother had come to Park Place in hopes of finding Abby's grandparents who didn't know of her existence. Thinking her condition was terminal, she would ask them to adopt Abby. On her way into town with her little girl, Holly was critically injured in a car accident, but Abby wasn't hurt. The prayers of the good people of Park Place, a competent doctor, and a gracious God had contributed to Holly's complete recovery and she was now happily married to Abby's father and doted upon by his parents. She and Sonny were now expecting their second child.

"Holly, please don't ever feel nervous about talking to me or Reva. You've been a Godsend in our lives in so many ways. Your illness drew Liz and me together and brought to light our growing feelings for each other. And our precocious little boy thinks you're his second mother."

She smiled. "He's the reason I'm over here. Abby saw Liz and Matthew on the playground and wanted to go out to play, so I went along too. That's when Liz told me you were going to be hiring some help for the office. I've been thinking about working part-time to fill in the hours while Abby's at school." She patted her tummy. "But I don't think anyone would hire me knowing that in a few months I would be taking some time off for maternity leave. I'd love to work for you at least until the baby's born. You'd have more time to find someone permanent."

Rock was about to respond, but Reva jumped up out of her seat like the house was on fire. She'd been doing a lot of that lately, he'd noticed. Maybe she was on a miracle drug for her arthritis or something. She reached Holly in five seconds flat. "Hallelujah, thine the glory, hallelujah, Amen!" Her alto voice came out loud and clear.

"Child, you don't know how much of an answer to prayer you are. You were the first person I thought of when we talked about hiring, but I didn't think there was any way you would want to work with this crazy old woman and that hardheaded man!"

Hardheaded? Well maybe so, but for now, all Rock could think of to say was, "Thanks be to God! You're hired."

HE CLOSED and locked the office door after everyone left and gravitated to the angel fountain that had come to represent the quiet and peaceful moments in his day. He sat down on the bench and reflected on the day's happenings. Two people, right here within easy reach, and he had overlooked what they had to offer. He felt humbled that God was looking out for him even when he hadn't had faith enough to see the path clearly for himself. He got down on his knees, and that's where Liz found him when she ventured out to collect him for supper knees bowed, head low and cell phone turned to the off position. He hadn't heard her footsteps. She stood there for a moment, watching the humbleness of his posture. She sent up a heartfelt plea for God to provide him with patience and grace and the spiritual strength to overcome the challenges of his ministry. And she prayed that he would soon lead again with the joy and thanksgiving that was so much a part of him. She thanked God for him as she stood there, this man she loved with all her heart. Then she tiptoed away without interrupting him, knowing that his hunger pangs would eventually lead him home. She had made him a peach pie from her *Eating Healthy* cookbook. In her opinion, it wouldn't hold a candle to Maura's with its buttery crust and filling, but maybe Rock would never know the difference.

CHAPTER TWENTY-FOUR

MAISY

"Perfume and incense bring joy to your heart. And the sweetness of a friend comes from their honest advice."

—PROVERBS 27:9

Two weeks and two counseling sessions had passed since Momma almost gave me a heart attack that morning after she'd taken two pills instead of one. Mrs. Clark and I had counted the pills in the bottle and according to the notebook Momma kept, there was one pill unaccounted for. It made me wonder if I'd spend the rest of my life worrying about whether she was taking her pills right. I had my own private counseling during the last fifteen minutes of each session and I mentioned it to Dr. Barnes, our counselor.

"Maisy, it may be a while, but someday you'll learn to trust her ability to take care of herself. She's doing very well, and I suspect she would have improved years ago if the staff in Columbia had arranged for follow-up care when she was released from the hospital. There are so many things that should have been done; the county could have assigned you a *guardian ad litem* to represent your best interests when your mother was unable to care for you or herself."

"But the county people might have taken me away from Nana Zell and Papa Tom."

"It's possible."

"Then I'm glad they didn't. They're my grandparents and I wouldn't have been happy living with anyone else."

"I know, Maisy. We won't dwell on what might have happened; we'll just go forward from here."

"I'm trying. There are so many things I wish would happen."

"Tell me about those wishes."

I hesitated. "Promise you won't tell Momma?"

"Maisy, what you and I talk about is confidential."

"What I'd really like to do is find my daddy, but I don't where to start looking. I'm afraid it would hurt Momma if she knew. Like maybe she would think my wanting to see him would be a betrayal or something."

"I understand."

"You do?"

"Yes, it's natural to want to know your father but what if he wouldn't want to see you? How would that make you feel?"

"No worse than I feel already. I've already thought of that."

"But you would want to see him anyway?"

"Yeah. I think if he saw that I'm a pretty okay kid, he would like me, but if he doesn't...." I shrugged my shoulders. "I've grown up thinking he doesn't like me anyway, so what would I have to lose?"

Dr. Barnes coughed and turned his head away. I saw his eyes were a little wet and I figured he must have summer allergies like Sabrina does. She's always coughing and sneezing, and her nose runs like a faucet when something triggers it. After another cough or two and blowing his nose, Dr. Barnes seemed to feel better and smiled at me.

"Maisy, you are a pretty okay kid, and don't listen to anybody that would ever tell you different. But I want you to promise me something?" I nodded. "Don't try to find your father without first telling your mother."

I laughed. "I thought you were going to repeat what Papa told me."

"What's that?"

"He said that before I go trying to find him, I should try to find myself."

"Your Papa is a wise man. You've spent a lot of your life trying to meet the needs of other people without thinking of your own needs being met. That's the sort of thing that can make you lose your own identity. You try to measure yourself by someone else's standards rather than your own. Finding yourself simply means to know who you are. When we have a sense of self, it's easier for us to make personal decisions that are beneficial to us rather than harmful to us."

"I guess I understand. So, it may be more harmful to me than good to find my father?"

"Again, I think that's something that's best left up to your mother."

"You don't think she would be upset? I mean, he hasn't exactly won any father of the year awards. I wonder if it would offend her."

"No, I think she would understand. She's a reasonable and compassionate person, Maisy." He looked at his watch, then looked back at me. "We've run a little bit over. I could sit and talk to you all afternoon, but I've got another appointment at 3 o'clock. Talk to your mom about your dad. She just might be waiting for you to ask questions."

I jumped up from my chair. "Okay, I'll let you know next week. And by the way, Doctor Barnes, Happy 4th of July!"

"Ah, that is this weekend, isn't it? I can do without the firecrackers, though. My poor dog goes into panic mode."

I smiled. "But you're a psychotherapist! Surely you can fix that!"

He laughed out loud. "I'm afraid dogs can be just as complicated as humans. And cats are even worse. I could never be a pet therapist."

~

MOMMA WAS ROCKING on our front porch with Mrs. Clark making plans to take her new paintings to the gallery. She had them lined up trying to decide which ones to take.

"Why don't you take all of them?"

"Some of them are a little too personal, don't you think?" Momma pulled one out. "Besides, we want to keep this one," she said, holding it up. It was of Zell and Tom sitting at our kitchen table. She had taken a snapshot of them the last time they had dinner with us. And from that snapshot, she had captured them perfectly with her paints on canvas, right down to the mole on Nana Zell's chin.

"It would be such a shame not to show it," Mrs. Clark said. "Maybe you could exhibit it and put a 'not for sale' sign on it. I've seen that done before at art shows."

"That's a good idea." She picked another one out of the stack. "I'm keeping this one too."

"Oh, I love it!" Mrs. Clark looked at me. "Did you pose for this one, Maisy?" It was a portrait Momma had painted of me sitting on the dock at Papa's pond.

"Yes! She wanted the light just right, so I had to sit on that dock for two hours. At least I got a little fishing in while she was sketching the background."

"We're keeping that one too," Momma said, "but I'll put it in the exhibit." She winked at me. "I'm rather partial to it, for some reason."

They put the paintings aside and started talking about childhood memories. Matthew was napping inside, and I was in sort of a daze sitting on a lounge chair half-way reading a magazine and thinking how nice it was to have friends visiting. I felt like I was in the middle of a Hallmark movie just doing normal, with a capital N, summer things. Mrs. Clark seemed fascinated by Momma's tales of growing up as a missionary kid in places like Papua, New Guinea, Central Africa, and Nicaragua. I had never paid much attention to her stories before. But now I was beginning to realize that she'd lived a much more exciting life than I had stuck here in Baker's Grove.

Max was filing down the splintered boards underneath the swing with his dad's wood planer. The night sounds and the easy conversation were about to lull me to sleep, but I perked up when I heard Mrs. Clark mention my name.

"Mandy, you and Maisy should come with me and Rock to the festival in town tomorrow."

I could tell Momma was pleased. "What do you think, Maisy?"

"I'd love to go! Hey, I know! I can push Matthew around in his stroller."

Momma laughed. "How many teenagers do you know who are so eager to help with a toddler?"

"Not a single one," she said. "You're welcome to help with Matthew. He'll be a little cranky in this heat, though, so be prepared. It's supposed to be in the mid-90s tomorrow."

"I'm on the early shift at work in the morning," Max said, "but I'll be off by noon. Maybe I could meet you there after lunch. I read that all the food vendors will be set up on the town square. Is it okay with you, Mrs. Martin?"

"Of course, you can, Max. Maisy, do you think Sabrina would want to go?"

"She'll already be there with the school band. They're marching in the parade. We're going to meet up afterwards."

Max made one last swipe at the plank with the planer. "I think that's smooth enough," he said, and got up from the porch floor. "I'll get the broom and sweep this up and you can try it out, Maisy." He started into the house.

"It's in the laundry room, Max," Momma said. "You won't

need the dustpan. You can just sweep it off the porch, or better yet, let Maisy do it. You've done enough already."

"Oh, I don't mind," he said and headed into the house to get the broom. When he'd finished, he watched me swing back and forth. The floor was nice and smooth. I wondered how it would be to have a daddy to fix things around the house. Papa Tom had helped us out when he was a little younger, but now it was all he could do to look after his own place.

"Thank you, Max," Momma said. "That's needed doing for a long time."

"You're welcome, Mrs. Martin." He turned to me. "I'll see you tomorrow, Maisy. You'd better wear that hat or your freckles will all run together." I threw my magazine at him and he ran down the steps laughing. "Just kidding," he said, but kept running. Boys! They can be nice one minute and infuriating the next.

CHAPTER TWENTY-FIVE

CHRIS

"For Your name's sake, O LORD, pardon my iniquity, for it is great."

—PSALM 25:11

It had been an emotional week for the man living in the basement apartment of Miss Marple's B&B. He was lucky to have found such a quiet place to live out his final days in solitude. But it had proved to be more, much more. The people living at the inn were kind and compassionate. His own mother had been suffocating and had made his dying all about her. She had put him six-feet-under while he was still alive and had played out her "poor little me, my son is dying" role to the hilt with all her friends. He marveled at how she could even have friends, but he suspected it was because of the money she donated to buy herself into the good graces of the organizations she belonged to. Even though it wasn't genuine, it was the most attention she'd ever paid to him. Well, no, not really. There were the drama years she had spent trying to ruin his marriage. If he'd only had the sense and maturity to have dealt with her then, things could have been different. When he had picked up his belongings from his parents' house, he'd told his father where he would be staying, extracting a promise from him that he wouldn't tell his mother. Mrs. O'Malley, the owner of the inn had his father's contact number and would let him know when things got worse.

He wondered how other people reacted to knowing they were dying. Did they, like him, look back through the years, dredging up every single detail, good or bad? Were their last days filled with regret like his were now? Not that the feeling of regret was new; he'd lived with it for ten years. He had abandoned his wife and child. It had torn at his conscience every single day since he left. He was convinced they would never forgive him. He doubted he would ever even have a chance to ask for forgiveness.

Chris had never believed in miracles until this very afternoon when he got caught in the crosshairs of two preachers. The first was John, the man Mrs. O'Malley would be marrying on Sunday. He hadn't realized John was a retired preacher until today. He'd never got close enough to ask, but he knew he wouldn't have been as likely to listen to him if he had known. His poor opinion of preachers started when he was just twelve and their own overbearing pastor had been the cause of their church being split apart. He'd refused to go to church at all after that, a sign of his own immaturity.

Mandy's parents had been missionaries. He cringed as he thought of the times he had made fun of them and called them goody-two-shoes and holier-than-thou. And they weren't. They were good people who lived their faith daily. His words had hurt Mandy deeply, and just a few short months before he left her for good, her parents had died in the missionary field.

It was still hard for him to believe that God could forgive him. He thought back to the day last week when John walked into the B&B's library and caught him reading one of Mrs. O'Malley's books. Chris had been embarrassed and walked out before John could talk to him. But after that, Bibles and books seemed to multiply around the house. They were in the library, in the drawer of his nightstand, and even on the table in the reading nook where he sat having his coffee every morning. The words seemed different from how he'd remembered—clearer and easier to understand. He wondered if that's the way it is when people are dying. The words full of hope and promise; an urgent message that kept drawing him into a realm he had never thought possible.

It was while he was in this state of mind that John had found him with a Bible in his hand this morning sitting at a chair in the small English rose garden at the back of the house.

"A good book", John said as he plopped down on the chair beside him.

"I'm beginning to see that," he'd answered. "Enlightening and confusing at the same time."

"Any questions?"

"Do you know it well? The Bible, I mean?"

John laughed. "I've spent a lifetime studying it, but I don't think there's a man alive who can honestly say they know it well. Every time I pick it up, I seem to find new answers in there."

"All I seem to find is more questions," Chris said wearily. "I guess it's because I haven't given it much more than a glance since I quit going to church at an early age. Since then, the only time the Bible has even remotely played a part in my life was during my marriage vows, and I'm afraid I didn't take them seriously enough, even then."

"So you divorced your wife." John had said it as a simple statement, not as an accusation and not judgmental which made it easier for him to confess the obvious.

"No, I did much worse than that. I abandoned her at the worst possible time."

"I see. Do you want to talk about it?"

"I know I should talk it out and get some advice, but I'm not ready yet."

"Just don't wait too long, son. You have too much to lose."

"How can I have more to lose than what I've already lost?"

"Believe me, there's so much more to life than that. When you're ready to talk, I know just the right person."

Chris's raised eyebrows expressed his doubt. "That's what the guy on the plane said, and I even gave him my phone number. Never heard a word back." His tone was sarcastic. "I guess I had religion pegged right all along."

John gave him a long, thoughtful stare. "Chris, one thing I've learned in life is not to underestimate God's timing. When we truly seek to find the answers, He will provide them."

They both heard it at the same time. A car door slammed shut around the corner near the carriage house. John smiled. "That must be Aggie back from picking up my suit we took to be altered. I've put on a few pounds since I've been here. I'm sure she'll want me to try it on."

"Oh, I forgot. You two are getting married on Sunday, aren't you? You're a lucky man, John." His look was wistful.

John stood up and patted him on the shoulder. "I think I'm pretty lucky, but if I'm going to stay in her good graces, I'd better get upstairs and see if that suit fits. If not, I'm in trouble."

He started to walk away but turned back. "I hope to see you upstairs tonight, Chris. Aggie's meeting the florist over at the church and there's no telling how long they'll be. She told me to fend for myself. Kevin and Anna are going out so maybe you and I can order a pizza and play some chess. Kevin says you're good at it."

"I'm not that good. He and I are pretty much even, I'd say. Sure, I'll come up and share a pizza with you. I've been spending too much time alone and it's depressing."

"Great, I'll see you then." As John walked away, Chris thought about what he'd just said. Depression; it was an ugly word. Poor Mandy, she'd suffered from it for years. And leaving her when he did. My God, what kind of man was he? He sat there with his head in his hands sobbing. When the sobs subsided, he felt cleansed, and with the tears had come a softened heart.

He remembered Mandy's tears and how they would come without warning and for no reason he could see. When they'd first married, he would hold her through her crying spells wanting only to protect her from what she was going through. But as time went on, those spells began to get under his skin. He told her she just needed to think positive and she'd get over it. His mother had harped to him that Mandy was crazy and asked how could he live with someone like that? And somewhere along the way, he'd let his mother influence him to the point that he felt the same way. And he left.

With his face still down, he shook his head to clear his thoughts and reached into his back pocket for his handkerchief. It wasn't there. He sniffled and raised his head. Through his hazy tears he thought he saw an outstretched hand. He wiped the tears away with the back of his knuckles and looked again. It wasn't an illusion after all. A man was sitting on the same seat John had vacated and he was holding out a handkerchief.

"Here," he said. "It's clean. I always carry a spare because in my profession, you never know when you'll need one."

The sun had come out from behind the clouds and was shining directly behind the man's head. With the refraction effect of his still moist eyes, the man looked almost ethereal. He took another look and with a hint of mischief asked, "Your profession? A clean hanky? You must be a funeral director. Am I dead yet?"

The man's laughter was spontaneous. "I've been called a lot of things but funeral director is a first." He put the handkerchief on the table between them. Chris picked it up and wiped his eyes. The man reached out his hand for Chris to shake, and he took it. "No, I'm not a funeral director. I'm Rock Clark and I'm the pastor of Park Place Presbyterian Church." Chris let go of his hand, but Rock held his gaze. "And if I'm not mistaken, God timed my visit just right."

Chris couldn't think of a single comeback or joke about preachers, and he'd had plenty of practice telling them over the years. All he knew was that his heart was raw with emotion. The fog in his mind was lifted and there was a burning desire within him to find some answers. And find them he did. Before the next hour was over, he and the man named Rock Clark would have been fighting over the handkerchief if John hadn't been watching out the upstairs window and brought down a box of tissues.

And in the end, Rock had declared to him, "Chris, thank you. My heart has been opened today just as much as yours has. God sent me to minister to you, but in turn, you ministered to me."

After Rock left, Chris had gone inside to rest. Later he and John had sat easily together eating pizza and talking, without even playing a single game of chess.

The day had been a good one, he thought as he turned back his covers, but now, back to reality. God must have a big heart to be able to forgive him. But Mandy? How on earth could *she* ever forgive him? He had been stunned to find that Rock knew Mandy and Maisy, and, equally stunning to Rock, that he was Maisy's father. Chris had plied him with questions and Rock made no promises but said he would pray about how to handle it from here. Maybe he'd been right saying that God had orchestrated the whole thing. It gave him hope.

Anna and Kevin had invited him to go with them to the July 4th festival tomorrow, but he had declined, saying it was too hot. But maybe he would go after all. Anna was a nurse and would know what to do if he got sick. The thought of one last hurrah in his hometown was appealing. After all, it was his last 4th of July celebration on earth. Somehow, with his newly found faith, that no longer seemed a bad thing.

CHAPTER TWENTY-SIX

REV ROCK

"You are the God who works wonders; You have made known Your strength among the peoples."

—PSALM 77:14

Rock sat in the brown leather arm chair in his study with his feet propped on the ottoman in front of him. His Bible lay open on his lap, but he wasn't reading it. The answering machine on the phone line that had recently been installed was blinking, but he hadn't even noticed it; his thoughts were elsewhere. In his twenty-five years in the ministry, he had never experienced a day quite like today. The door to the study opened and Liz walked in, closing it softly behind her. She sat in the office chair behind his desk and looked at him. He looked back and gave her a weak smile.

"What are you going to do now?" she asked.

"I'm not sure."

"I'd like to be with you when you tell them, as a support system." He nodded again. "It's going to be a game changer for both of them."

"Yes, I'll need you there. He wants to see them; did I tell you that?" It was her turn to nod. "Do you think she'll allow it?"

"I don't know."

He laughed softly. "We're talking in whispers and hushed tones as if there'd been a death in the family. Instead of looking at it so grimly, maybe we should be looking at it as a blessing. From what you've said, Maisy has been curious all along."

"Who wouldn't be after all this time? I just wish the circumstances were different."

He took a deep breath and let it out. "I know. That's why it's going to be hard to tell her. How do you tell a child who has been wondering about a father who disappeared, that he's right here in town and he's dying?"

Liz was quiet. Rock looked down at his Bible, then started thumbing through the pages. This was the same Bible he'd thumbed through with Chris Martin as they sat and talked that afternoon. It was the same Bible where they'd read the 23rd Psalm together and where Chris's tears had fallen, temporarily staining the opaque paper to the point where the text was almost luminescent.

The fact that Chris Martin, the man who had been pushed upon him by both Alan Carter and Agatha O'Malley, was Maisy's father, had shocked him to the core. The turn of events and the reluctant part he'd played in those events was something he would marvel at for the rest of his life. God had planned it down to the most minute detail. Alan had started the ball rolling. John Newman had initiated conversations and placed reading materials within easy reach.

He felt his own part was minimal; it was all in the timing, but in reality, Chris had found him easy to talk to and had sensed that Rock was a person he could trust to help him find the answers. Chris was eager for God's grace and it was only after he prayed the prayer of forgiveness and accepted Christ, that Rock found out that he was Maisy's father.

He closed the Bible and looked over at Liz. She had been watching him and he could see the emotions playing across her face. Maisy and Mandy were both very special to her.

"When did you realize who he was?" she asked.

"It should have jumped out at me when he told me his last

name, but it didn't. Martin is a relatively common surname, so I didn't even give it a thought. He said his disease was terminal and he came back home to apologize to two people he had hurt terribly. He said he knew they would never forgive him, but he just wanted a chance to tell them how sorry he was.

"I asked if they had accepted his apology. He said he hadn't seen them yet. He said he was torn now about whether he should try to see them because his resurfacing after ten years would likely hurt his wife and daughter worse than if he simply disappeared. That's when I knew."

"Oh, Rock! You must have been floored."

"Almost as floored as he was when I told him that we know Mandy and Maisy well."

"All I can say is that it was definitely God-inspired."

"Without a doubt. You said Mandy and Maisy are coming here in the morning?"

"Yes, we're going to walk downtown from here."

"We could tell them then."

"Why don't we hold off telling them until after the holiday. Maisy's looking forward to the festival and I don't know how she's going to react to the news." Liz looked up at Rock. "You know, this is going to be hard on Mandy. She's done so well, I keep forgetting that she's still vulnerable to setbacks."

"I think Chris has mellowed out a lot since he's been sick. I didn't know him before, but the fact that he kept on supporting them financially proves he isn't a total jerk."

"Yes, Mandy said he was a good husband to begin with, and when Maisy was born he was a good father at first. She thinks his mother's interference made something snap inside of him. It sounds like he needed a good psychiatrist too."

"I'm sure. Mental illnesses are not always recognizable. Some people can operate normally to the outside world, but inside they're a mess, and I've got a feeling that's how Chris has been for a long time."

"What does he look like, Rock? What if he comes to the festival tomorrow and Mandy sees him? Would she recognize him? That might be a problem."

"I asked him if he was coming and he said no, so we won't have to worry about that happening. How does he look? Well, his hair is thinning, he's pale and much too thin, and I don't how else to say it, but he looks sick. I would guess from Mandy's age that he's in his late 30's, early 40's, but he looks older."

"This breaks my heart, Rock. Here he is back in town wanting to see his wife and child to ask for forgiveness. If he had just done this before, their lives could have been so different. Let's tell Mandy after the festival."

"That's going to be a problem. We have the wedding rehearsal and the dinner party afterwards. How about we just go by their house Sunday afternoon after the wedding?"

"You're forgetting the reception. It's supposed to be a big affair with Greenbriar catering it."

"Ahh, cake; my favorite part of a reception."

Liz laughed. "I had a feeling that would cheer you up. Agatha didn't want a big wedding cake, so she asked Betty Ann Williams to make three of her caramel cakes."

"Only three?", he said, looking dejected.

She rolled her eyes. "I'm sure there'll be enough, Rock. She knows how many people a cake will feed."

"When it comes to her cakes, if you snooze, you lose. Besides, the first piece Betty Ann cuts off the side has more icing on it, so I plan to be the first in line."

They laughed together; the moment was lightened, but underneath it all, they were on edge. They would have to tell Mandy, and soon.

CHAPTER TWENTY-SEVEN

ROCK AND LIZ

But he said, "What is impossible with man is possible with God."
—LUKE 18:27 ESV

To everyone's relief, the humidity was at a tolerable level as the festivities began on Saturday morning. The day was off to a good start when the marching band began their descent down Main street as the crowd of onlookers watched. All four faces of the old town clock silently announced ten o'clock on the dot. As the color guard and drum majors approached the spot where the two families were gathered to watch the parade, Rock lifted Matthew up on his shoulders so he would have a better view. Liz's attention was more focused on watching Matthew and his reaction to the instruments than watching the band itself. He clapped as the trombones and french horns marched by but was startled at the sound of the cymbals. As the drummers passed, she smiled when he used Rock's head for a drum. The flutes were last and by then he was squirming to get down. Liz lifted him from Rock's back and put him in the stroller.

"Don't you want to see the fire truck?" Rock asked.

"Fire twuk!" He wiggled around, eager to get back out of the stroller. By the time the Sun's Up Convertible Club came riding through proudly displaying their American flags, he had fallen asleep on Rock's shoulder. He laid him gently in the stroller and pulled the sunshade over his face.

Maisy had waved at her friends in the band but had grown bored with the convertibles. Sabrina joined them after she changed out of her band clothes and handed her flute off to her mother.

"Can we take turns pushing the stroller?" Maisy asked.

"Be my guest!" Liz said, handing it over. "I think I could use a lemonade; how about y'all?"

"Inside or out?" Rock smoothed his hair back in place where Matthew had been holding on tight. "Carter's Drug Store has the best lemonade in town, but the youth from the Catholic church have set up a booth down on the south end of Main to raise money for the homeless shelter."

"Let's help out the homeless shelter," Mandy said. "And speaking of shelters, I hope they have a canopy set up for shade. I forgot to bring my hat."

"Momma!"

"What, Maisy?"

"You reminded me ten times to wear my hat, and you forgot yours!"

Mandy laughed. "That's stretching it a little bit. I only reminded you six times."

"I'd give you mine, but you'd look a little funny wearing a Braves baseball hat."

"No way you'd part with that hat anyway." She made a move as if to take the cap off Maisy's head, but Maisy jumped back, almost tripping on the sidewalk.

Liz smiled at the light-hearted banter between mother and daughter. She had grown to love them both and offered up a silent prayer that their happiness would continue. She couldn't help but worry about how the news about Maisy's dad would affect them. But no need to worry about it on such a pretty day, she thought. Let them enjoy the festivities.

St. Gabriel's had chosen to set up their vendor tent under a massive oak tree, the shadiest and most coveted spot on Main Street. "It pays to be ahead of the lunch crowd," Liz said as she picked out an empty table where they could all sit together. She left the others sitting so she could help Rock bring the food and drinks back to the table.

"Apple turnovers and lemonade, a strange combination," she said as they placed the food on the table. "They don't start serving lunch until 11:30, but this will tide us over for a while."

"Those are the biggest apple turnovers I've ever seen in my life," Mandy said. "But I'm not complaining; I'm starved."

"So am I," Maisy said. "Who's going to bless it? Want me to?"

"Please do."

"Lord, bless this food to the nourishment of our bodies and bless those who prepared it. Amen."

"Short and sweet," Rock said, laughing.

It didn't take them long to devour the turnovers and bemoan the fact that they'd eaten every crumb. Maisy and Sabrina went back for refills leaving the others sitting at the table. Matthew was still asleep. Liz looked up as a young couple walked past with a tray of food, carrying it to a bench under another canopy where people were scattered around in lawn chairs.

"Oh look, there's Kevin and Anna. I guess John and Agatha are getting a little frantic right now. The rehearsal dinner tonight and the wedding and reception tomorrow; I'm surprised they don't have those two running errands for them."

"I think Agatha has it all under control," Rock said. "You know how organized she is." He glanced in the direction Liz was looking, then his face turned ashen. Just then, the girls came back with their lemonade and sat back down at the table. Rock got up and stood behind Liz. "Girls, you've made me change my mind about a refill." He put his arm on Liz's shoulder. "What do you say, Liz? We need to walk the apple turnover off anyway."

"Sure, why not. We don't want to get dehydrated." She looked at Maisy. "Do you mind watching Matthew?"

"He's not going to require much watching," Maisy said as she pulled back the sunshade and peeked inside the stroller. "He's out like a light."

"Thanks. We'll be back in a few minutes."

"Or maybe a little longer. I saw someone walk by that I want to speak to."

"Take your time," Mandy said. "If the girls decide they want to move on, I'll be glad to watch him. I'm perfectly content sitting under this shade tree."

Rock took Liz's elbow and guided her to the food stand. "You turned so pale, Rock. What's wrong? Are you sick?"

He pulled her along until they could no longer see the picnic table. "Liz, we're in trouble. We need to go back and get Mandy and the kids and head off in a different direction."

"Why? You're not making any sense. What's going on?"

"Chris Martin is sitting on the other side of that tree with Kevin and Anna. They must have talked him into coming after all. That's why I wanted to get away; I thought they might see us and come to our table."

"Oh no! What are you going to do?"

"Me? I was hoping you'd have something in mind?"

"Oh Rock, I should have told her earlier. I'm her best friend and I feel like I've betrayed her by not trusting her mental stability. She deserves to know, but I just didn't want to rock the boat. Everything was going so well."

"It's my fault. I'm the one who said we should wait. Neither of us wanted to rock the boat, but it looks like God's saying it's time to jump out and either sink or swim."

She grabbed his hand in hers. "Let's pray about it. Maybe God has a plan we don't know about." She took his other hand and they bowed their heads, unaware that people were watching, and if they had been aware they wouldn't have cared.

After their prayer, they squeezed hands and smiled at each other. Liz spoke first. "Now what?" she asked.

"I don't know; let's leave it in His hands."

"So no running away?" she teased.

"Not unless He sends a hive of bees our way," he said. "That would get our attention. I may run some interference though. As soon as we refill our lemonade."

"What will you do?"

"I'm going over and speak to Chris. I'll let the natural progression of things determine what I say. It could be the opportunity he needs to see them from afar. He's been hoping to get a glimpse of Maisy without her knowing it since he came back to Park Place."

"Maybe his time is running out. You said yourself that he's looking pale and frail. You know, we've made all these plans about when and what to tell Mandy and Maisy, but we forgot that God is in control. I'll go back to the table. He'll guide us in what to say and do. I love you!"

LIZ STAYED under the refreshment tent for a while after Rock walked away. A game of horseshoes had attracted some onlookers and she watched the players and the good-natured ribbing from the crowd. In another grassy area, a cornhole game was in progress and the soft thud of the corn bags hitting the boards contrasted sharply with the clanking steel-on-steel sound of the horseshoes. It was a carnival-like atmosphere with squeals of laughter coming from the children and friendly back-slapping from the adults.

It was the one day of the year that the kids were allowed to play in the water fountain in the middle of the square. Adults parked their chairs as close as possible to the fountain where their children splashed around trying to stay cool. No one complained, and many parents egged on the wayward splash now and then giving some welcome relief to the bystanders. Park Place was the ideal town to raise a child and she found herself hoping that Rock would never be called to preach anywhere else. Standing there as if rooted to the spot, she sipped her lemonade through the red and white paper straw, smiling and nodding when someone spoke to her. She shivered and wondered if it was a reaction to the icy cold drink or a premonition of what might happen when the two different worlds of the Martin family collided. She hoped with all her heart it would turn out okay.

Taking a few steps forward, she stopped again as Mandy came into sight. The world felt surreal somehow as she took in the scene before her. Mandy had taken Matthew out of the stroller and was holding him in her lap. He was drinking from a juice box and was laughing at something she said. What a peaceful and serene expression on Mandy's face, she thought. Peaceful now, but what about later? Liz stayed where she was, afraid that taking even one more step would speed up the inevitable and turn the lives of those she loved upside-down.

She thought back to her own life and the feelings of fear and uncertainty she'd faced and tried to compare it to Mandy's life. When her first husband, Ron, had died of a heart attack at the age of forty-two, she thought her life was over. Then when she fell in love with Rock, she felt she was betraying Ron's memory until God made it clear that she needed to move on with her life.

But these were all small snippets in time in an otherwise happy life compared to Mandy's ongoing battles. A debilitating mental illness that began early in life, the tragic loss of her parents, and a husband who abandoned his family—all were life-altering events. And now this.

Then she remembered who was in charge and started walking again. If this was part of God's plan, He would get Mandy through it. Under normal circumstances, the return of a remorseful prodigal son, or in this case, prodigal husband would stir feelings of hope and reconciliation. But the hope would only be short-lived because of Chris's terminal illness. Maybe it would bring answers, and with the answers, forgiveness. And with forgiveness, a sense of closure for both Mandy and Maisy. There was such irony in it—the man who returned with a change of heart, but so little time to make amends.

Liz watched Matthew as she approached the table. When he saw her, he began to squirm and wiggle trying to get down. "Mommy!"

Mandy held on to him tightly so he wouldn't fall and smiled at Liz. "He just woke up with a healthy appetite." She shook the empty juice box. "And he wolfed this down along with the container of sliced grapes I found in your bag."

"He's always hungry," she said. "It must be a growth spurt. I hadn't planned on keeping him out much longer. We'll go back to the house whenever you're ready."

"I'm ready anytime you are. I'm a wimp when it comes to weather this hot." She looked around. "Max came by and the girls walked with him to Pizza Loco to get lunch. I told them if we weren't here when they got back, we would be at your house. Is that okay?"

"More than okay," Liz said, breathing a sigh of relief. If she could get Mandy home, she would somehow find a way to tell her about Chris. She looked across the grassy area and saw Rock sitting on a lawn chair beside the man who must be Chris Martin. He apparently hadn't told him yet because they were not looking in their direction. She hurriedly gathered their belongings and put Matthew back in the stroller. "Let's get out of here before we melt," she said. "Rock got tied up with some folks from church. I'll call him on his cell phone when we get home and let him know where we are."

"I guess I'm just not a 4th of July person," Mandy said, "unless I can experience it from an air-conditioned room."

"We have way too much in common, my friend. Let's go soak

us up some cool air." Liz started pushing the buggy forward, but Mandy called her back.

"Hey, look. I see the kids. Max is carrying a pizza box and they're all heading in Rock's direction where he's talking to his friends. Maybe I should let them know we're leaving."

Liz froze in place and lifted another silent prayer, but Matthew's restlessness saved the day. He started crying and Mandy turned her attention back to him.

"Poor baby. It's too hot out here for him. Let's go on back; the kids'll know what to do."

ROCK HAD WANTED a few moments alone with Chris, but Kevin and Anna had been excitedly discussing an upcoming camping trip to the mountains. The two of them had been volunteering with the church's youth group. Holly and Sonny, the youth directors, had planned a weekend camping trip and had asked Kevin and Anna if they could go along as chaperones. It was heartwarming for Rock to see these young adults get so involved in the life of the church.

"Oh wow," Kevin said, looking at his watch. "Chris, we promised you we'd have you back at the house by 1. It's so hot out here, you must be exhausted." He looked at Rock. "He wasn't planning to come out today, but we convinced him being around people would be good for him, but I think we've overdone it."

Anna chimed in. "And I promised I'd help Mrs. O'Malley get ready for the rehearsal dinner. She thinks she's got everything all together, but I can tell that underneath that facade, she's a mess!"

Rock smiled. "I'm sure you can straighten her out, Anna. Why don't you two get back. I want to talk to Chris for a few minutes and then I'll walk him home."

"Sure thing," Kevin said. He stood up and folded his chair, then reached for Anna's.

"I've got it. I'm not helpless you know."

"How well I know," he said, laughing. "This is Miss Independence herself. I think this day must have been made just for her."

"Right!" she said, putting her hands on her hips. "The day the Continental Congress declared their independence from Great Britain, they named the day for someone who would be born two-hundred years in the future. I'm flattered!"

"You should be," he said. "We'll see you later, Chris." He nodded at Rock. "And thanks, Rev Rock. I guess we'll see you at the rehearsal."

"We'll be there. Go take care of Agatha and John." He looked at Anna. "And what are you going to call Agatha after tomorrow? She won't be Mrs. O'Malley anymore."

She grimaced. "I know! I can't call her Agatha; it's too informal. I'll think of something."

Kevin looked at her tenderly. "Looks like I'll be calling her Grandmother. Maybe you could too?" They finished folding their chairs and walked away, still talking.

Rock watched them as they made their way across the grass and onto the sidewalk. "That sounded strangely like a proposal," he said, laughing.

"They're sweet on each other, that's for sure," Chris said. "I don't know how I got so lucky to find my way to the Bed & Breakfast. They've all treated me like family."

Rock looked at the man sitting in the chair beside him. His frame was thin, too thin and his complexion so pale. "It wasn't luck, my friend."

"I know that, now," he said. He looked intently into Rock's eyes and Rock could see the pain and exhaustion there. "I am getting tired, Rock. What did you want to talk to me about? Is it Mandy or Maisy?"

"Yes, but it can wait. You look tired. Maybe I should get you home."

"I'm okay. Please tell me. I'm anxious to hear anything you can tell me about them."

"Okay, but then I'll walk you home. They're both here at the festival. They came with me and Liz."

Chris's hands started shaking. He put them on the armrests of the chair and tried to stand up. "Where are they?"

"When I saw you sitting here with Anna and Kevin, I was afraid you would all run into each other unawares, so I decided to come over. I thought the shock might be too much for you and for Mandy. I came to tell you so you'd have a chance to see them before they could see you. Liz and I are going to talk to them today. We can't wait any longer." He looked toward the picnic table where they'd been sitting. "It's hard to see with all the people between us, but there's Mandy and Liz. It looks like they're leaving."

Chris looked, then put his hand over his heart and closed his eyes. "Oh Mandy," he said, with tears running down his eyes. He looked again. "She hasn't changed a bit. Still as beautiful as ever." He stopped talking and took some deep breaths. "Where's Maisy? I don't see her. But I wouldn't recognize her anyway, I'm sure."

The sun was shining through the tree branches at an angle, making it hard for Rock to see. "I don't know where she is now. She was with them earlier." As he was staring through the crowd, he felt a hand on his shoulder and jumped. He heard a laugh behind him.

"I didn't mean to scare you, Mr. Clark. Do you mind if we spread our blanket here and eat our pizza? This is my friend, Max. He had to work this morning but got off early and met us for lunch."

His heart was pounding as he stared at the little group of three standing before him. "Maisy!" he said, shocked that she had slipped up on them without his seeing her. As soon as he got her name out of his mouth, he heard a thud behind him and when he looked, Chris had fallen and lay flat upon the ground. He got down on his hands and knees and checked his pulse.

"He's fainted," he said softly. He shook his head to clear the confusion. How had this happened so quickly? One minute Chris was fine and the next minute he was out like a light. It must have been the shock at hearing Maisy's name. By then a crowd had gathered and he heard a familiar voice. He looked up at the sea of faces around him and honed in on Lonnie Welch, one of the medics that worked for the county. His first thought was that God Himself must have made Lonnie materialize right in front of him. It was too good to be true.

"Lonnie, call an ambulance, please. This man is very ill."

"I'm already on it, Rev Rock. The van is parked right here on Main Street. I thought we might have some heat-related problems today. I'll run get the stretcher."

"I'll go with him", Max said, and started running behind Lonnie. Then Rock remembered Maisy. He looked up to find her standing there with her mouth open.

"I'm sorry, Mr. Clark. I hope it wasn't something I did. I wasn't trying to sneak up on you or anything."

"No, it's not that at all, Maisy." He hesitated for a moment, then made up his mind. It was now or never. He patted the ground beside him. "Sit down here beside me for a minute." She looked confused but sat down as he asked. He took a deep breath.

"Maisy, this is not how I pictured telling you this."

CHAPTER TWENTY-EIGHT

MAISY

"Finally, all of you, be like-minded, be sympathetic, love one another, be compassionate and humble."

—1 PETER 3:8

It couldn't be. Surely it was just a bad dream. This wasn't the happy ending I'd always imagined would happen when my daddy came back. He would be handsome and strong and would come barreling down Baker's Grove Road in a red Jeep kicking up a dust storm behind him. He would knock on the door and when Momma answered he'd get down on his knees and beg her to take him back. She would run to the bedroom and close the door, and I would try to be tough and tell him to go away, but he would take my small hands in his big ones and look so remorseful, I would forgive him. Then Momma would come out of her bedroom and the three of us would hug, with me in the middle and Momma crying softly. That's the way I had imagined it.

The minute Mr. Clark got the words out of his mouth, I almost fainted myself. My daddy was on the ground and this was my reality, not my imagination. My daddy, not handsome, not strong—I had heard Mr. Clark tell the medic that he was very ill. And yet he was still my daddy. I leaned over and patted his face. It's hard to describe, but I felt an instant connection with this man I hadn't seen in ten years. I never would have recognized him, but I could feel the kinship. It was then I noticed it. On the inside of his arm was a tattoo of a heart, and written inside the heart, *Mandy*.

"Daddy," I said, as I touched his cheek. It's me, Maisy. Wake up." His eyes fluttered open, then closed again.

I looked up at Mr. Clark. "There's something bad wrong with him, isn't there?"

He looked at me with sad eyes and I saw then what a good and caring man he was. "Yes, Maisy. He's not well at all. He has cancer."

I know I looked pretty dumb, but I just sat there on the ground and cried, not worrying about what people were thinking. Sabrina stooped down and patted me on the back which made me cry even more. I heard someone tell the crowd to back off, then Max and the ambulance driver were there with the stretcher. By then another man in an EMS uniform had joined them and together, the two men lifted him up onto the stretcher. He looked so helpless. "Can I go to the hospital with him?" I asked.

The man named Lonnie spoke up. "I'm sorry. It's against policy. But if he's your dad, you can get someone to drive you to the hospital. We'll be there with him in about ten minutes. You just ask for me when you get to the hospital, honey. I'll make sure you get to see him." He turned towards Mr. Clark. "He's stable enough, Rev Rock. His vitals are good—his oxygen may be a little low, but we'll take care of that in the van."

Max took my arm and helped lift me up from the ground. "I can take you to the hospital, Maisy. I left my truck just a couple of blocks from here."

"We'll go by the house and talk to your mother first, Maisy." It was Mr. Clark. "Max, you and Sabrina can come too if you'd like."

"My dad is picking me up on the corner at the post office at 1:45, Sabrina said. "I'll walk that far with you and I'll wait for him. He'll be worried if I'm not there."

"I'll wait with Sabrina," Max said. He looked at me with

concern. "I'm sure you and your mom want to be alone, Maisy. Call me when you get home."

"I will." They were my friends, but it would be awkward to have them around. I felt like I was in a bubble and this wasn't really happening. Maybe I was the one who fainted and was just dreaming the whole thing. It would have made more sense.

"Momma!" I jumped at my own voice. I hadn't meant to call her name out loud. What was she going to think about all this?

Mr. Clark lightly touched me on the shoulder to get me moving in the right direction. "That's where we're going now Maisy, to see your mom. She'll know what to do." The way he said it made me feel proud. Yes, she would know what to do. I sighed. It was a relief not to have to be in charge. There had been a metamorphosis in my momma, and the change had happened gradually, one day at a time. This was the first time I realized the huge burden had been lifted. *Momma would know what to do.*

Metamorphosis; I love that word. It's another one that rolls off the tongue.

CHAPTER TWENTY-NINE

LIZ

"Give thanks to the Lord for he is good, his love endures forever."
—PSALM 118:29

Liz and Mandy entered the house through the kitchen door. "What a relief," Liz said. "Thank God for air-conditioning. I'll take this sleeping beauty to his crib and hope he stays asleep for a while. He's had an exciting morning. There's some iced-tea and sandwich makings in the fridge. Why don't you make us a sandwich while I put him to bed? I'd like a pimento cheese, but there's ham and turkey too, so help yourself."

Mandy opened the refrigerator door. "Ah, this is even cooler," she said, fanning the refrigerator air onto her face. "You go ahead, I'll get things started."

Liz walked in the bedroom and gently laid Matthew in the crib. She stood looking at him for a minute. He was beginning to look more and more like his daddy. His wispy hair and long eyelashes were more like her own, but his features were definitely Rock's. She tiptoed out of the room hoping he would stay asleep long enough for her to talk to Mandy. She wondered if Maisy had seen Rock sitting beside Chris. And with her personality, of course she would have spoken to him.

Liz was glad she hadn't been in Rock's place, but now she

found herself in a similar predicament. If Rock had introduced Maisy to her dad, she would be here soon with the news for Mandy. It had to be done. She may as well get it over with.

A glass of iced tea and a sandwich was waiting for her when she walked back in the kitchen. "That was fast," she said. Mandy had already spread mayonnaise on her own bread and was putting a slice of ham on top. Liz opened one of the cabinets. "Here's a bag of chips. Do you like pickles?"

"I'll pass on the pickles, but I'll take some chips."

With their food on the table they both sat down. Mandy looked across the table at Liz. "Do you mind if I say the blessing?"

"Please do." She bowed her head and Mandy did the same.

"Lord, thank you for the blessings you bring into our lives every day; for the food we eat and the company we keep. Thank you for Liz, that she accepted me as a friend, flaws and all. Thank you for letting that friendship flourish. Most of all, Lord, thank you for healing my mind that I may be a better mother to Maisy. In Jesus' name, I pray. Amen."

Liz smiled. "If you weren't sitting on the other side of the table and I wasn't so stinking hungry, I'd get up and hug you, Mandy Martin. That was such a sweet prayer. I'm thankful for our friendship too."

They were hungry and ate their sandwiches quickly. Liz got up and put the dishes in the dishwasher and hurriedly tidied up the counter. "I'm sure Rock will want a sandwich when he gets in. I'll finish cleaning this up later. Let's go into the living room, Mandy. I've got something I want to talk to you about."

Mandy smiled, unaware that her world was about to change. "Hmm, that sounds mysterious. I hope it's something good."

"HERE? NOW?" Mandy's look was incredulous but her reaction to the news wasn't nearly as bad as Liz had feared. It made her question if she and Rock had been wrong to wait. There were a few tears but no drama, and it was compassion, not hysteria that was fueling the tears.

"I always knew he would come back someday, but not like this. The last couple of months I've felt normal again and I've had the chance to honestly assess my feelings for Chris. I've thought about what I would do if he did come back. I came to the conclusion that because my trust in him is so completely broken, I'd never be able to reconcile the fact that he so casually walked out on us."

She put her hands up in the air in frustration. "He didn't care enough to even call and tell me where he was. Don't get me wrong, Liz. I'm not poor-mouthing about me. It's Maisy who has been so deeply affected. An absent father, an off-again on-again mother; it still grieves me that she's had to cope with all that. I thank God every single day for the Bakers. And for you too, Liz. You've been my calm in the midst of a storm." She smiled.

"What you must be thinking! My husband is dying and I'm sitting here talking calmly. Yes, I have compassion for him and I'm sorry for what he's going through, but in my mind, it's almost as if he died ten years ago. Poor Maisy. I think she's always dreamed of him returning and being a father to her. But now ... that will never happen."

"That's another thing, Mandy. According to Rock, he's full of remorse for how he treated you. He has recently accepted Christ and he's hoping for an opportunity to ask for your forgiveness."

"Liz, this is so hard. There's a tiny part of me that still loves him, but if his coming back hurts Maisy in any way, I would have a hard time forgiving him."

"I know it's hard. I can't even pretend to know how you feel, but I'm here for you. I just want you to know that."

"I do know, and it makes such a difference." She got up from the chair.

"Do you mind calling Rock to see if Maisy did in fact run into her father? I'm so worried about how she's going to take it."

They both heard the outside entrance door to the kitchen open at the same time. "Maybe that's them now," Liz said.

"Momma? Where are you?"

Liz called back, "We're in the living room, Maisy."

She walked in with Rock right behind her. He motioned to Liz and silently mouthed the words, "She knows."

She mouthed back, "So does she"

Maisy's outside demeanor was calm and her expression solemn. She looked at her mother and with a small quiver in her voice said, "Momma, I've found Daddy." They both stood still for a moment, Mandy transfixed by Maisy's revelation.

"But Momma, he's really, really sick." Mandy gathered her into her arms and the tears flowed, cleansing tears for both of them. After a moment Maisy's tears turned into snuffles and she pulled away from her mother.

"He's in the hospital, Momma. He fainted when he saw me. Mr. Clark said it was probably the shock of it all. Can we go see him?"

Mandy looked to Rock for validation and he nodded. She pulled Maisy gently to the sofa and patted the seat beside her. "Let's sit down so you can tell me about it."

"I felt a connection to him, Momma. He didn't look at all like the pictures you have of him, but I could feel it in my heart that he was my daddy. I've got to go see him. What if he dies before I get a chance to talk to him?" She looked up at Rock. "You tell them about it, Mr. Clark."

Liz spoke up. "First, why don't the two of you sit down. It looks like you both got too hot out there. I'll go in the kitchen and pour you some iced tea. I'll be right back."

CHAPTER THIRTY

MAISY

"For the Spirit God gave us does not make us timid, but gives us power, love and self-discipline."

—2 TIMOTHY 1:7

Mrs. Clark was right. I was about to melt. Iced tea would hit the spot. I thought about asking her for a sandwich but thought it might be rude. There had been no time nor appetite for pizza after the scare about Daddy. I spilled my soft drink in the confusion and left the pizza for Sabrina and Max to eat while they waited under the shade tree at the post office.

I sat beside Momma on the couch and Mr. Clark sat on the closest arm chair. I wanted so bad to go to the hospital to see Daddy and figured he would do a better job of explaining why to Momma. She didn't know how sick he was. I sat and watched them talk.

"Mandy, I don't know if Liz had a chance to tell you yet, but Chris has cancer and his condition is terminal."

Terminal—it sounded so final. I decided that was not a good word. It didn't roll off your tongue. It just hung there in the air like sticky glue.

"I hope you don't mind that I told Maisy how serious it is?"

She looked at me, then looked back at Mr. Clark. "I think the way it all unfolded, it was the only thing you could have done.

I've never sugar-coated anything with Maisy because she always seems to know when something's wrong anyway. She's a smart girl."

"I've already gathered that," Mr. Clark said. "Anyway, back to what happened today. Chris had walked down Main Street with some other guests at the inn where he's lodging and stayed longer than he intended. He was exhausted, so, along with the heat and surprise of meeting Maisy so unexpectedly, it was all too much for him. When EMS arrived, his vital signs were fine, but they took him to the hospital to rule out a heat stroke."

Mrs. Clark came back in the room. She handed me a sandwich and glass of tea with a big slice of lemon tucked on the rim. I took a big bite of the sandwich and gulped the tea. I wiped the condensation off the glass before I set it down on the coaster. I had noticed that coaster during my first visit to the Clark's. *Be still and know that I am God*, it read. It was a passage from Psalm 46:10. Being still is well and good, but right now I wanted to go see Daddy. There was another passage from Proverbs, but I couldn't remember how it went. Something about being as bold as a lion. That's what I needed right then.

"And I want to go to the hospital to make sure he's okay," I threw in for good measure. "Lonnie Welch, the EMS driver said we could get in to see him."

Momma sighed and looked from Rock to Liz as if asking for their guidance, but they remained quiet. Then I remembered the word metamorphosis and I looked at her proudly. "Mr. Clark brought me back here because he said you would know what to do."

It was the right thing to say. She smiled and gave me a quick hug. "Rock is right. I know exactly what we'll do. We're headed to the hospital, so hop up and go find my purse. I think it's in the kitchen." I grinned and bolted from the room in search of the purse. From the dining room, I heard her speaking to Mr. Clark.

"Thank you so much for believing in me, Rock. And for

boosting me up in the eyes of my daughter. My self-confidence wavers from time to time, but I'm getting there."

I smiled when he replied, "You're already there, Mandy. I have no doubt."

~

THE DOOR to the emergency room slid open as soon as I stepped in front of it. Momma had dropped me off at the door while she went to park the car. July 4th must be a magnet for accidents. The waiting room was full. The woman at the counter must have read my mind because she pointed to the crowd and said, "Sprained ankles, a near drowning and a knife that slipped while cutting a watermelon. But most of them are heat exhaustion. What can I help you with?"

"I came to see my daddy," I said. "He came in by ambulance about thirty minutes ago."

Her sympathetic look seemed genuine. "I'm sorry, Honey. Where's your mother?"

"She's parking the car."

"What's your daddy's name?"

"Chris, Chris Martin. I think his problem was heat exhaustion also. He fainted at the festival in town." Momma walked in and came up to the counter. "And this is my mother, Mandy Martin."

She nodded at Momma and looked on her computer screen. "Yes, here's his name. *Chris Martin*. He's in Room 4, second room on the right beyond these doors. But I'm afraid you can't go back yet. The doctors are swamped with all the emergencies and there's no room for visitors. It could be up to an hour."

I looked at the double doors looming in front of where she pointed. An hour? I had waited ten years to see Daddy and now they were going to make me wait another hour when he was no more than fifty feet from where I was standing. My shoulders slumped, and I headed for the nearest chair thinking Momma would follow me.

"Wait, Maisy," I heard Momma say. I turned back around, and she was speaking to the lady behind the counter. "Could you tell me if Lonnie Welch is here?" Why hadn't I thought of that?

"I think so," she answered and gave Momma a curious look. "Do you know Lonnie?"

"My daughter does, and he told her to ask for him when we got here."

The lady looked a little skeptical, but she got up from her chair and started walking toward the doors that no longer seemed so far away. "Hold on, I'll be right back."

And she was. Within two minutes a hospital orderly was leading us through the double doors. "I didn't know it would be this fast," I told Momma, squeezing her hand. "I'm nervous."

She stopped in mid-stride, taking both my hands in hers. "It's not too late to turn back, Maisy," she said. "Do you need more time to prepare for this?"

"There's no turning back now," I said. "They may not let us in again." I took a deep breath. "I'm ready."

Momma walked in first and I was right on her heels. She stopped abruptly and gasped. The momentum of moving forward made me run into her from behind. I caught my balance and moved around beside her.

"I think we're in the wrong room," she said quietly. "This can't be Chris."

I looked at the man lying on the hospital bed in front of us. "It is, Momma. Or at least it's the same man who fainted in front of me. The one that Mr. Clark said was Daddy."

The orderly was adjusting the monitor and looked up at us with an odd expression. "I thought this was your husband. Does he look so different?"

"We've been estranged," she explained. "I haven't seen him in almost ten years."

"Oh, that explains it. People change a lot in ten years." He smiled. "The photo on my driver's license was taken eight years ago and if a police officer pulled me over now, I'm not sure he would believe it's me." He rubbed his hand through his hair. "I had a lot more of this back then."

He was being nice and trying to put us at ease, but I really didn't want to listen to small talk, so I walked around Momma and went to stand beside Daddy. There was an oxygen tube in his nose and an IV hooked up to his arm, but other than that, he looked peaceful.

"Is he conscious?" Momma asked.

"He did regain consciousness, but he was agitated when they brought him in, probably from the ambulance ride. The ER doctor sedated him, so he may sleep for a while. His oxygen was low, and he was dehydrated, so we started fluids."

Momma moved a little closer. "What happens next?"

He looked at the chart. "He came in about an hour ago and was seen right away. He'll be evaluated again soon, and they'll decide whether to keep him overnight or send him home." He blushed, realizing his blunder. "Or wherever he's staying."

Momma ignored the comment. "Can we stay in here?"

"I don't see why not. There's only one chair, but I can get another one."

"That's okay," I said. "I don't mind standing."

He walked toward the door. "I've got to check on another patient now. If you need anything, push the call button." He left but just a minute later, quietly came back in with another chair and set it near the door. "Just in case," he said and left the room again.

Momma had hesitated about coming closer, but she finally got up the nerve to come stand beside me near the bed. She looked almost as pale as he did, and I could see conflicting emotions playing across her face.

"Do you think he can hear us?" I asked, turning to look her in the eye.

"It's possible. During the times I've been sedated in the hospital, I've heard voices fading in and out."

"So we should keep our voices low if we talk about how sick he looks?"

Momma smiled gently. "I think he knows how sick he is, Maisy. I have a feeling that's why he came home."

"Do you think he came home to see me?" I asked. I could hear the hope in my own voice and felt a little foolish after I said it. I sighed. "He's never wanted to see me before, so why should he now?" I hated it, but I had a big old lump in my throat. At least no one but Momma was there to see the emotional mess I was in. She hugged me, and it felt good to be in her arms.

"M-Ma...." We both heard the small voice coming from the bed. We looked and there was Daddy looking straight at Momma. "M-Mandy!" He finally got it out. Then he looked at me. "Maisy, all grown up." It had taken a big effort to talk and he closed his eyes again.

I walked up to the bed and took his hand in mine. It just seemed like the natural thing to do. All the resentment bottled up inside me just seemed to melt away as I watched him struggle to stay awake. I looked at Momma. She was wiping away tears and trying to blink them back into her eyes, but she couldn't catch up with them. They were falling faster than she could blink. I felt Daddy's hand tighten on mine and I looked down at him again. His eyes—they were like I remembered them so long ago. I'd always nurtured a faint memory of him looking at me with laughing eyes and singing the itsy-bitsy spider song. Mine began to fill with tears again and he spoke to me weakly, "I'm so sorry...."

"That's okay, please rest, Daddy." Daddy—the word had been in my mind a thousand times, but it hardly ever made its way out of my mouth. And calling a real person that name seemed totally weird. I practiced saying it one more time. "Daddy." He looked at me and gave me a weak smile. I smiled back. I heard someone walk into the room and turned around. It was a doctor.

He nodded at me and then at Momma. "Mrs. Martin?" he asked, looking at her. She hesitated for a minute and nodded.

"And I'm Maisy Martin," I said. "His daughter."

"I'm glad to meet you, Maisy. Now if you'll slip over there with your mother, I'll take a look at our patient." I did as he asked.

"His blood pressure and pulse are good," he said after he examined the chart and poked and prodded for a few minutes. "I understand from speaking with him when he first came in that he has other health issues." He looked at Momma and she nodded. "I would feel more comfortable keeping him overnight. We'll get him hydrated and his oxygen level back up and then we probably will be able to send him home tomorrow." He looked at Daddy once again.

"Is that okay with you, Mr. Martin?" Daddy nodded, his eyes still closed.

The doctor keyed a few notations into the computer, then looked back at us. "You two can stay a little while longer. They'll be here in a few minutes to take him upstairs to a regular room. I would prefer that he not have any visitors for the rest of the day. If all goes well, he'll be released before noon tomorrow."

He flipped through the chart and looked again at Momma. "I don't have your contact information anywhere on the computer, Mrs. Martin. Can you give me your phone number?"

I was expecting Momma to explain again that Daddy didn't live with us, but she didn't, she just gave him our number and he left the room. I pulled the chair up to the bed and sat down beside him. Momma stood there with her hands on the back of the chair, not knowing quite what to do. Daddy's eyes opened again, and he called her name. "Mandy?"

She walked around the chair and stood at his bedside. "Yes, Chris. I'm still here."

He reached to take her hand, but she didn't give it to him. I couldn't read the expression on his face. I wanted to reach over and put her hand in his, but I didn't. She had her own struggles to deal with. He had hurt her terribly and I wondered if she would ever forgive him. It was so much harder for her. I'd been just a little kid when he left, and even though I had felt his absence, I'd never experienced the downright slap-in-the-face kind of rejection she had.

"Mandy," he said again, this time pulling his hand back to his side. "I'm so sorry. I didn't come back to cause you any trouble."

"I know Chris. I know. You rest now; we'll talk later."

"Thank you for coming. It means a lot."

"It was Maisy's idea," she said. "She was worried."

"And you?"

She gave a heavy sigh. "My worry ran dry a long time ago, Chris."

Come on, Momma, I thought. Don't make him feel any worse than he already does. He's sorry, for crying out loud. But Daddy sighed too and closed his eyes.

I DON'T KNOW what I expected to happen. Maybe that we could go pick him up the next day from the hospital and take him home. But the hospital called in the morning and said he'd be staying at least one more day; they needed to request his medical information from the Charlotte oncologist. I wanted to go visit him again after church, but Momma insisted that we wait until the next day.

"The hospitals are flooded with visitors on Sunday, Maisy," she said, but there was a far-away look in her eyes. There was more to it than just that. I saw her talking to Reverend Thatcher after church and he and Mrs. Thatcher came to visit right after lunch.

Before I could get settled in the living room for their visit, Momma pulled me aside. "Maisy, I'd like to visit with Rev. and Mrs. Thatcher by myself, if you don't mind. Mr. and Mrs. Clark are busy with a wedding and reception all afternoon and I need a little spiritual counseling."

"I don't mind," I said, and I didn't. I would do anything to make her feel better. The far-away look in her eyes was haunting me. "Nana Zell told me in church that she made two peach cobblers yesterday, so I'll go over and have dessert. I'll bring you some back." I had taken off my shoes when we came home and instead of trying to find them, I hurried down the path to Nana and Papa's house barefoot, still wearing the sundress I'd worn to church.

∽

THE PICTURE I had in mind of having Daddy living in our house so that I could take care of him and ask him a zillion questions didn't materialize. On Monday, Anna, the nurse who rents a room at the B&B picked him up and took him back to his apartment there. Momma seemed to be acting more like herself.

That Sunday afternoon when the Thatchers were visiting, Papa Tom and I sat out on the front porch steps and talked. I asked him why Momma seemed so mad at Daddy. He said that ten years worth of hurt was hard to wash down the drain like so much dirty dishwater, and I couldn't resist saying, "or down the road ditch to puddle up in the red clay." He smiled and said, "yes, and that."

"Your momma has a soft heart, Baby Girl," he said. "Just go easy on her. It's not only that he left her that's keeping her from forgiving, it's the consequences of his actions. After he left she went into a downward spiral and she had no one to pull her out of it. The deeper she went, the more you suffered. That's weighing heavy on her mind."

"That makes me mad at him all over again. I'd never thought of it that way—you know, that because he wasn't around, she couldn't get well. Maybe I shouldn't be so quick to forgive him after all."

"I didn't mean for it to upset you, Baby Girl," he said, patting me on the back. "I'm just trying to make you understand how it's very hard for your momma to just up and pretend nothing ever happened." He put his thin arm around my shoulders. "It makes me proud to see what a forgiving heart you have."

I grinned up at him. "I got that from you, Papa" I said. Right then things couldn't have been clearer in my head. Blood kin didn't have much to do with shaping a person. If it had, I might have turned out like my daddy and his side of the family—not the kind of people you can depend on. But Papa, on the other hand, led by example. There wasn't an unkind bone in his old body, and I wanted to grow up to be just like him.

On Tuesday, Mrs. Clark came over to the house to pick me up. Momma had gone to get a haircut. "Mr. Clark thought you might like to ride along with him to visit your dad at the B&B. I talked to your mom on her cell phone and she said it was okay. Would you like to go?"

"Yes! Just give me a minute to comb my hair and get some shoes on." After I combed my hair, I looked in the mirror. The grungy tie-dyed t-shirt had to go. I pulled it off and rambled through my drawer to find another. Ah, there was the Neil Diamond shirt. I put it on and looked again. It didn't match my shorts which were last year's gym shorts, so I changed into a decent pair of jeans. They barely came to my ankles. I folded the hem up to make them look cropped. Teeth! I had to brush my teeth.

"You look nice," Mrs. Clark said when I finally made it into the living room.

"Thanks!" She stood there with her keys in her hand. I remembered just a couple of months ago I'd been wishing I had a mother like her. Now I felt guilty that I could have ever had such bad thoughts about my own mother. I had the best momma in the world all along; she just needed some tender loving care. Thoughts of Daddy running away and leaving her like that flooded my mind again and I decided that this forgiveness thing is complicated.

WE PULLED into the driveway of Miss Marple's Bed & Breakfast. I wondered if the owner's real name was Miss Marple or if she named the place after Agatha Christie's detective. I expected Mr. Clark to stop but he kept driving around the house. "Your dad lives in the basement apartment," he said when he finally stopped. "Just one thing I want to say before we go in."

My hands were trembling. "Anything to delay going in," I said, "I'm pretty nervous."

"I know you are, Maisy. Calm down. I think you'll find him easy to talk to. I haven't told your dad about how hard your mother took his leaving. He doesn't know anything about her hospitalizations over the years or that you had to live with the Bakers because of it. Under normal circumstances, I would have, but your father is dying, and I couldn't bring myself to make him even more miserable than he already is. It's up to you and your mom if you want to share the details of your life since he left. I don't know your state of mind, Maisy, but if it's any consolation to you, he's grieving terribly for what he's done to you and your mother."

I held my shoulders a little higher and stared at him as if he had two heads. "I'm not here to condemn him or to console him, Mr. Clark. I'm here because he's my Daddy."

He sat there, still as a mouse. I was beginning to think I'd hurt his feelings. But then he smiled, and I knew he was okay. He bit down on his lower lip and shook his head. "Maisy, Maisy, Maisy. I keep forgetting how incredibly honest and kind-hearted you are. You put most adults to shame." I started to spill the beans and tell him that I wasn't so kind-hearted after all. I'd been teetering back and forth about my feelings since I'd seen Daddy at the festival. I was sad for him one minute and ready to crucify him the next. But I didn't. I just sat there soaking in the compliment he had paid me and wondered if smugness was a sin. I would worry about that later.

He took the keys and got out of the car, but I just sat there as if frozen in place. I guess he thought I expected him to open my door because he walked around the car and did just that. It was like I had stage fright or something. I didn't want to move, but he stood there waiting for me to get out, so I did.

"I was here earlier this morning, Maisy. I think you'll be surprised at how well he's doing. He's up and about and doing pretty much everything on his own." I felt relieved because I was picturing him still being in bed with tubes running everywhere. The news that he was better made me step a little faster.

Mr. Clark rang the doorbell and I could hear footsteps. I held my breath and waited. He opened the door and I still held my breath. At this point I was wondering how long a person can hold her breath and not die. Mr. Clark made sure I didn't find out by slapping me on the back; well, not really a slap, but bigger than a pat on the back.

"Are you okay, Maisy?" How could I be okay? My daddy was standing right in front of me and I didn't know what to say. Then he smiled.

"Come in, Maisy." I breathed a little easier. I guess I'd been afraid he would try to hug me or something, and I wasn't quite ready for that yet. "I like your shirt," he said. He'd noticed!

"You sure look better than you did Saturday," I said as I walked in the door. It was an icebreaker; not much of one but everyone seemed relax.

A tall counter with some bar stools separated the foyer from the dining area and I followed Daddy as he led us into the living room. He was walking with a cane. Mr. Clark made small talk for which I was thankful. I didn't feel like I had anything to say just yet.

There was a sofa, a recliner and a wingback chair and they were arranged with the sofa in the middle. "I hope you don't mind sitting on the sofa, Maisy," Daddy said. "The recliner is easier for me to get in and out of." It was the first time I'd noticed how stooped he was. The only other times I'd seen him, he'd been crumpled up on the ground or lying in a hospital bed. I wondered if he was in much pain, and with that thought came a new wave of compassion. I sat down first, followed by Daddy and then Mr. Clark who sat with me on the sofa.

"I'm glad you came, Maisy. There's so much I want to tell you."

"And I'm glad you came back, Daddy. There's so much I want to ask you." Suddenly I couldn't think of *what* I wanted to ask him. "You go first," I said.

He smiled. "First, I want you to tell me a little about yourself—about school and your friends." He hesitated a second. "And about your mother."

What could I say? That my life had been hunky-dory without a care in the world? That Momma and I had gone about business-as-usual when he left? That she'd been the perfect mother sticking little love notes in my lunchbox every day? That she had an active social life with friends galore?

But then I thought of how indignant I'd been just a few minutes earlier when I told Mr. Clark I wasn't here to judge him. So much for being kind-hearted. No, I wouldn't lie, but I wouldn't tell him about all the bad stuff either. He was my daddy and I wanted something good to come out of the time we had left together.

I told him about my good grades, about Papa Tom's pond and how we loved to fish together. I told him about babysitting for little Matthew, about my friends and our church family and about Reverend Thatcher. I told him about Momma's art and how proud I was of her. And I politely ignored the tears that were running down his face because I knew they were tears of sorrow and regret.

When it was his turn, he told me about his job and how it had taken him to far-away places. He told me about working hours of overtime so he wouldn't have time to think about all the mistakes he'd made. He told me he'd been lonely and there had never been anyone else to fill that loneliness. He showed me a worn-out photo of me and Momma from his wallet.

Then he told me about his own childhood with a demanding father and a delusional, self-centered mother who cared more about keeping up appearances than she did about him. He told me about seeing his best friend's leg blown to bits by a landmine in Afghanistan. And how eventually he was diagnosed with post-traumatic stress disorder. He told me how sorry he was, and that he realized that Momma and I could never forgive him, but all he wanted was to see us again and tell us how stupid he had been and how sorry he was for the hurt he had caused us.

And finally, he told me how undeserving he was for God's amazing grace of forgiveness, but how thankful he was that God does forgive. And in the telling of it all, he politely ignored my tears over *how different our lives could have been* running down my face.

"I loved you and your mother, Maisy. I focused on just sticking a Bandaid on her bouts of depression instead of seeking help for her. I became angry at her, at my mother, and at the world in general, and all I could think to do was run away from it all.

"I didn't know anything about PTSD. I had no idea that feelings of anger, anxiety and feeling all alone in the world were all classic symptoms. Years went by before I was diagnosed, and by that time I felt it was too late to come back home and ask for forgiveness.

"But none of that is an excuse for what I did. Rock tells me what a great kid you are and how wise you are beyond your years. I just want you to know how proud I am of you. I would like nothing better than to spend some time with you, but I'll understand completely if you don't want to do that. And I can't begin to tell you how much it means to me that you agreed to see me today."

I looked at the man sitting in that chair, the daddy I'd been looking for, broken in body and in spirit. His eyes begged for my forgiveness even though in his heart he didn't think it could be done. He was a newbie in the Jesus compartment of the heart that really knows what God's grace is all about. I was a seasoned pro, and it looked like it was going to be left up to me to have to train him.

I scooted up on the sofa so that I could reach over and take his hand. With a shocked expression on his face, he reached out and took mine.

"You've got a lot to learn in a short time, Daddy, so I need to get busy. Can I come over tomorrow and start teaching you?"

It's a good thing I had run out of tears. There were enough from the men in the room to float a boat.

CHAPTER THIRTY-ONE

REV ROCK

"Let your gentleness be evident to all. The Lord is near."
—PHILIPPIANS 4:5

"You should have seen her Liz! What I would give to have a heart that clean and uncluttered!"

Liz had been so touched as Rock's story unfolded. "I told you from the beginning that she was something special, didn't I?"

"How did she get that way? I mean, seriously, I really want to know so I can bottle it up for Matthew. You would expect a child who had such an unstable childhood to rebel or at the very least be a little bitter about things."

"Rock, you've met the Bakers, but you haven't had an opportunity to get to know them. Because of them, Maisy's childhood hasn't been nearly as unstable as you would think. Mr. Baker, or Papa Tom as she calls him, has a heart of gold. Of course, Nana Zell's heart is enormous too, but she doesn't want you to know it. They love that child like she's their own, maybe more so."

"The relationship they have reminds me of the kind of relationship that God wants to have with us. Like in Philippians 4:7 where it says, *and the peace of God, which surpasses all understanding, will guard your hearts and your minds in Christ Jesus.* Paul is telling the people of the Philippian Church that in order to be content and at peace, they need to rely upon the power of Christ. Mr. Baker is a content follower of Christ and that contentment is contagious. God certainly sent Maisy to the right place when He sent her to be loved and nurtured by the Bakers."

"I think I could learn a lot from Papa Tom. We need to visit them more often. But since you're so wise, oh wife of mine, how *do* we bottle that up and hand it down to Matthew?"

"We just have to learn to be content no matter what our circumstances and let him learn by example. I think Paul mentions that a little further down the chapter."

"And why didn't you point me to Philippians 4 when I was struggling with burnout?"

"I'm just the counselor, my dear. You're the preacher."

"I love a wife that always has the last word. Especially when she's also beautiful."

"Hmm," she said, and pulled him close. "Flattery will get you everywhere."

CHAPTER THIRTY-TWO

MAISY

"For if you forgive others for their transgressions, your heavenly Father will also forgive you."
—MATTHEW 6:14

Summers have a way of crawling by when you're a kid, especially when you live in the country. This summer had been different. It was flying by and it didn't help knowing that along with the days getting shorter, my time with Daddy was growing shorter too. Momma had been real hesitant about sitting down and talking to Daddy, and it was almost a week before she would agree to it. To be honest, she seemed a little resentful that my first visit with him had gone so well. She listened quietly for a few minutes, then excused herself to her room saying she had a headache. She came out at supper time and asked if I wanted a sandwich. I offered to make her one but she said she would just eat some ice cream so she could take her medicine, and then she went back to bed. It made me feel a little uneasy. I couldn't help but think of other times she'd gone to her room and hadn't come out for days.

I talked to Papa on the phone that night and he said maybe I should have toned down my excitement after my visit with Daddy. He said not to worry because at least she had taken her medicine. That was a good sign. I woke up the next morning to the smell of bacon frying and that was an even better sign. She was pretty chipper that morning and even offered to drop me off at the Clarks' house on the way to the art studio in Charlotte to drop off the paintings she had promised. Mrs. Clark was riding with her, and her neighbor was watching Matthew. So, I could walk to Miss Marple's B&B to visit Daddy if I wanted to. I knew she was coming around, and I wasn't going to push it.

She dropped me off again on Thursday and Friday, but she didn't ask any questions and I didn't talk about our visits.

Saturday was Max's birthday, and his family invited me to go to Carowinds amusement park with them. Mama teased me about going on a date. It didn't feel much like a date though with Max's little sister following us around everywhere. We finally got wise and told her we were going to ride The Intimidator, and she begged us to take her back to their parents—which we did with gusto.

I was beginning to think that Momma wasn't going to talk to Daddy at all, but Monday morning while I was getting ready, she came into my room.

"I called your Daddy last night. I'm going over there today, but I'd like to do it alone. I hope you understand, Maisy."

"Sure. I'll go over to Nana and Papa's. I haven't seen them all week."

"Good. They'll be happy to see you. I made oatmeal and it's on the table ready for you. I've already eaten." Her voice was trembly. I figured she was about as nervous as I was the day I rode with Mr. Clark to see Daddy for the first time at the B&B. I held my arms out and she hugged me.

"I love you, Momma. It'll be alright."

She hugged me tighter. "I know it will be, sweet girl. I have you to come back home to."

I spent the morning helping Papa mow the grass. Nana Zell fed us lunch and then I came back home and found Momma already there. I had worried the whole time I'd been at Papa's house about how they would get along. Would it be as awkward for her as it had been for me? I walked in the door not knowing what to expect. Either she would be crying, or she would be happy. I found her in the kitchen and she was neither. She turned to me and said, "There you are. Would you pick some okra from Papa Tom's garden? Your Daddy's coming for supper tonight and his favorite food is fried okra." She smiled. "Isn't it funny how you remember things like that?"

"Yes, ma'am! I'll be right back!" I flew out the door as fast as my long skinny legs would take me and I felt like I was floating all the way to Nana and Papa's house. I ran in their front door shouting, "Nana! Papa! You won't believe what's happening!"

I almost bumped into Zell as she was walking out of the kitchen. "Lord a'mercy, Maisy! You scared me half to death. What's wrong?" She was wiping her wet hands on a kitchen towel and I grabbed it out of her hands and flung it in the air. I would have danced around the room with her if she hadn't jerked back her hands when I tried to grab them in mine. Her big hazel eyes opened wide. "What's got into you, Child? Did you get snake bit or something?"

"No ma'am! My daddy's coming to supper. I need some okra from the garden. It's his favorite food, you know."

Her eyes got real moist and she turned away so I wouldn't see her tears. "There's a bucket on the back porch. Be sure to put your garden gloves on and get that stainless-steel paring knife from the drawer to cut it off the stalks. You'll need it."

I grabbed the knife and started out the back door for the bucket and my gloves. "Pick a good mess now. Once you slice it and fry it up it shrinks down to nothing, so be sure you get plenty of it. You don't want your daddy going hungry!"

DURING THE NEXT TWO WEEKS, Daddy ate supper with us every night. Then we'd sit on the porch talking until the mosquitos ran us in and he would go home. One Saturday night, he announced that he would be going to church with us the next day. He'd been going to Mr. Clark's church with Agatha and John. There are no secrets in Baker's Grove so when we walked into church that morning, everyone knew who the man with Mandy and Maisy Martin was and they greeted him kindly. It was a perfect Sunday morning. I was so proud; now everyone could see that I really did have a daddy.

Church was an effort for him that day though, and as soon as we got home, Momma told him to go take a nap on my bed. He didn't protest. He seemed to grow weaker overnight, and the next night when he came for supper, he pushed the food around on his plate taking only a bite or two. Momma began making protein milkshakes for him; it was the only thing he would eat.

On Thursday afternoon Agatha called and said Daddy was in too much pain to come over, so we drove to his apartment. Anna called his doctor in Charlotte to make him an appointment for Friday. Momma volunteered to take him.

After the appointment, she came home and went straight to the kitchen table and sat down. I could see something was wrong. Her eyes were red; she'd been crying. She motioned me to sit down beside her, and she took my hand.

"Maisy, I'm not going to hold anything back from you. Your daddy won't be able to drive anymore, so we've decided he'll be moving in with us. As you know, we saw the doctor this morning and the news is not good. The nurse in his office called and made arrangements with Hospice to send a hospital bed out tomorrow and we'll set it up here in the living room. John and Agatha will drive him over here in their van."

I tried to hold back the tears, but they somehow escaped and ran down my face. Momma squeezed my hands a little tighter.

I had watched with my own eyes as Daddy was growing more and more frail. Even though I knew it was coming, I didn't like this Hospice news one bit.

"How long?" I asked, but I wasn't sure I wanted to know.

She sighed, and her eyes filled with tears too. "Not long, Maisy. Weeks at the very most." She looked down and then back up into my eyes. "He's going to be on some heavy pain meds. He's been hiding how much pain he's been in from us, but it's to the point now that he can't hide it any longer."

"Thank you for bringing him here, Momma."

"He's going to be needing round the clock care, and I know he'll be happier here with us than back at that lonely apartment with a full-time nurse that he doesn't even know." I looked at my momma with new eyes. I had always thought of her as a fragile flower, so easily blown over with any little wind. Now she was facing a cyclone and was holding up just fine. She would be caring night and day for the man who walked out on her when she herself needed caring for in a bad way. When she forgave him, she never looked back.

She cupped my chin in her hand just like she always did when she was about to tell me something important. "It was through God's grace that I found the strength to forgive, Maisy. I didn't do it on my own."

I understood.

I HAD LULLED myself into thinking that this could go on forever—this paradise of having a daddy in my life—but now I knew we wouldn't have him with us much longer. He slept a lot; Momma said it was the morphine. It was the only way to ease his pain. When he realized how weak he was getting he asked Mr. Clark to call his parents.

"I'll understand if you don't want them to come here, Mandy," he said. "Rock can drive me back to the apartment and they can visit me there. I promised Dad.…" He left the sentence unfinished but we both knew what he meant.

"You're not up to riding anywhere, Chris. Maisy and I will go stay with Tom and Zell while your parents are here. I'll ask Rock if he minds coming over for a while when they're here."

"Can I stay?" I asked. "They're my grandparents, and even if they don't want to see me, I'd like to see them. It may be my only chance."

I thought sure Momma was going to say no, but she looked long and hard at Daddy. "It's your call, Chris. But if Maisy stays, don't let your mother say anything to hurt her."

"I promise. If she does, I'll tell them they have to leave."

"Okay, she can stay. But I'm still calling Rock to see if he'll come over and give you some emotional support."

The look he gave her was tender. "Thank you, Mandy."

The next morning, Mr. Clark came by shortly after we had eaten breakfast. My grandparents had said they would arrive at 10. I went to my bedroom to pick out something nice to wear. I tried on just about everything in my closet because I wanted to make a good impression on this woman who had once said I was crazy. Momma came in as I was checking myself out in the mirror. "Are these jeans too short?" I asked. I had decided to wear my white jeans with a pink t-shirt.

"I don't think so. They look nice, but we do need to go back-to-school shopping, don't we?"

"I could roll the hem up."

"You look beautiful just the way you are." She studied my reflection in the mirror. "You're nervous, aren't you?"

"A little bit. I want them to like me."

She sighed. "I wish you would go with me instead of staying here. I spent too many years wanting your grandmother to like me, Maisy, and it never happened. She's a different sort of person. Just try not to be disappointed if she's rude."

Momma's words turned out to be prophetic. The first words out of my grandmother's mouth were rude. She came huffing into the house like the queen of Sheba, only she wasn't bringing gold and precious stones to Solomon, she was spewing hate and bigotry to anyone in her path. And I happened to be first because I opened the door. I had rehearsed what I was going to say. *Hi Grandmother, I'm Maisy*, would be my first line, but I didn't even get out, *Hi* before she cut me off.

"Where's my son?" she asked as she marched into the room. She looked me up and down, then looked around the room as if she'd walked into a homeless shelter.

"There you are, Chris. Oh my, you look awful, just awful. And why on earth would you choose to stay here when you could have your own private bedroom and round-the-clock nurses at our house. You must come home with us immediately!"

"Mother, please!" Daddy said. He had the strength of a mouse, but he said it like a lion. "I'm happy here. Mandy and Maisy have taken good care of me, far better than I deserve. And look at you, Mother. You march in here and totally ignore your granddaughter.

"That's Maisy. She's a beautiful, smart and loving child and she and her mother have made me happier these past few weeks than I've ever been in my life. And if you're going to stay and visit with me, you are going to acknowledge my child."

My grandmother didn't even look my way but went on with her rant. "Son, I'm sure Mandy's only doing this hoping you'll change your will. Why else would she take you back after all these years?"

"It's called forgiveness, Mother, but you wouldn't know anything about that."

She ignored what he said. "But *surely* you're smart enough that you haven't changed your will already, have you?" Daddy just sighed and shook his head sadly. "Good! Don't you do it. Your dad and I would contest it anyway since you can't be of sound mind when you're doped up on all those painkillers."

I could tell Daddy was real upset, but he didn't have the energy to get worked up. He tried to stay calm, I'll give him that.

"I don't plan to change it, but I'm afraid you'll be disappointed when you see what's in the will. I set up a trust years ago. Mandy and Maisy are the beneficiaries of that trust, and I've put every dime I've saved into it."

My grandmother's face turned red, but Daddy kept talking.

"My funeral expenses have already been paid in advance—I did that when I first moved back. And since Mandy is still my legal wife, it will be up to her to decide where I'll be buried." He paused for a minute and took a deep breath. This was taking a lot out of him.

"But," he said, dragging it out a little, "I did leave you and Father something. The two of you are named the beneficiaries of a $1000 life insurance policy. I trust it will be enough to reimburse you for any expenses for the week I stayed with you."

I stood there feeling very awkward but proud of my daddy. Grandfather had walked in unnoticed while she was going about her tirade, and he looked as if he would prefer to be swallowed up by the floor.

Mr. Clark was sitting on the sofa with his mouth open. I don't think he'd ever seen anyone as hateful as my grandmother before. I doubt that many people show their mean side in front of preachers. She apparently hadn't noticed him yet or she would have been nicer. And I was right.

She looked as if Daddy had slapped her or something. Then she noticed Mr. Clark. And Daddy *noticed* that she *noticed* Mr. Clark and he smiled smugly. He had her number.

"Mother, this is my friend, Reverend Rock Clark. He's the pastor of Park Place Presbyterian. I'm sorry I didn't make introductions earlier, but you came in like a thunderstorm and it couldn't be helped."

Then it was Grandmother who looked like she wanted to be swallowed up by the floor. She had revealed her true colors to a preacher, of all people.

"Oh, Reverend Clark, I didn't see you sitting there. Forgive my going on like that, but a mother can get very rattled when her son is so ill. I'm sure you can understand my state of mind seeing how much he has deteriorated. He's not in his right mind right now, and this is not the place for him. My home is much better suited to look after him, and I'm afraid my former daughter-in-law is quite lacking in giving him the care he needs. You do understand that, don't you?"

"No, I don't understand, Mrs. Martin. Mandy is a fine young woman and she's also my wife's dearest friend. I can't imagine anyone who would be more kind-hearted in caring for your son than she. I'm sorry you haven't taken the time to get to know her better.

"And your granddaughter! Wow! Maisy is one of the most amazing kids I've ever met. She's our son, Matthew's babysitter.

"And as for Chris not being in his right mind? I think you have it all wrong, Mrs. Martin. His mind is now focused on God, and God's promise is true. In Ezekiel 36, we hear what He promises. *I will give you a new heart and put a new spirit in you; I will remove from you your heart of stone.* Mrs. Martin, He'll do the same for you if you'll only ask."

When Mr. Clark finished his speech of a lifetime, Grandmother's face had turned so red I thought it was going to catch on fire.

"Well, I never!" she said. "Come on Walt, it's apparent we're not wanted here," and she stomped out the door.

Walt didn't follow her. Instead he walked over to Daddy and sat down on the chair beside him. He took his son's hand in his. His glasses were all fogged up, so he took them off and wiped his eyes. "Chris, I am so sorry. Your mother is harsh. I hope you can find it in your heart to forgive us. I love you, son."

"I love you too, Dad. If God can forgive me for what I've done to Maisy and Mandy, I can forgive you. Mother hasn't asked, but I can't take bitterness to the grave. Tell her I love her."

Walter laid his forehead on the side rail of the hospital bed. I supposed it was to keep us from seeing him cry. After a few minutes, he got up and walked to the door where I was still standing. I had been too stunned to move. He stopped beside me, and his red-rimmed eyes looked into mine. I was almost as tall as he was. He had looked so intimidating when he first arrived, but he didn't now. He took a small card case from his pocket, opened it up and handed me a card.

"Maisy, I'm ashamed of our actions, or maybe I should say inactions. I want to get to know you if you'll let me. I'll understand if you don't. My cell phone number is on this card." I nodded my head and he walked out the door. I felt sorry for him having to go back to the car and deal with that old battle ax. I looked over at Daddy to see what he thought about our exchange. He had fallen asleep and Mr. Clark was standing over him checking his pulse.

I STOOD without taking a breath until Mr. Clark finally looked up and nodded his head. "He's okay. Just exhausted."

About the time I finally breathed again, Momma came walking in the door. She had watched for their car to leave, and when it did, she came rushing back over. When Mr. Clark and I finished telling her the whole story, she was upset.

"I knew I should have insisted you come with me, Maisy. You didn't need to witness that."

"Maybe she did, Mandy" said Mr. Clark. It's best she saw for herself what her dad had to endure as a child. It sure opened *my* eyes."

"Daddy and Mr. Clark are both heroes, Momma. You should have heard them defending you. But I felt really sorry for Walter."

"Walter?"

"You know, Daddy's daddy. Walter. I don't feel right calling him Grandfather yet. But he was nice to me on the way out—said he wanted to get to know me. I pulled the card out of my pocket and showed it to her.

"See, right here," I said, pointing to his name. *"Walter Martin, retired and tired.*" I laughed. "See, he's got a sense of humor at least. Maybe I'll call him sometime."

She and Mr. Clark both laughed, and Momma pulled me close. "My amazing little Maisy," she said. "You find the funny in everything."

I sighed. "I didn't find much funny when Grandmother was here. I guess I'll have to ask God to work overtime on getting rid of my bad thoughts about her. Poor Daddy, he didn't need that."

"How is Chris?" Momma asked Mr. Clark.

"The exchange took a lot out of him. He went to sleep just as soon as they were leaving."

"I wonder if he's in much pain? It's almost time to give him his meds again."

"How much has he been sleeping, Mandy?"

"A lot. For the last two days, I would guess he's been awake maybe six hours out of twenty-four. And he forces himself to do that. He's eating so little. About all I can get in him are milkshakes. He took a few bites of grits this morning but couldn't handle the eggs. I'm really worried."

Mr. Clark started to say something, but stopped, looking at me.

"Whatever you were going to say, Rock, Maisy can hear it. She needs to know what to expect."

"Talk to the Hospice nurse when she comes out this afternoon. I've been around many people in their end stages of life over the years, but everyone's different. She can tell you more."

"Thank you, Rock. You've been a good friend."

"And so have you. I'll be leaving in a few minutes, but first we'll pray. Let's stand around Chris. Maybe he'll wake up long enough to hear our prayer."

It was a good prayer he prayed. Daddy didn't wake up, but we stood on both sides of his bed putting our hands on his arms. Mr. Clark called it "the laying on of hands", and he asked God to hold Daddy in the palm of His hand, to keep him from pain, and to give him peace. And God did.

CHAPTER THIRTY-THREE

MAISY

"and the dust returns to the ground it came from, and the spirit returns to God who gave it."

—ECCLESIASTES 12:7

The sun doesn't shine quite as bright in Baker's Grove now, and the honey from Papa's beehives isn't nearly as sweet. There's a small part of me that wonders if the grief that came from losing Daddy was worth the small amount of time we had together, but the bigger part of me screams, *Maisy, you know it was!* I would have never known the joy of finding him, forgiving him and loving him. That's the part that will stay with me; the grief will fade with time, or that's what Papa says anyway.

We had a few more days with Daddy after the visit from my grandparents. When the time came, he slipped away peacefully with Momma's hand on his brow and me holding his hand. It was a hard thing to let go.

I used to have recurring dreams that I was putting together a puzzle at Nana Zell's kitchen table. It was a scenic landscape of a valley with two houses, a church, and cows in the pasture. The puzzle box showed people in the scene—a woman sweeping the porch, a man mending a fence and a little girl on an old tire swing. But when I finished the puzzle in my dream, the house with the porch was there, the fence and the tire swing were there, but there were no people. I would look inside the box and under the table, but they weren't there. In my dream, Nana would always say, "Clean off that table, Baby Girl, and set it for supper."

"But I've got to find the people," I would say.

She would study the puzzle for a minute, then put her hands together, intertwine her fingers and make a church. Then she would laugh and say, "This is the church, this is the steeple, open the door and there are the people. Look in the church, Baby Girl."

Now I wonder if that dream was God telling me that someday we would be together again, and even in the same church together like we were that one perfect Sunday. And I can still hear Nana Zell's words in the dream, "Look in the church, Baby Girl."

SOMEHOW IN THE finding of Daddy, I found myself. Not the Maisy Martin who by all outward appearances had it all together. Not the overachiever Maisy who thought good grades were the key to escaping a life of upheaval. Not the *yes ma'am, no ma'am* Maisy who thought appeasing others was the only way to win their approval. And not the fairytale Maisy who thought if Daddy would just come home, we'd all live happily ever after.

The Maisy I found knows that it's okay to laugh in the midst of sadness and cry in the midst of joy. That happiness is being with the people you love. That there's more to being a grandparent than just sharing the same gene pool. That people can change, and sometimes it takes a team effort to help them along.

The New Maisy no longer feels a need to escape. I'm not so naive to think Momma is cured forever. Bipolar doesn't work that way. There will be setbacks, of that I'm certain, but we can deal with those when they happen. And when I go away to college, I will feel at ease knowing that her friends will be looking out for her.

Daddy's decision to come home brought peace to me and

Momma. We finally understood how the chaotic household he grew up in, the anxiety and flashbacks from his military days, and the added stress of a wife whose mental illness he couldn't understand had pushed him over the edge.

There's a lightness of heart that comes with forgiveness, and I'm not talking about the superficial lip-service forgiveness where you say you forgive but keep the bad things bottled up inside you. It's the deep-down in the soul forgiveness that comes when God's grace pours out love, kindness and a forgiving heart.

If you're ever in Baker's Grove, turn right on the gravel road beside the filling station. You'll pass two white houses, a pasture and a pond. The next driveway leads you into the church parking lot. There you'll see a tall granite cross on a new grave in the cemetery behind Baker's Chapel. The words engraved upon the stone say, *I was lost, but now I'm found; was blind but now I see.* That's my daddy.

The End

RECIPE: TOMATO PIE

Ingredients
1 (9-inch) pre-baked deep-dish pie shell
4 tomatoes sliced thin
8 - 10 fresh chopped basil leaves
½ cup green onion, chopped
1 cup grated cheddar cheese
1 cup grated mozzarella cheese
1 cup mayonnaise
Salt and pepper

Directions
Place the tomatoes in a colander in the sink in 1 layer. Sprinkle with salt and allow to drain for 10 minutes.
Layer the tomato slices, basil, and onion in the baked pie shell. (Don't skip pre-baking the shell or the pie will be soggy) Season with black pepper.
Combine mayonnaise and grated cheese, then spread mixture on top of tomatoes and bake for 30 minutes or until lightly brown.
Cut into slices and serve warm.

ALSO BY THE AUTHOR

The Southern Grace Series
    Book 1 - Sweet Tea and Southern Grace
    Book 2 - Lighting the Way
    Book 3 - High Tide at Pelican Pointe
    Book 4 - The Melancholy Moon
    Book 5 - The Sweet Tea Quilting Bee
    Book 6 - Miss Marple's B&B
    Book 7 - Finding Maisy

AUTHOR'S NOTE:

Thank you for reading Finding Maisy. I hope you enjoyed it and if you did, please take a look at the other books in the series.
In writing Maisy's story, I got stuck in some hard places. Depression is a tough subject to write about, especially for one who has experienced it. It was not what I set out to do. I had something a little more light and frivolous in mind following Agatha's fun story in Miss Marple's B&B, but God had other plans. He kept putting Maisy and her mother in the forefront of my mind—so much so, that I gave up on my other project and dived in. Who am I to argue with God!
While I was praying for direction in writing this story, one scripture kept showing up in daily devotionals and social media news feeds. Philippians 4:8. "Finally, brothers and sisters, whatever is true, whatever is noble, whatever is right, whatever is pure, whatever is lovely, whatever is admirable—if anything is excellent or praiseworthy—think of such things." As I pondered upon the verse, I changed it in my mind to "WRITE such things" rather than THINK such things". True, noble, right, pure, lovely, admirable, excellent and praiseworthy; I hope I've done justice in writing

some of these attributes into the lives of my characters in Finding Maisy.

If you or someone you love is suffering from depression, bipolar disorder, or any mental health condition, I pray that you'll find a message of hope, love, joy, and inspiration in Maisy's story. To learn the symptoms and ways to support a friend or family member with a mental illness, I urge you to check out the following links.
https://www.nimh.nih.gov/health/topics/depression/index.shtml, and the National Alliance for Mental Illness (NAMI) at https://www.nami.org/.

I love hearing from my readers. If you enjoyed reading Finding Maisy, please leave ratings and reviews on Amazon and Goodreads to let others know that it's worth the read. I hope you'll visit me on my Facebook page, **Glenda C MANUS**, with my last name all in caps. On that page, I post inspirational messages and give periodic updates of books that I'm working on. I can also be contacted by email at gecm1948@yahoo.com.

Happy Reading!
Glenda Manus

ACKNOWLEDGMENTS

A special thank you to my editors, Dorothy Pennachio and Laura Whittaker for their keen observations and helpful suggestions.
To my husband, for his love, patience, and understanding.
To my friends and family, for their encouragement and support.
To my pastor, Reverend Carson Overstreet, for the glimpses of God's grace she shares in her Sunday morning sermons.
To our neighbor, Hadleigh, for posing as Maisy for the front cover.
To photographer, Cherie Steele, for capturing the perfect pose for the cover, even wading knee-deep in water to get it!
To my readers, who continue to reach out and give me the affirmation I need to keep writing.
And to God, the One who gives me strength and whose grace is sufficient.

"For I know the plans I have for you," declares the Lord, "plans to prosper you and not to harm you, plans to give you hope and a future."

— JEREMIAH 29:11

Note: The scripture verses used throughout are from the New International Version unless otherwise noted.

Made in the USA
Columbia, SC
10 November 2018